Acclai...

of JOSEPH KOENIG!

crime

Anniesland Library
833 Crow Road
Glasgow G13 1LE
Phone/Fax: 276 1622 / 276 1623

This book is due for return on or before the last date shown below. It may
be renewed by telephone, personal application, fax or post, quoting this
date, author, title and the book number.

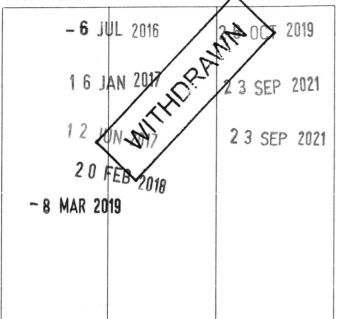

Mollie came out in the robe, and de Costa showed her where to stand. She shrugged the robe off her shoulders, surprising Jordan as it fell around her feet. De Costa showed no expression while Mollie's confidence melted, a woman naked in every way.

De Costa gave her a second look through the viewfinder of a Nikon. "You've been startled," he said, "and are trying to locate the source of a disturbing sound."

De Costa fired off a handful of shots, then removed the camera from the tripod. "Let me see you cognizant of danger, but not panicky, prepared for anything."

Expression flickered across her face, and was extinguished at de Costa's command to clear the slate for their next experiment. Jordan knew the edgy look he wanted from the shooting on Park Place, when Mollie had walked past the dead body on the floor. De Costa would refine it into something glamorous, keeping readers in mind that they were paying for a detective magazine.

De Costa changed lenses and came close, barking commands. Jordan saw tears on Mollie's cheeks. De Costa ordered her to stop crying, mocked her, browbeat her while he captured each drop. Then he unloaded the camera, and gave her a towel to dry her face, brewed a cup of tea for her, and thanked the other girls for their time.

"That was a terrific impersonation of quiet fear," Jordan said when she was dressed.

"What impersonation? I was scared to death..."

FALSE
Negative

by Joseph Koenig

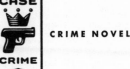

A HARD CASE   CRIME NOVEL

A HARD CASE CRIME BOOK
(HCC-107)
First Hard Case Crime edition: June 2012

Published by

Titan Books
A division of Titan Publishing Group Ltd
144 Southwark Street
London
SE1 0UP

in collaboration with Winterfall LLC

Print edition ISBN 978-0-85768-580-3
E-book ISBN 978-0-85768-740-1

Design direction by Max Phillips
www.maxphillips.net

Typeset by Swordsmith Productions

The name "Hard Case Crime" and the Hard Case Crime logo are trademarks of Winterfall LLC. Hard Case Crime books are selected and edited by Charles Ardai.

Printed in the United States of America

Visit us on the web at www.HardCaseCrime.com

For Naught

FALSE NEGATIVE

CHAPTER 1

Flynn from the *Bulletin*, dead earnest over a four-martini lunch, said he had a ticket he was looking to get rid of. "Front row, center. You'll taste ozone when the lights dim."

A younger man drinking Schmidt's moved his head noncommittally.

"Best seat in the house," Flynn said, "aside from Conrad Franklin Palmer's, and he would gladly change places with you."

The beer drinker looked at his watch. In the United States courthouse across Market Street a lackadaisical jury was deliberating racketeering charges against stewards from the Atlantic City racetrack. "Where will you be?"

"New Haven." Flynn peeled back a lapel, uncovering yellow pasteboards in an inside pocket. "Be a crime not to use these, too. I was talking to Professor Einstein on the anniversary of his coming to America, and I mentioned, I asked him did he know a way I could be in two places, the same time. Not with the technology presently available, he said, but see him again in thirty, forty years."

The beer drinker, whose name was Adam Jordan, said, "While you're watching the Yalies roll over Princeton, who's the *Bulletin* got to see Palmer die?"

Flynn turned a swizzle stick around the lip of his glass. "I thought you might make that small gesture."

"I work for the competition."

"Loyalty's overrated, you want my opinion."

Jordan shook his head at the waiter who asked if he was ready for another Schmidt's.

"Con Palmer will sell a lot of papers for the *Atlantic City*

Press," Flynn said. "Would it kill you to do two thousand words under my byline for the *Bulletin*, or pull an old death house story from the clips, and slap a fresh lead on it?"

Flynn turned the stick the other way. To Jordan it looked like he was determined to separate the martini into its individual parts again.

"This is a story that's begging for you," Flynn said. "*Bulletin* hacks don't know what to make of a divinity school student standing to inherit twenty-five million who poisons his parents so he can marry a big-titted Steel Pier hostess. Rita Snyder says Adam Jordan's the only reporter in our circulation zone worth reading besides myself."

"Who is she?"

"Our ladies page editor. Big, big fan of yours," Flynn said. "The Snyders are major stockholders in the *Bulletin* corporation. Show us what you can do, and there'll be more pinch-hitting assignments down the road."

He put a ticket to the execution on the table, and moved it to Jordan's side. "You might even be hired away from the *Press* by a paper that pays better than beer money."

Flynn captured a waiter by the arm, held him while he finished his drink before sending him for a refill with a gentle shove.

"Eddie Fisher's opening at the Steel Pier next week," he said. "Rita's nuts for Eddie Fisher. If she doesn't get to see him, she'll make a scene more disturbing than what you can expect from Con Palmer. *Press* reporters are comped at the Steel Pier. Give me your freebies, and you won't have to feel you owe me anything."

Palmer's girl, there to watch him die, left Jordan uninspired—the massive chest failing to make the case for a forgettable face. He left Trenton State Prison racking his brain for a better angle.

Late for a deadline at the *Press*, he called the *Philadelphia Bulletin* switchboard indentifying himself to a dictation operator as Thomas Flynn.

"The green room in reality is a soothing shade of buff with indirect lighting and sound-proof panels on the ceiling," he began. *"The executioner is a grandfatherly fellow who looks like the florist he is when not moonlighting for the state. But 'old sparky,' a straight-back oak seat—No, make that 'throne'—tricked out with leather straps and ankle restraints is a nasty prop out of a nightmare set in a torture chamber..."*

He started home trying out a fresh take from the point of view of the lovestruck heir to millions with minutes left to live. In his room above a law office in Absecon he reviewed his notes, then rolled copy paper and two carbons into his typewriter. The words came in bunches, as they always did when the work went well, his fingers racing to keep pace with his ideas. When he dropped into bed two stories for the *Press* were on his desk, the one he liked best a dry-eyed interview with Conrad Palmer's sister for the Sunday features.

At 8:15 he kicked off the covers. Congressman Theodore Garabedian would deliver his Armistice Day Speech at the American Legion Hall in Brigantine in forty-five minutes. Jordan dangled his legs off the mattress, and then he crossed them and lit a Lucky. Holiday boilerplate from a windbag politician was not worth getting out of bed for. He doubted that many *Press* readers would blame him if he went back to sleep.

But his editors would. They had a news hole to fill, and were counting on him for twenty column inches. A call to the Legion Hall was answered by a woman with a stuffed nose. "God Bless America" blared from tinny speakers in the background.

"I'm Jordan with...with the Garabedian party," he said, "running late in Absecon, and trying to catch up to the congressman. Do you know if he—?"

"Speak louder, will you? I can't hear you above the commotion," the woman with the stuffed nose said. "Representative Garabedian just entered the hall."

Jordan got back under the blankets to finish his smoke. A medical columnist advised that cigarettes weren't as healthy as advertised, but it wasn't Luckys that were choking him. In his first year as a police reporter for the *Press* he had written every kind of story that he ever would, and he had been on the paper now for close to four. Crime on the Jersey Shore followed the seasons. Con artists appeared on the boardwalk in summer, and were joined by hotel thieves around Labor Day when the Miss America pageant came to town. By Christmas the chiselers were gone, and Jordan kept busy with assaults and drunken brawls until the horseplayers returned from the Florida meets with pickpockets in tow. He had covered fires, drownings, fatal drag races and other car crashes, stabbings, shootings, knife fights, suicides, murder-suicides, three wife-murders, two murders for hire, and now an execution.

He'd interviewed elected officials in prison, and broke news of the indictments of the good government types appointed to replace them. Three times he had heard Theodore Garabedian's Armistice Day valedictory. Nothing but a headache would be accomplished by a visit to the Legion Hall to hear it again.

On his way to work around 2:00 he stopped to pick up a *Bulletin*. His death house story was on the front page in the favored spot in the extreme right-hand column above the fold and under a four-column headline and three decks. Any tickets passing hands between Tom Flynn and himself should be moving his way for a job well done.

He parked in front of the *Press* building and went upstairs. At deadline the city room became a madhouse, but on a Saturday afternoon in late November he had the third floor almost to himself. There was little on his calendar besides the speech in Brigantine. He dialed the Legion Hall for someone who could give him the gist of Garabedian's remarks, but hung up before the call went through. It was easier to go to the clip file instead.

Last year's story, updated with a new opening graph, was on the city desk in fifteen minutes. One dupe was on his spike, and the other in the basket for the *Press'* radio station to be turned into a 30-second spot. None of his readers would suspect that he hadn't been near Brigantine today. Professor Einstein could learn a thing or two from Adam Jordan. It was not impossible to be in two places at the same time, if no one checked.

The rest of the weekend was his. The thing to do was to get started on the novel that would pave his way out of Atlantic City. Facing down an empty first page held no terror for him. He'd been doing it for years. A quick run to New York would be more rewarding. Charlie Parker was at Birdland, and there was time to make the early show.

Rain sprinkled with ice pellets turned to sleet as he reached the parkway. Carefully, he felt for the brake. He could forget the early show. And if he stayed for the midnight jam, he'd be returning half in the bag on slick roads. Another crack at the novel wasn't a bad idea.

Illinois Jacquet was on the radio, his choppy tenor interrupted by static from another speaker under the dash. Jordan had installed a Bearcat police scanner when he'd come to the *Press*. Not every cop car was equipped with something as good. Frequently he beat troopers to the scene of major accidents.

More static accompanied a dispatcher's call that faded under a bridge. Jordan cruised the shoulder till the 10-54 was repeated, a report of a possible dead body on the beach at Little Egg Harbor. A dog-walker who had made the discovery would be on hand to point out the spot. Jordan moved the gas pedal closer to the floor. On that miserable afternoon his new '53 Hudson Hornet was the only car headed toward the shore.

There were no cops at the beach. No dog-walker. He pulled off the pavement, keeping out of the soft sand. From the dunes he watched a cruise ship strung with colored lights sailing to warm waters. A black pup was hunkered by the tide line. He kept an eye out for its master until the animal wriggled into the surf on stubby flippers, and dove under the waves.

This wouldn't be the first time a 10-54 had led to nothing. The body might be a driftwood log, or not that much. A prankster's day at the beach.

The funny pages swirled around his ankles with the debris from picnic lunches and Coney Island whitefish. Plenty of those. In a cleft in the dunes he spotted a blanket spread over brittle beach grasses. The sea breeze fluttered the corners, threatened to carry it away. But it was anchored by a woman curled on her side.

Wet sand coated her face, which was turned away from the rain. She was barefoot, in a pleated skirt and cashmere sweater. A silk kerchief was tied across her mouth, and her ankles, knees and thighs were bound with a single piece of rope that was also looped around her throat. If she had tried to free herself she would have strangled, and it seemed to Jordan that was what she had done. Handcuffs cinched her wrists behind her back. Jordan pictured her killer crafting the tableau on the blanket, stepping back from time to time to appraise his work.

He scraped the sand from her cheek, and tilted it toward himself. She was a beautiful woman dead for several hours whose looks hadn't begun to fade. He reproached himself for being sentimental. Beauty was the cheap accolade that newsmen rewarded automatically to female victims of murder.

Adam Jordan didn't have a sentimental bone in his body. The dead woman had flame red hair, and a shape on the neat side of voluptuous. Her skin, colorless now, was unblemished, and he would write also about her fine jaw and the sensitive cast of her features. If he drew back her lids to inspect the color of her eyes, who would reprimand him for doing his job?

But his readers would have to get along without that information. Perhaps a sentimental bone or two.

A couple of men tramping across the dunes made him think of *The Lost Patrol*, his favorite desert movie. A Mutt-and-Jeff team in blue uniforms with yellow piping. They waved him back from the blanket, and then told him not to move. Troopers Michael Brannon and Dennis Riley were attached to the state police barracks in Absecon where Jordan prowled for fatal accidents around the winter holidays when drunk drivers terrorized the roads.

"You called it in?" Brannon was the tall one.

Jordan shook his head.

"Who did?"

"She was alone when I got here. I don't know."

Riley, pouring sand from his shoes, said, "What were you doing with her?"

"Keeping her company while she waited for you. Long wait."

"Have the M.E. see if the corpse was sodomized," Riley said to Brannon.

The needling was not good-natured. The real crime for Brannon and Riley was a reporter beating them to the scene, and mentioning it in his paper.

"She's hog-tied," Brannon said. "You were in the Navy, Jordan. You must be handy with a rope."

"I was an MP at Fifteenth Army headquarters in Vienna under General Clark," he said. "All thumbs. I washed out of the Cub Scouts because I couldn't tie a slipknot."

Brannon and Riley were adept at chasing speeders, and refereeing domestic disputes. In their largely rural county homicide was a rare occurrence for which they prepared with a three-week course in forensic investigation. Usually it meant one of the family squabbles getting out of hand, and a remorseful spouse in a bloody nightgown or pajamas waiting by the phone for arresting officers. A murder entailing a search for the killer came along a couple of times in a decade. Riley went back over the dunes to radio for assistance.

The rough wool blanket was khaki-colored. Two of them together hadn't kept Jordan warm in his billet in Austria. The troopers were not interested in his observations. They had observed the wind picking up, and that it was unnecessary for both of them to freeze while waiting for back-up. Brannon took cover in the lee of the dunes, while Riley sat in their car. Adam Jordan remained with the woman on the blanket.

A fierce gust blew the pleated skirt above her hips. She was wearing sheer panties several inches below the line imprinted in her waist by the elastic. They were on front to back, the label on the outside. Jordan turned his back to the wind, and scribbled in his notepad.

He would eulogize her with tenderness. In the squalid circumstances of her death was a story more compelling than Conrad Palmer's. He would polish its lurid detail into a cautionary tale, every parent's nightmare. It would be his ticket out of Atlantic City and into journalism's major leagues. His and hers.

Brannon hadn't quit flashing him dirty looks. Something was wrong with a man who kept close to a corpse. A creep who got his thrills looking at murdered women. Riley might not be off the mark about him. A car door slammed. Brannon elbowed him aside, and stood closest to the blanket.

Coming across the dunes with Riley was a man pressing a fedora against the back of his head. He was ruddy and beer-swollen, Irish—as were most state police in New Jersey—Irish and something else. The wind snapped back the brim, and Jordan got a look at a crumpled pompadour sprinkled with gray.

Detective Lieutenant Ralph Day knelt beside the body as the troopers filled him in. He plowed the sand with his fingers, lifted the corners of the blanket, and swept underneath. He climbed to the top of the dunes to view the wider scene, and sent Riley and Brannon to hunt for evidence before their curiosity ran out. "This is how you found her?" he said to Jordan.

The wind had straightened the dead woman's skirt. Jordan didn't tell Day what he'd seen under it. "I know better than to interfere with a crime scene."

"I didn't ask if you know better."

Day did not like having reporters around. Cases were blown cozying with the press. Pensions were lost. If it were up to him the Bill of Rights would be revised—the article guaranteeing Freedom of the Press—and while they were at it he would also tell the states to narrow the rights of suspects in criminal cases.

"Just like she is now," Jordan said.

Unlike killers and their victims the police were all of a type, taciturn men from working class families innately suspicious of the civilians who paid them. Fair game for Jordan to coddle, massage, flatter, bribe, pressure, threaten, trick—whatever it took—into giving up their secrets. In the city room where he was admired for being a fast writer careful with facts, he accepted kudos only as an expert at manipulating cops. And also for protecting them from prosecutors and judges by refusing to discuss—even under subpoena—what they told him.

"What do you make of it?" he asked Day.

"It would be pure speculation."

Speculation put men in prison. From a conscientious investigator like Ralph Day it was often closer to fact than anything heard in court. "I'll take what I can get."

"So you can use it in quotes with attribution?" Day said. "I'll pass."

He might do that. He'd burned sources before. Anything he could get out of a cop at a crime scene was gold.

"The body is bound with rope, cuffs, and a silk gag. That must tell you *something*."

"Okay, here's what I have for the *Press*," Day said. "Foul play suspected."

Two men wearing Eisenhower jackets were making the trek from the road. One of them battled the wind to keep an umbrella over the head of an older fellow toting a doctor's satchel. Sam Melvin, the Atlantic County coroner, put down the bag on the dead woman's hips, and invited Day under the umbrella. Jordan stepped close to listen in.

"...Cornell by two and a half touchdowns," Melvin said. "Princeton's gone soft since Kazmaier left."

"Who do you like tomorrow?" Day said.

"Tomorrow? Tomorrow's Sunday. Oh, you mean the pros. I don't follow them. They're soft, too."

They talked about the weather while Melvin had a look at the corpse.

"Evidence of petechial bleeding," he said as he raised the eyelids.

Jordan made a note that the eyes were light blue.

Melvin lifted her head, started to undo the gag.

"Hold off," Day said. "We haven't taken pictures yet."

The coroner wiped off his hands on his coat, and offered Camels all around. Brannon shot a roll of film, discarded the burned flashbulbs among others in the sand.

A worm of ash fell in the woman's hair as Melvin worked off the gag. Her mouth was agape, frozen in a smile that Jordan planned to describe as hellish if a better adjective didn't come along. Melvin forced two fingers between her teeth, and pinched out some gauzy material. He unrolled a nylon stocking, fished in her throat till he had its mate.

"She must have put up an awful squawk," Brannon said, "to make him want to shut her up like that."

Jordan didn't think the killer had tired of hearing her scream. He'd seen stranger objects retrieved from the bodies of murder victims, not always from the mouth. Not only from women.

"I'm going to remove the rope now, and palpate the limbs for a preliminary time of death," Dr. Melvin said.

"Cut around the knots," Day said. "I want them."

As the coroner looked in his bag for a scalpel, the men in the Eisenhower jackets rearranged the body. Day noticed the handcuffs, pointing them out to Melvin.

"Why don't I bring her to the morgue before everyone comes down with pneumonia?" Melvin said. "Stop by with a locksmith. Unless you've got someone in your jail who's good at picking cuffs."

The attendants opened a canvas stretcher. Melvin stopped them before they could transfer the body from the blanket.

"There's no wedding ring," he said to Day.

"It shouldn't be hard to get her ID'd, even if she's single."

Jordan knew that Day would give him the quote he was looking for. He'd been figuring a way to get it in his story if no one actually said it.

"She's a good-looking girl. Somebody wants her back."

None of the other Sunday papers had anything about the body on the beach at Little Egg Harbor, but Jordan didn't credit himself with a scoop. Away from a mile-long strip along the Atlantic City boardwalk the competition maintained a slight presence on the Jersey Shore.

Jordan had been working on a Bronx weekly when he was hired away by the *Press*. It was a step up from the Grand Concourse, an opportunity to make his name trailing after movie stars, and big band singers, and the gangsters who ran the clubs where they entertained. But he almost never saw a hoodlum outside court. Whores, bookmaking and loan sharking brought in too much profit for the mob bosses to jeopardize by calling attention to themselves. The luxury suites above the hotel nightclubs were a no-man's land for reporters. Frequent rumors of fights, drunken orgies, drug use, and of midnight visits by abortionists were impossible to confirm. Publicists threatened libel. Jordan's editors told him to dig for dirt somewhere else. If Atlantic City couldn't keep its secrets, the stars would stay away, leaving a swell place to buy salt water taffy, and build sand castles on the beach.

Jordan was expected to write a Sunday feature every week—an extended piece on an odd aspect of life in "America's Ocean Playground." And where did you come up with fifty-two of those each year? The fetishist murder of a beautiful girl was a gift. With luck the cops would go through twists and turns in getting her identified and finding evidence. The investigation would drag on, and he'd live off it till the bathing beauties returned in the spring.

A quarter past eleven, and he was having breakfast over the Monday paper when the phone rang. He didn't know anyone up so early. Nightside reporters didn't start work till five. No one called unless a calamity required his attention, usually a boardwalk fire or drowning worth a few paragraphs on the local page. A fire at a crowded restaurant, a hotel robbery, another killing would be a welcome change of pace—any story that didn't involve the Coast Guard. November was too cold to go out in the cutter, and get sick to his stomach chasing after fishermen who'd been caught overnight in strong currents.

But the voice on the other end wasn't from the paper. "Adam Jordan, this is Ed Pelfrey."

"Do I know you?"

"I'd like to talk to you about something that ran under your name in the *Press*."

Jordan had been meaning to remove his number from the phone book. *Press* readers weren't shy about bothering him at home to ask what right he had to put something they didn't like in his paper. He'd point out that it wasn't *his* paper, and that

Thomas Jefferson had given him the right, but *Press* readers weren't listeners. Rather than continue the civics lessons, he'd change to an unlisted number.

"I was out late, Ed, tracking down more stories for you, so if you'll excuse me I'll be getting back to my Rice Krispies."

"Don't hang up. There are a couple of articles we need to discuss."

Only two? Readers who didn't appreciate his reporting normally had a gripe with every word he wrote.

"One," Pelfrey said, "is the execution of Conrad Palmer. The other is the body on the beach."

"What didn't you like about them?'"

"There was nothing I didn't like. They were excellent accounts with lively writing, and good insights into the thinking of a pathetic killer, and the detectives hunting the murderer of a beautiful girl."

"Thanks for the kind words, Ed. I really do have to get off the phone."

"I haven't told you who I am," Pelfrey said. "I'm the editor of *Real Detective* magazine at Turner Men's Group in Manhattan."

"You're calling from New York?"

"That's right."

"To say you like my writing?"

"To ask if you'll do some work for us."

Jordan pushed away his breakfast. He reached for his cigarettes.

"*Real Detective* is Turner Men's lead title. We publish four fact detective magazines a month. Ever read us?"

"I don't look at pulp—don't get to read many magazines. You were big before the war."

"We're still big," Pelfrey said. "Circulation is over a million for each title. Four books a month, twelve stories in each issue, eat up close to six hundred homicides a year. We're starved for copy."

"What's six hundred murders in a country of a hundred-fifty million people?"

"Six hundred too many," Pelfrey said. "That's one way of looking at it. For us it's barely enough. We can't use just any case. The old man comes home with a load on, the wife kicks him out of bed, and he slaps her around till she stops breathing, our readers aren't interested. Ditto for any murderer who's not smart enough to keep out of the hands of the police for three days, the time it takes to get a good homicide probe working. We want stories with good dick-work, and sympathetic victims. Young, nubile, and attractive don't disqualify them either. We can't be picky with our killers. Maybe one in a thousand is an appealing character. Conrad Palmer, for instance. We'd like you to do his story for us."

"I've never done magazine work."

"Pick up a stack of dick books at a cigar store, and study the formula. Begin at the beginning with the victim gone missing, and the discovery of the body, and proceed through the investigation, arrest, and legal process. Our readers aren't fans of literary experimentation. Tell the story in short, declarative sentences. They'll think you're Hemingway."

"I don't know," Jordan said. "I'm pretty busy."

"We pay fast, Mr. Jordan."

"So does the *Press*. Every Friday."

"We also pay well."

"What do you call well?"

"A nickel a word. Five thousand word stories are the norm. Six or seven thousand well-chosen ones are okay, if the case merits it. What do you make on the *Press*?"

"That's not any of your business."

"We pay better than the papers, because good crime writers are harder to find than inventive killers. We don't want just one story from you. Keep an eye on every promising murder in your neck of the woods. The first story or two will take most of a week to write, and give you fits. After you get the hang, you'll knock them out in no time. Our best regulars pull down two, three thousand a month."

"Where did you get my name?"

"People send us clips on potential stories. It surprised me I'd never seen your byline before. Can I count on you for the Palmer case?"

Jordan was slow with an answer because he was doing math in his head. At a nickel a word he figured on a four-hundred dollar payday. How could a novice who hadn't learned the formula tell Con Palmer's story in fewer than eight thousand words?

"Did I mention that we also need photos?" Pelfrey asked. "The victim, of course, and the crime scene, and investigating officers digging up evidence. Gruesome is okay, but no close-ups of a morgue slab. We want pictures of the suspect when he's apprehended, and another on his way to court or behind bars. Payment is ten dollars for every one we use. Shoot them yourself, make a deal with a staff photographer, or steal them from the police like most of our writers do. It can add another hundred or two hundred dollars to your fee."

"When do you need the Palmer story?" Jordan asked.

"Yesterday."

"I think I can give you what you want."

"Some very fine reporters can't," Pelfrey said. "They look down their nose at the pulps. It shows in their writing."

"How will I know if you like my story?"

"There'll be a check in your mailbox."

At a candy store on his corner the pulps were racked with slick girlie magazines away from *Life*, *Look*, and the *Saturday Evening Post*. A dozen or so detective titles all seemed the same. On the cover of each one was a tough guy and/or babe with a gun, or a doe-eyed innocent in the clutches of a fiend.

Easy to snicker at, but he'd never look down his nose at five cents a word, or a formula that for all he knew was as difficult to master as Professor Einstein's.

Real Detective readers did not like being teased with red herrings. They did not want policemen who were conflicted about sending killers to the death house. Investigators were not deductive geniuses, but bulldogs who fastened on a suspect and didn't let up till they had a confession. The victims of murder were naïve and trusting—in particular those with money—unless they were prostitutes, strippers, or wayward youngsters asking for trouble. Lawyers were not mentioned by name, which was how the *Press* also tried to cut down on lawsuits. Killers were irredeemable monsters. Those who cheated the electric chair cheated justice.

Not every murder victim Jordan had written about for the *Press* was as uncomplicated as she would be portrayed in the pulps. He knew killers who were worse than others. On the Jersey Shore homicide came in various gradations of gray. *Real Detective* paid better than newspapers because there was an art to telling a story in just two colors—black and white—and keeping readers riveted for five thousand words.

Jordan read three magazines from cover to cover before sitting down at the typewriter. Color and authenticity were essentials of the formula. Invention was not. Pelfrey didn't want literature, but morality tales, and maybe that wasn't a bad thing. *Real Detective*'s grit was lacking from Jordan's sensitive death house piece for the *Press*.

By 4:00 he'd completed three and a half pages. He could have written two long Sunday features in that time, and knocked out a couple of obituaries. He wanted to count the words, to know to the penny how well he'd spent the afternoon, but he had to leave for work.

◦

"Mr. McAvoy's asking for you," a copy boy said as he ran up the stairs to the city room.

Ken McAvoy had started at the *Press* as junior varsity sports stringer during his sophomore year in high school, and risen through the news ranks to editor. He was divorced, without children, a semi-reformed alcoholic who worked seventy-hour weeks and never took a vacation. His cubicle under the south window was his only perk. He didn't smile when he looked up at Jordan, but McAvoy almost never smiled now that he almost never drank.

"What do you want, Ken?" Jordan asked him.

McAvoy's desk was buried under news clips and copy paper held down with linotype slugs. On the walls were historic *Press* front pages cast in lead, the attack on Pearl Harbor, D-Day, V-J Day, FDR's death, and Bobby Thomson's shot heard round the world. Jordan liked it here in McAvoy's place in the sun, and occasionally let himself think about what he'd hang on the wall.

"The Palmer execution was as good a piece of writing as I've seen in this paper. I don't know how you wormed your way into the death house," McAvoy said, "but it's where you belong."

His faint smile puzzled Jordan, who didn't smell alcohol on his breath.

"We've gotten dozens of calls and letters. Opponents of the death penalty say you deserve a Nobel Prize—and so do those in favor. I wish I had more reporters who saw things with your eyes."

"I took dictation. The story told itself."

"One of your others didn't."

"The killing at Little Egg Harbor?" Jordan said. "I caught a break. I was in my car when they called it in."

"Not that."

"What else—?"

"Garabedian's talk at the Legion Hall."

Jordan didn't blink. McAvoy knew he'd fudged the piece. How many times had McAvoy pulled the same stunt himself?

"What about it?"

"You made him sound almost intelligent," McAvoy said. "Something else you got wrong, too. We're fielding calls on it, non-stop."

"I got back late from Trenton. I was in no shape to drag my-self to the Legion Hall to listen to that hack spoon out garbage. What happened? He get off a few zingers I left out?"

"Wasn't that," McAvoy said.

"I quoted something he didn't say?"

"Several things. He never gave the speech."

"Oh, crap."

"That's your poker face, right?" McAvoy said. "How can it be the whole town's talking, and my ace reporter hasn't heard?"

"Mea culpa, Ken. Quit looking at me like my back was turned while the Hindenburg burned."

"Nobody gives a rat's ass about the speech," McAvoy said. "But Teddy Garabedian dropping dead ten minutes after he walks inside the Legion Hall is a huge story."

"He did *what*?" Jordan said.

"From what I read in the *Cape May Times* and the *Vineland Journal* it was a grisly performance. Four or five people who saw it needed ambulances themselves."

The way he felt, Jordan might be the sixth.

"For us to get beat because we went with an account of the remarks he didn't make doesn't do a lot for our credibility."

"What can I say, Ken?" Jordan pressed his hand over his heart. "It'll never happen again."

"No," McAvoy said. "No, it won't."

"I don't suppose," Jordan said, "you're asking me to cover the funeral."

"You're a newsroom legend," McAvoy said. "The hot shot who filed copy on a speech after the congressman who gave it, or rather didn't, choked on a fried egg sandwich. The day will come when you'll have a good laugh, too. Laugh loudest."

"When do you think?"

"Five years? Ten? Not any time soon. I'm letting you go."

"There's got to be something I can do to put things right."

"Not by me," McAvoy said. "I could fight to keep you, but it means going up against the board, and probably losing my job also. Bad judgment is not a strong selling point for either of us."

"Goddamn Garabedian," Jordan said. "He almost went last summer eating oysters he dug up out of season. I prepared an obit on him for when we'd need it. All you need is a graph telling how he died."

"We found it when we cleaned out your desk. We're going with it today. Nice piece of work."

"Might as well run mine alongside it."

"It's not the end of the world," McAvoy said. "Someone else will want to take a chance on you. When they ask for references, have them call me. I'll be happy not to pick up the phone."

CHAPTER 2

Jordan hadn't come to the *Press* with ambitions to be a great reporter. Of the things he did better than ferret news, none paid. Journalism would serve as an apprenticeship for his real life's work, the writing of novels. But he'd begun to have doubts. Scott Fitzgerald was churning out his best stuff when he was the age Jordan was today. Same for O'Hara. Norman Mailer was a literary sensation with a big book under his belt by twenty-five. At the end of his twenties Jordan had plenty of false starts, and shoeboxes filled with news stories told in a sure, incisive voice. He had quit believing these were evidence of failure. A newspaperman was what he wanted to be.

Few reporters who screwed up as spectacularly as he had found work on other papers. He was grateful to have something to ease his transition into he didn't know what. He reviewed his notes on the Palmer case. He lit a Lucky looking at the empty page. He adjusted the ribbon, and picked dirt off the type. He studied the clips, and then he got up and fixed himself a sandwich.

Writing for the pulps didn't feel right. He was a newspaper reporter, an important novelist about to be born. Anything else was just killing time. But the words wouldn't come, and how could he kill the time without them? He opened a can of beer, and drank it at the typewriter. His mind remained blank. He tried to pretend that he was working on a long piece for the *Press*, nothing more ambitious. It didn't help. He stopped thinking, and began to type.

The words poured out. He wrote without let-up, afraid of bottling them up inside. He brought his readers into Con

Palmer's head, transported them to the death house, and left them there looking through the condemned man's eyes. The difficulty was not in finding the words, but in restraining them—to keep from trying to make literature. He let the story tell itself in straightforward prose. All he had to do was to craft an ending, and get the manuscript on its way to New York.

He didn't count the words. A good editor, any editor, would trim a few hundred, and he didn't want to know exactly how many. Every cut was a nickel stolen from him. He corrected a few typos before slipping the manuscript into an envelope with a batch of clips to show that he hadn't wandered far from the facts. He inked out *Atlantic City Press* from the envelope, wrote his return address, and sent it off.

He was elated as the story left his hands, at loose ends before he was home from the post office. He had nothing to do. Nothing but to get back to his novel while the terror of the empty page seized hold of him again.

Three weeks ago an armed man in battle fatigues had taken hostages in a Park Place restaurant. Jordan arrived on the heels of the police, crouching behind a cruiser as they tried to talk the man into surrendering. After an hour they stormed the restaurant and killed him. A waiter and a busboy, badly wounded, were rushed to a hospital. Jordan had called dictation with what he had, and hung around for more.

The 23-year-old hostess told him that she'd hidden in the kitchen. The gunman hadn't noticed her, and she didn't see him die. It wasn't much of a story. She was a pretty girl, though. There was always room for a face like hers in the *Press*. Jordan had her in his viewfinder when a farm truck pulled up. The woman who rolled off the back in a wheelchair was the mother of the dead hostage-taker. Her son was not a soldier or disgruntled veteran, but a high school sophomore. He was somewhat slow—the woman touched a finger to her temple—and liked to play cops and robbers. A detective came out of the restaurant with his guns, a Daisy air rifle and a cap pistol.

The hostess began to shake. Jordan took her to a tavern where she guzzled orange blossoms to no effect. At his apartment she smoked pot for the first time, and slept till noon wrapped in his shirt. Today it was his nerves that were shot. He had her phone number in his notepad, pretty sure he'd saved it. She was leaving for the restaurant when he caught her.

"Mollie, it's Adam."

"Do I know you?"

It was a question he often heard from women he brought back to his place.

"I meant to call sooner. But working on the paper, my life's not my own." He didn't expect her to believe him, but intended to wear her down, his strategy for reluctant sources. "Things have been hectic. You saw my story on the execution?"

"Adam, did you say? I'm drawing a blank."

"We sat at the bar after the shooting in your restaurant," he said. "You couldn't calm down."

"I don't drink," she said.

"I wouldn't call it drinking. We ended up here."

"Wherever here is," she said, "you've got the wrong Mollie."

"That night I didn't."

"Now you do. Goodbye."

She wanted contrition. No big deal. Sooner or later every girl had him saying he was sorry.

"Don't hang up," he said. "There's a shirt in your closet with light blue pin-striping. The number from the Chinese laundry is D52."

"Is this a mind-reading trick?" she said. "Do you also saw women in two?"

"It's not magic," he said. "You wore it home from my place."

"It isn't in my closet."

"You didn't throw it away? It's a twenty-dollar shirt."

"It went back to the laundry. It's been waiting for you," she said. "You took good care of me, Adam. But you also took advantage. And then I didn't hear from you."

"You don't believe in second chances?" he said. "The judges I write about allow first-time offenders one mistake."

"They don't wake up in bed with them."

She exhaled into the phone. Jordan wanted to believe it was a sigh of regret.

"You're smart," she said. "And sharp. Very, very cool. I've been dodging guys like you since high school. I'm not looking for someone I hear from after a month with an invitation to hop in the sack."

"Uh-huh," he said. It was hard to say he was sorry while he was being eaten alive.

There was nothing but to tell her he'd stop by her restaurant for the shirt. But not right away. After he had it where would he come up with an excuse to call again?

He blew dust off the shoebox where he kept his novel, and read the last chapter. The characters were strangers. He'd forgotten why he had them do the odd things they did. His notes on the plot made no sense. He couldn't figure out what he'd had in mind, or how to get back on track. He opened a can of beer, and lit a cigarette. More terrifying than a blank page was having nothing to write.

He went to the corner for a *Press*. The man behind the counter was standing over him when he remembered to put a nickel on the counter. It was a peculiar feeling having to pay for a paper, *his* paper. He couldn't say he liked it.

The paper looked the same. He'd considered himself the glue that held the *Press* together, and was disappointed in a way that it hadn't fallen apart immediately without him. On the split page was a byline he didn't recognize. R. Peter van Pelt was working the murder in Little Egg Harbor. Van Pelt favored the inverted triangle style of newswriting taught in college—the most important facts at the top of the story followed by everything else in declining order of importance, and to hell with the human angle. Lieutenant Day was quoted as saying that his investigators were making progress. One thing van Pelt hadn't learned in college was not to take the police at their word.

The victim remained nameless. Attempts to identify her through fingerprints and dental records had gone nowhere. A police artist's sketch showed a woman of indeterminate age with a dirty face and stringy hair. She was sleepy-eyed, as if she'd been shaken awake and caught on paper before she could get herself together. There was little of the girl on the beach, of the prettiness remaining in death. Jordan blamed the police artist. Police artist struck him as an oxymoron. It was a funny notion that he could have built into a feature illustrated with a rogues gallery of unfortunates and wanted men. Too bad he hadn't thought of it sooner. McAvoy would have squirmed at poking fun at the cops. Readers would have loved it.

The dead woman's clothes, according to Lieutenant Day, were available in hundreds of modestly priced stores throughout the state. No description accompanied the story. Another thing they didn't teach in journalism school was a reporter's responsibility in keeping the police on their toes. Day was a cheapskate with the facts. Jordan would have reminded him that the *Press* had thousands of sharp-eyed readers, any one of whom might remember the clothing and the girl wearing it. He'd cultivated other sources in the state police and coroner's office who loved to talk. His man at the morgue could be bribed for a look inside an evidence locker or refrigerator unit. Jordan figured that McAvoy was already eating his heart out over letting him go.

Dr. Melvin had ruled that the victim died of strangulation. Several articles of clothing had been "introduced" into her throat. Her undergarments were "disturbed" by her killer, and she had been "ravished." Jordan would have used raped. McAvoy preferred attacked, but would go with criminally assaulted. Jordan re-read the article to see what he'd missed. Trying to learn what had happened on the beach at Little Egg Harbor, he couldn't get beyond van Pelt's sorry treatment of the language.

There was boilerplate from the police asserting that they were working with the coroner's office to have the victim identified. Vague mention of promising leads were a tip-off that the investigation was marking time. Jordan had been cultivating an assistant DA who would tell him what was really going on. What he'd do, he'd call him, and— What he would do was try to forget about the case. The murder wasn't his. Nothing was.

From the day he'd gone to work on the *Press*, Jordan's life had stopped being his own. He was a slave bringing home a decent salary, a night differential, and eight cents for every mile he used his car in pursuit of the news. He lived near the ocean, but didn't have time for sailing, rarely went to the beach when he wasn't called there for a look at a corpse. He showed up on the boardwalk to cover fires, and at nightclubs when he was assigned to provide free publicity. Atlantic City was a great place to visit. Unfortunately he was stuck here. It was one cliché he wouldn't blame van Pelt for using.

He had all the time in the world now. But the beaches were cold, the ocean made him seasick. He didn't fish. On his nightstand was a stack of books he'd been meaning to read, but writers who finished what they started gave him a sour feeling. Tuesday nights he liked to sit in a bar watching Milton Berle on the television. But it was too much time to kill by the hour.

He called the *Bulletin*. Flynn wasn't expected till the end of the week. He drove to New York to catch Charles Mingus in the Village, and returned to Atlantic City after dawn. Two nights later he was back for Billie Holiday on Fifty-second Street, and to leave samples of his writing at the *Mirror*, the *Herald Tribune*, the *Telegram*, and the *Brooklyn Eagle*. Everyone had heard of the

Press reporter who wore out a new Chevy in a year getting drunk every night on Third Avenue. Jordan put no faith in those stories. His Hudson—a better car—wasn't going to last six months.

His name was mud at the big city newspapers where he wanted to work. He wouldn't be caught dead in the backwaters that hadn't been reached by word of his disgrace. He tried the *Bulletin* again. Flynn picked up, and said, "I was beginning to wonder if you were still alive."

"Makes two of us," Jordan said. "What did you think of my— of the death house piece?"

"You spoiled my readers," Flynn said. "They expect everything flying out of my typewriter to be as good."

Flynn wasn't a professional Irishman. Jordan was put off by his easy flattery. "You heard—?"

"I just got back from three days in Punxsutawney. The whistlepig died. They enticed a successor from his lair, and I was there for his investiture. In those precincts there's not much to talk about other than the order of sciuridae. You were the second leading topic of conversation among visiting journalists."

"Then you know why I'm calling."

"You're searching for a new place to collect a paycheck," Flynn said, "and would be happier moving up rather than down."

"Put in the word for me with your editors," Jordan said. "Tell them the kind of reporter they'll be getting."

"They already know. I don't have enough influence to change their mind."

"Everyone who's ever worked on a paper does what I did."

"They don't all get caught," Flynn said. "I won't step out on a limb for someone who's going to saw it off under my feet."

"I remember something different when you were asking me to cover for you in Trenton."

"Haven't you made empty promises to get a reluctant source to give you what you need?"

How did you answer without admitting the *Bulletin* would

be crazy to want you? "Rita Snyder can snap her fingers, and I'll have a job just like that."

"She isn't a finger-snapper," Flynn said.

"I'll ask her."

"She wants to forget you," Flynn said. "It won't do to remind her. Fisher showed up drunk. He stumbled around the stage, and called her a tub when we walked out on him. Rita blamed me. You more than me for getting us a ringside table."

Jordan went to the beach, where he froze. He toured the boardwalk till he got blisters. He hung around bars when Milton Berle wasn't on the TV. He put down his novel, and worked on a short story that he threw away. He wrote two others as bad as the first. He learned that he didn't have a suicidal bone in his body.

The New York papers turned him down. He tried the *Post* and the *News*, and stayed in the city to hear Miles Davis at a joint off Sheridan Square. His mailbox was stuffed when he came home. A letter from Turner Men's Group stood out from the bills and the junk.

The way his luck was running, it had to be a rejection. But the manuscript came back with a rejection, didn't it? He dropped the envelope twice before he got it open, and a check for two-hundred, eighty-four dollars and sixty cents sailed to the floor.

Jordan kissed it. He wanted to show it to his friends, to frame it, but most of all to spend it. Until he lived off his earnings he wasn't ready to call himself a writer.

He phoned Pelfrey at *Real Detective*, who said, "Congratulations, welcome to the staff."

"When are you going with my story? I'll need to pick up a dozen copies."

"I'll put you down for two dozen," Pelfrey said. "It's how we maintain circulation, selling magazines to new writers. We've got you scheduled for March *Sensational Detective*, one of our best-selling titles."

"It's a long time to wait to see my name in print."

"March *Sensational* goes to the printer at Christmas. It hits the stands in January. When can I expect another piece from you? The body on the beach sounds promising."

"The cops are spinning their wheels. It'll be a while."

"You shouldn't have trouble finding good cases in South Jersey."

"I'm not with the *Press* any longer."

"You didn't quit when the check arrived?" Pelfrey said. "Let me give you some advice: Don't put money down on a new house just yet. There will be times when you curse the killers for not working hard enough for you."

"I'll go easy on them, I promise."

It bothered him that Pelfrey didn't want to know why he'd left the *Press*. Was *Real Detective* so hungry for copy that they accepted stories from anyone, no questions asked?

"Read all the papers in your neck of the woods, and clip the promising murders," Pelfrey said. "The Palmer case is one of the best first stories I've published. You have a future with us, if you want it."

"I'll start looking."

When he was a *Press*man, he'd barely glanced at the sub-urban dailies, didn't think of them as serious competition, if he thought of them at all. Coming back from the corner with a stack of them under his arm, he felt ashamed, the way he would bringing home dirty books.

They were lousy papers. He hated to consider that he might end up working on one. The coverage was terrible. Reporters stinted on the news in favor of garden parties, and bridge club meetings, and the churches. The only mention of murder was a squib in the *Margate Light*, a couple of graphs from the United Press on the investigation in Little Egg Harbor that was going nowhere.

It wasn't just killers that he faulted for not doing their job.

Potential victims were not making themselves easy prey. The cops had been struck blind. Poisonings were misdiagnosed as tummy aches, cases going begging because corpses remained undiscovered under freshly poured patios. Bumblers were preventing him from making a living.

He filled a thermos and drove south, stopping for the papers in every town. At Cape May he turned back along Delaware Bay. He steered clear of the police stations and newsrooms where he had no contacts. His interest in bloody murder would mark him as a suspicious character to the cops. Enterprising reporters would hear him out, then pitch Pelfrey themselves. If he learned of a good story, he'd introduce himself. In the meantime it was enough to find out what was going on.

At Dennisville he went into Cumberland County. The isolated farm country was an unlikely setting for skillful homicide. In the sticks husbands bludgeoned cheating wives and were stabbed in their sleep by them. Jealous boyfriends gunned down love rivals on the high school playing field. Straight razors mediated craps games in the migrant camps. Killers lacked the ingenuity that *Real Detective* demanded.

A wife-killing outside Vineland seemed promising. But with an arrest barely two days after the body was found, it failed Pelfrey's criterion for a *Real Detective* case. Jordan wanted Pelfrey to love his stories, to put them on the cover with his name in 96-point type. *Real Detective* was the springboard to… he didn't know what. But he wouldn't spring far as just another contributor. He took a pass.

In May's Landing a third grade teacher was charged with sprinkling arsenic in her husband's lunchpail. Jordan studied pictures of a bottle blonde in handcuffs and a torpedo bra. Not his type. But he'd make the readers fall in love with her, and break their hearts. He'd make Pelfrey love her, too. Love him.

The trial could go on for weeks before ending in a hung jury or acquittal. He'd sat in enough dreary courtrooms when he was collecting a check from the *Press* to know he didn't want to be in one on his own time. If there was a conviction, he'd write the story from clips. It was cheating—but Pelfrey hadn't said it wasn't kosher. He didn't anticipate a moral crisis.

Every hour he wasn't at the typewriter was an hour that he wasn't making a buck. He hurried back to Vineland. At the circulation department of the *Times* he bought the back issues for the last couple of weeks. The wife-killing violated Pelfrey's three-day rule between the murder and arrest. The pacing was sloppy, but Jordan gave the husband an A-minus for inventiveness, a solid B for the elements of high melodrama. Together they would craft a memorable story.

He called Pelfrey without reversing the charges. "I've got one for you," he said.

"Convince me."

"I'm in the boondocks," he said. "Manumuskin. The suspect's the undertaker here, Elmer Lambert—38, ex-B-17 pilot, POW, double Purple Heart winner. The victim's his better half."

"Why'd he do it?"

"I couldn't tell you. The cops are playing it close to the vest."

"Find out, and call me back."

"The story's not about why," Jordan said.

"They're all about why."

"This one's about how," Jordan said. "The Lamberts lived on Main Street next to the funeral parlor. When he wasn't embalming a client or burying him, Lambert liked to sit in the living room with the papers. Never drew the shades. People on the street would see a sober man in a dark suit content in his own home, and know God's in his heaven and all's right with the world. Never gave anybody a smile. But if they dropped dead they knew he'd take good care of them."

"How'd he kill her?"

"Used a .38 he found in a client's pocket."

"Undertaker's generally a cold fish," Pelfrey said. "I'd be shocked, the wife's anything to look at."

"Just listen," Jordan said. "Lambert told her they were getting stale, and how did a weekend at the shore sound? It must've sounded good because one morning her body came in with the tide at Ocean Grove. Lambert wasn't seen there with her, but I don't have to tell you he was the automatic suspect. He told the cops he hated the shore, had never been within a hundred miles of Ocean Grove, that his wife had wanted to get away a few days on her own, and while she was being shot he was home with the papers. He had plenty of witnesses to back him up. Twenty or a couple dozen passersby on Main saw him on his couch the same time Mrs. Lambert was in Ocean Grove. Too many alibi witnesses to argue with. Lambert was officially a non-suspect."

Pelfrey said, "So?"

"Thirty-six hours later the cops got a tip he'd killed somebody else."

"The wife's boyfriend?" Pelfrey said. "Lambert's? The story can use one."

"There's no boyfriend," Jordan said, "for which I apologize. Lambert had been seen outside the cemetery with a man's body slung over his shoulder. He was pleasant when the cops came to see him again, said they'd made a natural mistake. He hadn't murdered anyone this time either, just brought a corpse to the graveyard to bury it. The cops asked if he carried all his customers on his shoulder. Wouldn't it be easier to drive them in his hearse? Lambert stopped being pleasant, and said he wanted a lawyer.

"A fresh grave had been dug in the cemetery. The D.A. got a court order to open it."

"And?" Pelfrey said. "Who'd they find? Judge Crater? Amelia Earhart?"

"A mahogany casket," Jordan said, "belonging to the woman who was buried there. Stretched out on the lid was a clothes dummy in a black suit with a moustache and a wig parted on the right like Lambert. Lambert had dressed the dummy in old clothes, and painted his face on it the way he restored stiffs who went through a windshield. The same dummy he left on the couch before taking his wife to Ocean Grove. What do you think?"

Pelfrey said, "That was awful clever of him."

"You know what they say about truth being stranger than fiction."

"It's bunk," Pelfrey said. "If truth were strange, I'd go to Hollywood and get rich selling story ideas to the studios. Truth is bland, forgettable, and often ridiculous. It's the work of amateurs with spare imagination. That's why scriptwriters make the money they do. A story like the one you told me almost never reaches my desk. How much did you make up?"

"I have the clips in front of me," Jordan said. "Every fact is documented."

Pelfrey said, "Pictures?"

"I'll make some calls," Jordan said. "Let me tell you what else I'm looking at. A young schoolteacher in May's Landing poisoned her husband. She's been married before, and both previous husbands died under suspicious circum—"

"Nice-looking woman?" Pelfrey said.

He stopped for sliders, ate them reading through the Lambert clips for ideas. The case didn't require ideas beyond a good opening sentence. After that he'd get out of the way.

He got home at ten, and went straight to the typewriter. At three, when he pushed back his chair, he had to force himself not to drive the story to New York. He wanted to be there when Pelfrey apologized for doubting him. What he didn't want was

Pelfrey expecting door-to-door service for every case. He put the manuscript in an envelope, and went to bed.

He couldn't sleep. He turned on the lights, and had a look at the May's Landing clips. The hook was staring him in the face— the pretty teacher's hard-working husband wracked with stomach pains as doctors struggled to diagnose the mystery ailment. Other angles might be more effective, but he wasn't going to knock himself out trying to find one. Clever plotting was not the mark of a *Real Detective* staffer. Fast typing was.

After the principal characters took the stage, he didn't know where the story was going. Investigators hadn't revealed how they'd gotten on to the wife, or what she had told them. The detective work would remain under wraps until the witnesses gave evidence from the stand. If the testimony wasn't credible, where the story was going was into the garbage.

Jordan chain-smoked as he filled around the holes in his case. More than sleep he needed to write. In Princeton, John O'Hara, his literary hero, was up every night at the typewriter. O'Hara produced underrated art, and Adam Jordan was churning out copy for the pulps that no serious reader would see. He liked to think that what he was doing could also be called writing. That was where the similarities ended.

He quit beating himself up, and concentrated on his story. By six he'd gone as far as the facts would take him. A couple of hours of sleep were under his belt when he left for the post office. He came back with the papers, determined to make slow work of them. With nothing left to write he had a long day to kill.

Van Pelt was reporting that the state police had identified the Little Egg Harbor strangling victim. Twenty-two-year-old Susannah Chase, originally from Manalapan, had been a wait-ress at a Brigantine restaurant, the Rusty Scupper. There were typical quotes from family members devastated by news of her death. Not much else. Accompanying the short piece were photos of a gorgeous girl in a waitress' outfit, high school cheer-leader's uniform, and looking serious but no less attractive in cap and gown.

Susannah Chase's name had not come to the attention of the police without other facts. That was not the way investigations progressed. The cops were sitting on information, and van Pelt was too lazy or inept to pry it loose. Jordan looked out at a gray sky promising sleet. Before the roads turned treacherous he'd find out what else the troopers had learned.

The Absecon barracks looked like nothing so much as the suburban home of an unusually patriotic family. It was some-what larger than other houses in the area, red brick at street level and aluminum siding on the upper floor. The stars and stripes and New Jersey flag flew above a grassy triangle edged in gravel. On a petrified log a brass plaque was inscribed with the names of town residents who had fought in every military conflict since the Battle of Trenton. Jordan ran his fingers down a shiny roster from the Second World War, lingering at the asterisks awarded to those who had died in combat.

No one asked what his business was. Everyone knew him. Outside the basement lockup he had the run of the building. Security wasn't tight because there was no call for it. It was a theory of Jordan's that troopers who screwed up in sensitive postings were stashed out of the way in Absecon where nothing happened and it was impossible to resuscitate their careers.

He went along the corridor nodding to officers who didn't deliberately avoid him. From time to time the brass barred him from the station. Threats of legal action, and editorials he scripted himself, had forced a reversal of the bans. The heav-iest burden that democracy put upon the state police was having a reporter look over their shoulder. Adam Jordan in particular.

Day was in the communications room, watching the teletype. When the clattering stopped he tore off the paper, and saw Jordan looking in.

"What's new, Lieutenant?"

"We talked to the papers yesterday."

Jordan remained in the doorway. All he'd meant was hello, and Day had taken it the wrong way. How did you misinterpret hello? "I was busy with something else."

"Watch your rear. The other fellow from the *Press* has the right stuff."

"No hard questions?"

"Good questions," Day said. "He's after your job."

"I have one or two he forgot to ask. Where did you get Miss Chase's name?"

"It's *Mrs.* Chase."

Jordan made a note. "Where—?"

"You'll have everything when we're ready to give it out."

"I can't hang a story on changing Miss to Mrs."

Day held the printout between his hands as though it were a royal proclamation, and then he looked up. "You've done it with less."

From anyone else it would have prompted a smile.

"My next stop's the Rusty Scupper," Jordan said. "My readers are entitled to the stuff you're holding back. If it comes as an exclusive, they'll get the idea you're not trying."

"Does *everyone* tell you what an SOB you are?"

"I thought we were friends, Lieutenant. Did I spell your name wrong?"

"I can't stop you from going." Day went to his office with Jordan on his heels.

"Give it a shot."

Day hesitated before opening his door and letting Jordan in ahead of him. "The victim was ID'd by her husband."

"What took him?"

"The couple had stopped living together, but they talked several times a week. When he couldn't reach her, he went to her place on North Carolina Avenue."

It was good information that Jordan didn't think he'd have gotten at the restaurant. He looked at Day as though Day was wasting his time.

"The papers were on the doorstep...the mailbox was full... he let himself in, but didn't see anything out of the ordinary... till he noticed the drawing of the dead girl in the *Press*."

The pauses were becoming longer, invitations for Jordan to pick up his marbles and go. He pulled up a chair. "The husband have a first name?"

"In a few days I'll call back all the reporters for another heads-up."

"All of us are here now," Jordan said. "Van Pelt was pinch-hitting."

Day gave him a sour look. Jordan decided that van Pelt was entitled to part.

"Susannah Chase's husband is Hub Chase."

"Should I know him?"

"He does some pinch-hitting, too. For the Newark Bears. He's an outfielder, a .300 hitter with some power."

"You like him for killing her?"

Day shook his head.

"How come? The husband's always guilty till proven innocent. Estranged husbands are the gold standard of homicide suspects."

"He was with his club at the time of the murder."

"This much I do know about minor league baseball," Jordan said. "The season ended two months ago."

"The Bears were barnstorming with the Havana Sugar Kings. Hub's teammates, coaches, manager, a batboy, several batting practice pitchers, and about two hundred thousand fans will swear he was playing ball in Cuba while his wife was getting herself strangled. He says he still loved her. If it's okay with you, I'm going to give him the benefit of the doubt."

Jordan scribbled in his notebook. When he looked up, Day was watching the door.

"I talked to the Chase broad's sister," Riley said as he came in. "Nice piece of tail, but she doesn't have anything we don't—" His expression changed several times before settling on a sorry look that was entirely for Jordan. "What's he doing here?"

"Don't mind him," Day said. "I'm tossing him a few bones."

"Yeah, but why?"

"It's the price for having him say nice things about us in the *Press*."

"You won't get much," Riley said. "He doesn't work there any more. You didn't hear they canned him for making stuff up?"

Day's hand slapped against his side. To Jordan it almost looked like he was going for his gun. Not to shoot the messenger.

"I'm covering the case for another publication," Jordan said.

"What other?" Day said.

"It doesn't make a difference. The story's the same."

"Don't tell me what makes a difference to me," Day said.

"*Real Detective* magazine."

"Those rags don't print anything real," Riley said. "They're whaddayacallit, fiction."

"I'm just as careful with the facts."

"What's that worth?" Riley said.

"I'm not giving up on a good story because you don't approve of the publication I work for."

"A writer for one of those magazines came through right before the war," Day said. "He picked a young cop's brains on a big murder, and stiffed him for the pictures. It cost the cop his job, and I should know. He was my old man. Get out of my sight before I toss you in a cell."

"This isn't Russia. You can't threaten me."

"It is till I stand corrected. Who's going to read me the First

Amendment riot act now that you don't have the *Press* behind you? A fancypants New York editor?"

Jordan didn't have answers but was ready to argue. Riley hauled him out of his seat with an arm bent behind his back, and he was waltzed down the corridor smoothly and without a lot of pain except when he struggled hard. Outside, in the fresh air, it didn't seem like a bad argument to have lost.

CHAPTER 3

Jordan swung back around Atlantic City for the road through
the salt marshes to Brigantine. Summer's grassy tangle had decayed into muck, and he lit up against the rotten egg smell. On
the horizon, the picturesque Brigantine lighthouse, erected as
a tourist draw, warned the new money toward Cape Cod and
the east end of Long Island. Jordan, without money of any
kind, shied away from the sticky bungalows thrown up in the
pre-Depression boom and reshuffled by the mortgage compa-
nies ever since.

He kept the Hornet pointed down the center of oceanfront
streets where the pavement showed beneath drifting sand. The
Rusty Scupper, in the former Brigantine casino, looked to be a
greasy spoon with airs. The stop sign at the corner was the best
reason to stop. Half a dozen cars in back seemed too many for
late November, made him wonder if everyone was looking into
murder till the beaches opened.

He got as far as the cigarette machine before a woman poked
her head out of the kitchen and said, "Sit anywhere, Hon." He
followed her back through the swinging doors while she looked
at him as if he'd tied a handkerchief over his face and shown a
gun. "Anywhere," she said, "does not include here."

Flashing his press card, something he never did when he
was working on the paper, he felt like a high school kid buying
beer with a phony license.

"I don't suppose you're the restaurant critic," the woman said.
She grabbed a Pyrex pot, and brought Jordan to the booth with
the best lighthouse view. "I'm Horty Miller."

Her hair was the color of the coffee she put in his cup as he began adding cream. He couldn't guess her age. She wasn't old, a tired woman who had quit being young when she ran out of steam. She lit a Herbert Tareyton from his Lucky, and coughed trying to fill her lungs. "I was beginning to think no one gave a damn Suzie's dead," she said.

When he was a young reporter Jordan hated interviewing the friends of murder victims. Homicide's collateral damage, they'd suffered enough without being laid bare. But most wanted to talk, to set the record straight about a loved one caught up in a horrific crime, or else to cry on the public's shoulder. The others he peppered with questions sharpened in previous tragedies to elicit the heart-tugging narratives his readers demanded.

"Did you know Mrs. Chase well?"

"I'm sorry. Who?"

"I asked if you were good friends with Mrs.—"

"Are we talking about the same person?"

"How many Susannah Chases are there at the Rusty Scupper?"

"Ours wasn't married." Horty Miller puffed her cigarette, and waited for Jordan to admit his mistake.

Jordan didn't make mistakes with questions. Those that went off-track brought answers that didn't always make for the stories he tried for, but occasionally provided headlines. He tasted his coffee while he waited for another shoe to drop.

"She never told me about being married," Horty said. "She was a bright girl, Suzie. You wouldn't think she'd forget having a husband."

"She was separated from Mr. Chase."

Horty shook her head. "It wouldn't have helped."

"What wouldn't?"

"Being separated. It's a disqualifier right off the bat, beautiful as she was."

"I don't get you."

"Suzie was in Atlantic City to be Miss America," Horty said. "She was a former Miss Teenage Garden State and Miss Monmouth County. The next step was Miss New Jersey. She wanted to be a dancer, or a flight attendant if that didn't work out for her. Married women aren't allowed into the pageant. If she was ever somebody's wife, she didn't mention it at Rusty's."

"She was working here to support herself while she competed in beauty contests?"

"She was learning to dance, to sing a little, to apply makeup and work on her posture and smile, what they call her presentation. Every waitress, hostess, counter girl, if she's not too bad-looking, the restaurant's just a second job."

Jordan turned around in his seat.

"We're out of beauty contest material at the moment," Horty said. "Girls like those don't fall off trees, you may have noticed. We've got a summer waitress studying shorthand, and two that are starting up a door-to-door skin care business. Suzie was our only Miss America candidate."

"She never let on there might be a husband in the background?"

"Suzie had her share of admirers, and some she was more inclined toward than others. I'd have to see her husband to know she wasn't passing him off as a good friend."

"She had lots of good friends?"

"You saw how she looked."

"Not before she died."

"Her picture ran large in your paper," Horty said. "A girl that looked like her, how bad could she be starving for men?"

"Who were they?"

"Think I kept tabs?"

Jordan shook his head, but said, "Let's say you'd wanted to."

"I'd take notice who picked her up after work, which would be mainly older gents in youngish clothes with promoter written all over them. The line formed on the left."

These were not questions he would have asked working for the *Press*. They were scattershot, and produced answers that weren't useful to a news story. A homicide detective might lead with them. But Ed Pelfrey didn't pay more for solving a case than for writing it from clips. Jordan didn't know what he'd do with the information Horty Miller gave him, but he wanted to hear everything she knew.

"Did you get any names?"

"The state police, they didn't bother here," she said. "How come it's a reporter doing all the asking?"

The question was as good as those he had for her. Her anger wasn't for him. Not too much.

"I don't know that Suzie got all their names, and some she did get, who's to say how real they were? Miss America's that kind of business. You get forty-eight...I almost forgot there's some from the territories...you get that many gorgeous young girls together in their bathing suits that you can make a buck off of in addition to something else you might want from them, names get lost."

"What do you remember of the last time you saw her?"

"I can't tell you exactly what I did last night." Horty poked a finger against the side of her head. "I'm sorry for not being more helpful. I figured when the reporters came, they'd want to know did she like good music and how many kids did she want. They wouldn't need me to break the case."

Jordan nodded. He hadn't thought he'd have to solve the murder either.

"Was there one man in particular interested in her?" he said. "Did she sign with a manager, or tell you someone had made a proposition—a proposition to advance her career?"

"If there was, she kept it to herself."

A girl with a soiled apron over her waitress outfit smiled at Jordan as she tapped Horty on the shoulder.

"We need you in back," she said. "Now. One of the ovens keeps flaming out, and Pasquale, he's ready to quit on the spot."

Jordan sipped his coffee. Horty Miller was wrong about the Rusty Scupper's staff. The girl had his vote for Miss Congeniality.

"Got to go," Horty said to him. "If you want to talk more, come around any time in the next thirty years."

"Thank you for your help, Miss Miller."

"It's Mrs. Miller," she said. "I got made a proposition once, too, to advance my career."

Always in Jordan's mind were the things he planned to do if he ever found time. Now the time was his, and he was afraid of becoming lost in it. A talk with Hub Chase about his late wife might eat up several hours. But if Chase was smart (or at least not flat-out stupid) he was far from Atlantic City, where he would be hounded by the police, and one out-of-work reporter with time on his hands.

Jordan went home for a beer and to type his notes. His handwriting was illegible code, and today he seemed to have forgotten the key. He put together a rough typescript of his conversation with Horty Miller, and then compared the new information to what was in the clips, and studied the pictures that ran with them in the *Press*.

Suzie Chase was too good-looking to be Miss America. Miss Americas were the breed standard for the earnest wholesomeness Jordan believed was best left to kindergarten teachers, homecoming queens, and rodeo cowgirls for whom high-breasted, long-legged sauciness were professional poison. He imagined her as never having an awkward moment or looking less than enticing, from the genus of the magical creatures he'd worshipped in high school, but whose magic ran out on a cold beach at twenty-two. The credit line for all three photos was PixleyPix. Pictures of murder victims usually came from the reporter, who obtained them from the family. He wondered if someone at PixleyPix knew the Chases and could give him a lead to finding Hub.

PixleyPix Photographic Agency, Inc. was in the yellow pages with an address on New York Avenue. On the eighth ring the phone was lifted from the hook. Jordan heard it bounce against a bare floor, and then an unintelligible mutter before, "Pix."

"My name is Adam Jordan. I'm trying to—"

"I know who you are," a man said. "What can I do for you?"

"I don't know who *you* are," Jordan said.

"Charles Pixley."

"I'm following the Chase killing in Little Egg Harbor. Where did you get your pictures of Susannah Chase, Mr. Pixley? Were you acquainted with her?"

"Call me Pix. Actually," he said, "I'm acquainted with Rollo."

"Who?"

"Roland Peter van Pelt," Pixley said, "only don't call him that without putting up your dukes. He's a fair newshound himself. Not as aggressive as you in ratting a story, or what I'd call a literary stylist, but improving. He told me how he got your job. The *Press* gave you a raw deal, Jordan. Even Rollo thinks so."

Jordan didn't care what van Pelt liked to be called, or how to defend against him, or Pixley's opinion of his abilities as a reporter. He didn't care that van Pelt's name put him in a lousy mood, and was very aware of it.

"You haven't answered my questions."

"You didn't let me," Pixley said. "Rollo figured the *Press* would pay well for shots of the dead girl's roommates at their place, and he lobbied to use me instead of a staff shutterbug. The girls were blech. I looked around the apartment, saw the photos, and swiped them. Naturally, they'll be returned—"

"They were credited to you."

"All it means is PixleyPix provided them for the *Press*."

"Do you have others they haven't run?"

"Two," Pixley said. "McAvoy's saving them for the next break in the investigation."

"What are they?"

"One's Mrs. Chase with her husband on their wedding day. Not many people know she was married. I've got her in a white gown with him in his baseball flannels making their vows at home plate. The other is her in a swimsuit. *There's* something to see."

"At a beauty contest?"

"On a beach rubbing suntan oil on her legs. She's not wearing a regular bathing suit," Pixley said, "but one of those skimpy two-piece jobs from France. A bikini." He pronounced it *by-kini*. "You can just about see what she had for breakfast."

"I'd be interested in seeing them."

"I'll bet." Pixley's laugh was good-natured and lascivious.

"How about a preview?"

"My studio isn't far from the *Press*. Drop by some time, and I'll show you what I have."

"Give me ten minutes," Jordan said.

In eight he was a block from the Central Pier, looking up at a cast-iron-front building with Doric colonnades flaking in the salt air. He climbed the stairs to a jumpy Latin beat. On the second story, outside an Arthur Murray dance studio, he stopped to listen to the music and watch a conga line snake around the room.

One floor up a burst of light forced his eyes shut. They opened on a kaleidoscope of various shapes and colors, settling on the most interesting of them, a pink ball above an inverted triangle. As the other shapes fell away the ball was defined as the head of a man, the triangle as his torso. He wasn't a big man, and the large, round head seemed to grow out of his narrow shoulders. The impression was of a baby who had grown in size without changing form, soft features differentiated inconclusively between adult and child, male and female, so the baby had raised a sparse moustache to ease the confusion. Blond hair falling over one eye caused Jordan to think of a Hollywood celebrity, though the name wouldn't come. Reaching carefully for his hand, afraid of crushing it, he was seized in a leathery grip.

"I'm Pix."

"Adam Jordan."

Jordan went ahead inside a loft half the size of a city block, mostly empty space enclosed by white walls, rough wood planking, filthy windows under a stamped tin ceiling. A photographer's screen was the backdrop for a banana split in a sparkling silver bowl. Beside it was a Hasselblad 2¼-inch camera and flash.

"Don't let me interrupt."

"The hard part's done," Pix said. "Shooting ice cream's tricky. You have to construct the perfect sundae, set up the shot, and get the picture before the project turns to slush. This was a commercial job for Paolo's Boardwalk Creamery. Now for the payoff."

A corner of the loft was done up like a small apartment with an unmade bed, bookcase, and kitchen area. He rinsed a couple of spoons in a hand basin and brought one back for Jordan.

"No thanks."

"Sure…?"

Pixley didn't go more than 120-130 pounds. One thing Jordan knew about him. He didn't do many shoots of banana splits.

The walls were hung with his best work. No ice cream, but plenty of artsy landscapes Jordan didn't think were any good, dinghies, terns skimming the waves, and several of the sun coming up over the lighthouse at Barnegat that lacked a shrewd eye. There were portraits of children behaving cutely, and of animals, cats more than dogs, and pretty girls on the boardwalk. No nudes. Jordan looked at the stunted man meticulously blotting whipped cream from a corner of his mouth, and figured if there were any nudes they probably wouldn't be of pretty girls.

A series of Negro children on fire escapes filled the space around two windows, along with Chinese kids cooling off under a fire hydrant and Jewish boys with ritual fringes and sidelocks. One wall was covered by panoramic views of the beach between the Central and Steel Piers. A nighttime scene of a corpse leaking blood onto the running board of a big Packard limousine was more to Jordan's taste.

"Like it?" Pixley asked him.

"It's a great shot."

"Unfortunately it isn't mine." Pix looked up from the silver bowl. "Weegee's my idol."

He faulted Jordan for preferring Weegee's work, and was fishing for an apology. The apology, Jordan thought, should come from Pix for not taking better pictures. Pix was a sly sentimentalist with the camera. His idol's noir sensibilities were absent from the walls.

Jordan had an idea that the little man's personality was a product of the same gene responsible for his grip. His stature and shapelessness were a disguise, but he was too damn peculiar not to be appealing. Watching him put away the banana split like it was steak, Jordan remembered the celebrity whose name had eluded him. Not a movie star—a literary sensation. Truman Capote.

On top of a file cabinet were a jumble of photos which he spread out for Jordan to see. In addition to the three pictures of Suzie Chase that ran in the *Press* were two that were new. Pix had described the wedding scene without mentioning that the man marrying the Chases between the foul lines was an umpire. Hub was a lug with the shoulders of a lumberjack, and a mafia hitman's five o'clock shadow. A hitman crazy for his bride. The shot of Suzie in her bikini went a long way toward explaining why.

Suzie Chase was the wrong kind of beautiful. Jordan knew that she would never have made it to Miss America, probably gone no higher than a Miss New Jersey runner-up. She wasn't what the organizers wanted to parade before the public as a queen. She exemplified something that was not regal—was, in fact, the opposite—the blatant objective of any competition among beautiful women that would interest Jordan. If it were up to him, every contestant would be Suzie Chase. Pix handed him a magnifying glass to examine the picture of the girl in the tiny swimsuit.

"What do you think?"

"You know what I'm thinking," Jordan said.

"She's dead, don't forget."

"I saw her dead. I'm not thinking about her dead." Jordan frowned at Pix, who couldn't suppress a smile. Invited to ogle a murder victim, he'd been set up to play the necrophile.

Pixley looked back as though he'd been misunderstood. "I'm glad you see it my way."

Jordan didn't know which way that was.

"What a waste," Pix said.

Jordan didn't take the bait. "How'd you get the shot?"

"Stole it—it's part of the job. I've cut head shots out of high school yearbooks, swiped the only photo a seventeen-year-old widow had of her husband killed at Inchon. I could have had more of Mrs. Chase if I wanted to make a pig of myself. Like I told you, these will be returned."

"Did the roommates talk to you about her?"

"I was there for pictures. I posed the other girls in the kitchen to make them comfortable with me. After that, I had the run of the place."

"Where are the photos?"

"I threw out the negatives without developing them," Pix said. "They aren't pretty girls. Not bright either. Cows—dairy cows. They didn't know Susannah Chase was married, and accused Rollo of spreading lies. Those kind of girls."

Jordan wondered what made him an authority on girls.

"Do you know anything about Hub?"

"Rollo's seen him play. He says he's a natural hitter with a short, sweet stroke."

"Before you return the photos of his wife," Jordan said, "make another set of prints. Girls like her, they don't—"

"Fall off trees?"

"Get murdered every day."

"I should hope not." Pix went back to the banana split. When he finished, Jordan watched him lick the bowl. "What are the chances you'll get to write the case?"

"It depends on the cops."

"It isn't fair a twenty-two-year-old girl is dead for being beautiful," Pix said. "Is there something—anything you can do to help them find her killer?"

"You've got ice cream on your nose," Jordan said.

"I've got one from the Pine Barrens," Jordan said. "Am I poaching on someone else's territory?"

"His tough luck if you are," Pelfrey said. "Shoot."

"The Barrens are a million acres of wilderness smack in the middle of New Jersey that might as well be West Virginia. The locals have been cut off since colonial times. You've heard about the Jukes and Kallikaks the scientists studied for the effects of inbreeding?"

"What have they got to do with murder?" Pelfrey said.

"I'm giving you local color."

"The hell with color," Pelfrey said. "Who's dead?"

"A cranberry grower, name of A.B. Tyler. He lived in a shack his great-grandfather had put up on stilts by his bog. When berries weren't in season he got by as a trapper and a hunter.

"Tyler was thirty-seven when he married," Jordan went on. "His bride was fifteen. A.B. was content with his berries and his trap lines. When Mrs. Tyler complained, told him she wanted to step out, he took to clouting her. At least that's what the lawyer says."

"You haven't told me about the killing yet, and I know who did it."

"I can have the cops scratching their head before they get onto her," Jordan said.

"Mrs. Tyler anything to look at?"

"I'd go without pictures of the suspect," Jordan said.

"Strike two."

"Let me finish," Jordan said. "Mrs. Tyler had a young man on the side in Wading River. When she began shirking her matrimonial responsibilities, A.B. slapped her around more than usual. They were all alone in the woods, no cops, nearest neighbors miles away. Mrs. Tyler decided the prudent thing was to kill A.B., and make it look like something else."

"What something else? An accident?"

"Act of God."

"Keep religion out of your stories," Pelfrey said, "unless one of the principals is of the cloth."

"October's harvest time," Jordan said. "The growers flood the bogs to loose the berries from the bushes. Then they rake them up and pack them off to the Ocean Spray co-op. It's backbreaking work, leaves them bone-tired.

"A.B. came home from the bog one night and threw himself down on the bed. When Mrs. Tyler heard snoring, she cracked his head with a skillet, and looped a clothesline around his throat till he quit breathing. Mrs. Tyler is not a large woman. She couldn't carry her husband out of the shack to bury him in the woods, couldn't even move him out of bed. What she did, she built a fire under him, made it look like he'd been smoking in bed. She figured the flames would burn up the cabin, and destroy any evidence of murder, and she'd be in Wading River when news of her husband's unfortunate death caught up to her."

Pelfrey said, "But?"

"Did I mention that A.B. had flooded his bog? He must have had a seepage problem, because some of the water ran off into a depression under the shack, and collected there.

"When Mrs. Tyler saw the place going up in smoke, she cleared out without looking back. What she didn't take into account," Jordan said, "was the fire burning through the floor. Cops found the bed in the water under the shack with A.B. toasted on one side, and with rope marks around his neck and his brains out the top of his head. The widow's staring down a life sentence."

"Twenty years tops," Pelfrey said. "New Jersey's a progressive state. She's still a kid."

"Getting around the fact that Mrs. A.B. Tyler is not a handsome woman, what I have in mind is a compelling love triangle story. Are you interested?"

"You'll need pictures of the cabin, the victim, and some cops," Pelfrey said. "Don't bother about the suspect, if she's the dog you say she is. Describe her as being unconventionally beautiful."

"I'd be lying."

"You'd be exercising good judgment. The readers trust that beauty is in the eye of the beholder—namely ours. Otherwise, we wouldn't have what to fill our books. Ever get to New York, Jordan?"

"When Billie Holiday's on Fifty-second Street, or Bird—Charlie Parker is."

"I like your work. Next time you're in town, come by the office. Lunch on you. Meanwhile, stop wasting time on the phone. I'm dying for copy."

Jordan called Pix Pixley, told him to get the shots.

CHAPTER 4

In the prison movies that were Morris Wing's favorites before he went away the gates swung shut with a resounding clang whenever a convict was let out of stir. For sixteen-and-two-thirds years Wing had been waiting for that sound at his back. But after breakfast on his release date he was brought through the administration building to an exit as inauspicious as a crap-house door. What he heard were hinges that needed oil. The warden was not there to remind him to keep his nose clean. Not a single guard shouted *See you soon*.

Beyond the shadow of the walls the river ran clear and blue. There was never a time, glimpsing the Hudson through the bars, that Wing hadn't dreamed of crashing out. How he would make good on his escape was not detailed. He saw himself in the water, swept along in the current. Wing's dreams were short on specifics until he was in New York with a knife in his pocket.

The old bus was one of the few things on the street that looked the same. The sleek cars without running boards and headlight cowlings were designed for the people in sharp clothes going around with a spring in their step, a far cry from the Great Depression, when Wing was sent up. He was nineteen then. Nearly middle-aged now, he felt old. Little in this new world seemed as it should be, least of all himself. The only thing that hadn't changed was his hatred for the man who'd ruined his life.

Two cons from Wing's block sat at window seats and pressed their face against the glass. Wing shut his eyes. He didn't want to be distracted by new things. The way he figured it, the bus ride was the first leg on a round trip. The new things would create appetites that would frustrate him when he was on the inside again.

Wing was first off the bus at the terminal near Times Square. The newsstands were crammed with girlie magazines in full color. Flipping through one, he was surprised by how much skin they showed. A redhead with huge jugs was on the cover, and when you unfolded her picture in the center you even got a look at her nipples. Wing replaced the magazine in the rack. Big jugs were something he'd struggled to forget about in prison. No sense in stoking an appetite for them either.

Real Detective had gone modern, too. Painted covers of jewel thieves in evening attire had given way to photos of molls in tight sweaters. The pictures looked like news shots, but Wing was doubtful. Sweater girls didn't need guns to make a killing. He opened a copy to the contents page. Although the editorial offices had moved uptown, the name at the top was still Ed Pelfrey.

"This ain't the library, mac," someone said. "Buy it, or give it a rest."

Wing looked up at a newsdealer in a *Long Island Star-Journal* apron, gave him a slit-eyed stare fashioned after the old movies and distilled on the yard. The man turned away in a hurry to take five pennies from a sailor who needed Clorets.

Times Square had become more of what it was before. In a store with French decks and loaded dice and handcuffs and braided whips and stilettos in the window Wing asked to see a switchblade knife. The mechanism wasn't smooth; *Made in Japan* was stamped on the handle. He tried a gravity blade, flicking the steel till he found one with a nice feel. Then he put his release money, a hundred dollar bill, on the counter.

"Knife's $2.98," the clerk said. "You don't have nothing smaller?"

Wing snapped his wrist, and the blade locked into place with a soft click. "How'd you like to be smaller?" he said.

❖

Pelfrey had been blue-penciling stories since 8:30, and his head hurt. Few of his writers were writers in any real sense, and he had to re-work each sentence between the double-spaced lines of copy. Pelfrey did not take coffee breaks, or leave the office for lunch. Nights, holidays, and on weekends he brought home articles to edit. *Real Detective* had cost him his marriage and most chances at happiness, but he was too busy to think about it. A minute away from work had to be made up another time, and he didn't have a moment to spare.

Several times a year, when he was hurting for copy, Pelfrey named a cop as *Real Detective*'s police officer of the month. The award—a cheap plaque from a Hell's Kitchen trophy shop—was useful in getting tight-lipped detectives to open up about cases that stymied his reporters. Lieutenant Tom Podgorny of the Poughkeepsie, New York police was due in the office at noon. Pelfrey would have to write Podgorny's story under deadline, which was making his headache worse.

"Hi there," Pelfrey said when he noticed a stranger standing over his desk. "It's a privilege to meet you."

"So now it's a privilege?" Morris Wing said.

Pelfrey rarely met a cop with a sense of humor, but the man watching him work struck him as funny. His deadpan was better even than George S. Kaufman's, which was cracking up everyone who owned a TV.

"It's not every day a hero comes to visit us."

"So I'm a hero, too?"

Not that funny after you heard him twice, and the lack of expression was creepy. Podgorny had been asked to wear his uniform so a photographer could get some shots. Instead he had on a chalk-stripe suit with broad lapels twenty years out of style, a dingy shirt, no tie, and cracked leather shoes. Either he was working a plainclothes detail on skid row, or he was headed there on his own.

"The readers say you are. You took a vicious killer off the streets."

It wasn't just the ugly clothes and poker face. The man was wrong for a cop, gray and sullen in a job that demanded personality.

"You don't know who I am, do you?"

"Why don't you tell me," Pelfrey said.

"Morris Wing."

"Doesn't ring a bell."

Wing shut the door.

"Leave it open, if you don't mind," Pelfrey said.

Wing kicked the doorstop under the door. "You told the world everything about me, and you didn't know one damn thing."

"When was that?"

"Six thousand, a hundred and ninety-one days ago."

Pelfrey knew *what* Morris Wing was. Murderers he'd covered when he started on the magazine in the 1930s were being paroled in bunches. Wing wasn't the first to show up at *Real Detective* holding a twenty-year grudge.

"I don't remember you. Six thousand days is a long time."

"You're telling me?" Wing said. "I'll refresh your memory. I killed Becky Smart."

Pelfrey had written the story himself, a case that stood alone for the brutality directed at a child. Rebecca Smart was twelve, the daughter of one of the last commercial fishermen in the Bronx, when her body was found in a derelict tugboat in the mudflats off City Island. She had been stabbed, strangled, raped, subjected to an encyclopedic compendium of sexual tortures. The jury came back eleven to one for the chair. The holdout, a nun, insisted that the youthful defendant should be spared so that he would know God's love. Pelfrey had chided her for being a bleeding heart. Morris Wing was not interested in God's love and had not been sent to a place where it would find him.

"What do you want?" Pelfrey said.

"Those six thousand, one hundred ninety-one days I spent in hell, I want them back."

"Get out," Pelfrey said, "or your parole officer's going to hear you're harassing me."

"I did the whole beef," Wing said. "If I'm returned for another six thousand days, or sixty thousand, I can do the time."

Wing flicked the blade out of his knife, and pushed it back inside the handle, flicked it out, pushed it back. Pelfrey didn't believe Wing was going to hurt him. Morris Wing wanted to make him sweat, to hear the unscrupulous editor beg forgiveness from the simple child-murderer he'd slandered. Watching him play with the knife, Pelfrey wondered if he would be rid of Wing sooner if he peed in his pants. It wouldn't be hard to do.

He got up from his chair, and Wing pushed him down. The first he realized he'd been cut was when he felt blood running down his neck. The knife shot out again. Pain in his cheek was immediate. Pelfrey raised his hand as Wing swiped at him, and the blade pierced the flesh under his thumb. The next jab sliced through his sleeve. As blood erupted from his arm he shoved the desk at Wing, who danced around it and slashed his other cheek.

The Smart case came back to Pelfrey as precise in its details as if he'd written it the other day. The coroner had compared the killing to the Chinese death of a hundred cuts. When defense counsel pointed out that the Chinese had disposed of their enemies with ten times as many small wounds the coroner had testified that Becky Smart's killer was neither patient nor light-handed, inflicting ninety-five serious punctures before severing the carotid artery.

Pelfrey heard shouting, the different voices not coming from the same place. What got his attention were the loudest shouts, which were his. On the other side of the door the editorial assistant, Mary Glenny, demanded to know what was going on.

The door rattled, and several thumps might have been Mary throwing her shoulder against the wood. It was hard to sort out the sounds, impossible to see with his blood in his eyes.

Pelfrey had a good idea that he was dying, and was concerned that *Real Detective* would screw up the story. How he would play it was with a first person account by a staffer under Mary Glenny's byline, and a cover line above the title. He'd begin with Wing turning up unannounced at the office demanding to talk, then flash back to his trial and the years in prison, suggest an enigmatic character, somewhat sympathetic, before revealing the gruesome facts about the killing of Becky Smart, and tying up things with Wing having his revenge.

The thumping got louder. The door inched away from the jamb and skidded open. It wasn't Mary Glenny who stumbled inside but a stranger taking in the scene with wild eyes that made Morris Wing seem tranquil in comparison. There was a gun in his hand, and he was looking to use it. As the situation became clear he turned the gun around, and hammered Wing's head with the butt, hit him three or four times before the knife dropped and Wing went down. Stepping over Wing, he clamped his hand around Pelfrey's throat.

"Don't move," he said. "It makes the blood pump faster."

"Who are you?" Mary Glenny said.

Pelfrey held still as the stranger compressed his neck wound. He didn't have the strength for anything else. Drifting in and out of consciousness, he heard the man tell Mary, "Tom Podgorny."

"Who?" Mary said.

"Your hero for the month."

"You don't look bad," Lou Segar said. "If it weren't for the IV, and that tube in your nose, and all the stitches, no one would know anything was wrong. How do you feel?"

Pelfrey reached for the control on the railing of the bed, and raised himself into a semi-upright position. "Dead."

"What I'm telling you," Segar said, "is that you're not."

Segar was *Real Detective*'s managing editor, number two on the four-man staff. If Pelfrey did die, Segar would take over the editor's chair with a large increase in salary. Pelfrey was moved by Segar's feelings for him, but answered with a grunt. *Real Detective* staffers dealt with too much tragedy to admit being moved by it, even when it was their own.

"You left most of your blood in the office," Segar said. "The doctors were surprised you had any left when you got here."

"Change the subject, Lou."

Segar dropped a large envelope on the bed. "Here's the stuff you asked for."

Pelfrey shook out a few manuscripts and a smaller envelope containing flimsies torn from the wires by his stringer at the *Herald-Tribune*.

"If I were you, I'd stay flat on my back," Segar said. "No one expects you to do anything but get your health. The magazine is doing fine without you."

"I really will die if I don't work," Pelfrey said. "I can't wait to get back to the office."

"You're sicker than you let on. Wing wasn't the first Sing Sing alum looking to have a piece of you. Tom Podgorny won't be around for the next one."

"If I quit, my replacement becomes a target," Pelfrey said. "Ever think about that?"

"All the time."

"And still you're angling for the job?"

"I've been cooling my heels for ten years waiting to have your office, and your salary, and my name where yours is on the masthead," Segar said. "Not any more, it's too dangerous. We're paper-pushers, not sandhogs, or test pilots. But life expectancy on the dick books is about the same as theirs, these days. When you're back on your feet, you can start interviewing for a new managing editor."

"You're quitting?"

"Going into hiding," Lou Segar said.

Pelfrey was up past ten fixing the story of a cop-killing in Gary, Indiana. He was ready to start on another right away, but the nurses would give him hell. In order to get well, he needed to sleep. He shut off his light, turned it on again, and read flimsies.

In Savannah, an 18-month-old had been strangled by a pervert. Pelfrey crumpled the flimsy, and tossed it away. *Real Detective* had stopped covering cases in which the victim was less than four. The readers loved stories of twisted sex, the sicker the better. But not when the victim was a baby. Baby-killings turned the readers against murder.

A Reno pump jockey was shot by a motorist who drove off without paying for $3.40 of ethyl. Service station holdups also had no place in the magazine. Aside from the names the stories were interchangeable. Readers hated them because there was never a new wrinkle. Pelfrey gave his readers only the killings they wanted.

Shirley Faber, a 27-year-old mother of four, had been stabbed to death by an intruder who entered her bedroom in Yardley, Pennsylvania, while her husband, a family doctor, was out on a call. It didn't take a genius to know the police soon would announce the arrest of Dr. Faber for murder. Pelfrey thanked God that not many *Real Detective* readers were geniuses. The doctor would have a girlfriend, probably a nurse. He would have money problems that made it impossible to finance a divorce without cutting back on a costly romance. Mrs. Faber would be suffering from depression causing her to lose interest in sex shortly before her husband insured her life for a large sum. Pelfrey would bet a year's salary that this was how the facts played out. In a population of 150,000,000 there were 9,000 murders in the United States each year. Only a few big city police departments got to investigate more than one or two. Pelfrey, with killings coming out of his ears, could give lessons to most detectives.

Real Detective had two stringers in Pennsylvania. Stash Lopata covered the western part of the state from Pittsburgh. Tom Flynn in Philadelphia handled the east. Yardley was in Bucks County in the Philly suburbs, which meant the case belonged to Flynn. Pelfrey didn't care for Flynn's sloppiness with the facts and high-handed tone. Bucks was a silver dollar's throw across the Delaware River from New Jersey. He'd give Adam Jordan first crack. Better to piss off Flynn and get a good story from Jordan than keep Flynn happy and be stuck with lousy copy. He picked up the phone, whispered Jordan's number to the long-distance operator.

"It's Ed Pelfrey."

"Say again."

"Pelfrey. From *Real Detective*. Did you forget me?"

"You sound hoarse," Jordan said. "Bad cold?"

"It's the tube in my nose."

"What tube?"

"I'm in the hospital. Somebody tried to kill me," Pelfrey said. "I've got something outside your backyard, if you don't mind hitting the road."

"Shoot."

"It's from Yardley, PA. Bucks County."

"The Faber case."

"That's right. What do you hear?"

"No sign of forced entry, or sexual assault, nothing taken from the house. The children left unhurt in their room. In other words, the husband."

Pelfrey was glad he'd given the case to Jordan, who seemed sober and on top of things. It wasn't something he could say for many of his writers after ten.

"I'll talk to the cops and the beat reporter, and hurry back to the typewriter," Jordan said. "After Dr. Faber is booked, I'll slap a few graphs on the end, and you'll have it."

"Writing in advance of the arrest is not a good habit to get into," Pelfrey said. "Cases don't always turn out like they should. You'll wind up with a pile of stories we can't buy from you."

"What else have I got to do?"

"Before you hang up—"

"Yeah?"

"The local reporter, if it's Tom Flynn, he doesn't know yet I took the case away from him and let you have it."

"You're pulling my leg," Jordan said, "right? About someone trying to kill you?"

"Occupational hazard," Pelfrey said. "Don't let it bother you. It wasn't Flynn."

He came back from Yardley with enough for a book. When the arrest was made he would have a nice payday. Till then he'd cool his heels, unless another murder came along. He had no life until someone died horribly, but it beat having no life at all.

He steered past the Park Place restaurant where cops had shot the kid with the air gun. It was high time to get his shirt back from Mollie, the hostess. Smoothing his hair in the mirror, he saw through his lounge lizard smile. He didn't give a rat's ass about the shirt.

The girl handing out menus at the velvet rope wasn't Mollie, and didn't know where she'd gone. A waitress who looked familiar carried an empty tray into the kitchen, and Jordan dogged her to a twelve-burner stove.

"I'm trying to find Mollie Gordon," he said.

"You're the gent who told her he'd put her picture in the paper," the waitress said, "and then you didn't."

"Turned out it wasn't that kind of story."

"Same old story, you mean."

Why was it that every waitress in Atlantic City sounded like she was auditioning for a part in *Guys and Dolls*?

"I need to see her."

"Another job opened up. Finding off-season work is like musical chairs for us gals, and she didn't want to be the one left with no place to put herself. You'd think she'd remember to mention it to a classy fellow such as yourself." The cook scraped something involving an egg off the griddle. He slid a plate under it, and the waitress caught the plate in her tray. Jordan followed her out of the kitchen.

"Where?" he said.

"On the beach. In Brigantine. It's all I'm going to say."

Mollie was at the cash register when he walked into the Rusty Scupper forty-five minutes later.

"How did you know I work here now?" she said.

"Finding out about people is what I do."

"I thought they had to be dead."

"Not all of them."

"Or naïve."

"Do you have my shirt?"

"I never go anywhere without it."

The way she said it, not too sarcastic, he had a sick feeling she was going to hand it over on the spot, and he'd never see her again. And he wanted to see her more than he'd realized. She wasn't the only one who'd been tight the night at his place. Why else hadn't he realized how beautiful she was?

A couple came in shaking the sand out of their clothes. The woman was holding a book with an osprey pictured on the cover, and Jordan noticed other diners wearing binoculars around their neck. Mollie stepped around him, brought the couple to a banquette, and continued into the kitchen. Jordan had an idea she'd gone straight out the back till she put down two bottles of Rupert's at a booth for six.

"You should have called," she said. "You made a long trip for nothing."

"You'd've told me to stay away."

"I couldn't force you. Just like you can't make me talk about something that never should have happened."

So beautiful he must have had the blind staggers, because being tight didn't begin to explain it.

"I'd convinced myself it never did," she said, "till Horty Miller told me a reporter came by. I've kept your shirt in my car ever since."

"I didn't know I'd find you here."

"It's your lucky day. I'll get it now."

"It can wait."

"We can talk about the woman who had my job before me, Mrs. Chase." She filled her glass, let him pour his own. "That way you won't be wasting your time."

"I need a break from murder."

"Not with me."

"You don't feel uncomfortable taking over from a woman who was killed?"

"That's not about her," she said. "But I'll answer anyway. Suzie Chase was in Atlantic City for the Miss America pageant. I've been thinking of taking her place there, too."

"It's not for everyone," he said when he meant to say, *It's not for every beautiful girl.*

She grabbed her bottle by the neck, emptied it. "I'm a former Miss Jersey Shore," she said.

"You never mentioned it."

"We did talk at your place, didn't we?"

"Not much."

"Maybe you weren't listening. I've been on the beauty circuit since I was seventeen. I was Miss Delaware Valley 1951, and Miss Sussex County. Last year I was first runner-up Miss Poconos."

"What are you now?"

"Sick of the whole scene," she said. "Look at me. Look close."

He'd never stopped. "Why the long face?"

"It isn't long," she said. "If it was long, I wouldn't have gotten past the qualifying rounds. It's sad, which is no good either. My skin's a mess, so is my hair, and I put on six pounds I don't know what to do with."

"I wouldn't bet against you."

"You're handing me a line. Being Miss Delaware Valley counts for nothing. I've seen pictures of Suzie Chase. Dressed to kill, I'm not as attractive as she was getting out of bed in the morning."

"Don't expect me to go along with that," Jordan said. "There's nothing wrong with you I can see."

"What do you know about beautiful women?"

He knew that the prettiest girls he'd dated were the most insecure. None were as gorgeous as Mollie Gordon, or filled with as much self-doubt.

"Being Miss anything does come with side benefits," she said. "I'm thinking of dusting off the old swimsuit." She picked up her bottle again, and emptied it into his glass. "I have to lose six pounds, anyway. But you want to hear about Mrs. Chase."

Not before he made his play to have her back at his apartment. New information about Suzie Chase was sexy, too, but hearing it now meant letting Mollie off the hook, and he didn't know when he would find her so vulnerable again.

"You'll need a new portfolio," he said. "I may be able to help."

"You're also a glamor photographer?"

At last he had a smile from her. It didn't mean he'd gotten anywhere.

"Do you know what the side benefits are?" she said. "Rich gentlemen falling all over themselves to do me favors. Are you rich?"

"I have a friend with a studio."

"Pictures are expensive. I can't pay now."

"You can work out an arrangement."

"I'm sure I can," she said. "No thanks."

"Tell me about Mrs. Chase."

"We had something in common besides knowing how to stuff a swimsuit," Mollie said. "She was also broke."

"Where did the money go?"

"What money? The Scupper pays terribly. The owner, Rusty—his name is George Cochran, but that's what we call him, Rusty—docks us if we're a minute late, or we don't dress like he wants, or we go home a little early. He could have shorted her for not putting out for him. Those are the side benefits *here*."

"How do you get by?"

"Who says I'm getting by?"

"How did she?"

"She borrowed. She was gorgeous, sweet, and had her hand in the kitchen staff's pocket. They knew they could collect from Rusty if she tried to stiff them, so they gave her what she wanted."

"That's not what happened."

"Who's telling the story?" Mollie said. "She put the arm on everybody, and then she died. No one got their money. The busboys haven't stopped grumbling. The dishwasher who thought she had a crush on him is out a hundred bucks, and blames her for getting killed. No one had a motive for wanting her dead except for me, and I never met her."

"Why you?"

"I'm going to be the next Miss New Jersey, or catch a rich husband trying. Suzie Chase was standing in my way."

"A sugar daddy," Jordan said.

"I could do worse."

He pulled a face, drank his beer.

"Easy for you to say," she said.

"Did Suzie already have a sugar daddy?"

"If she did, he wasn't very sweet. Why else would she be borrowing from the kitchen staff?"

"I'd like to see you again," Jordan said, "before you find a rich guy."

"That night at your place, it was fun?"

"No complaints."

"Would you say I enjoyed myself, too?"

"You gave every indication—"

"You read me wrong," she said. "A good time for you isn't a good time for me. That goes double when I'm out like a light."

"You weren't—"

He let it go. He wasn't going to get anywhere telling her they hadn't slept.

"Old men, are they fun?"

"Rich old men?" she said. "I'll let you know."

She smiled. It was the second smile he'd had from her, and he began to think she wasn't as angry as she wanted him to believe. Then she drained her glass, and said, "I've got to get back to work now."

"When's your day off?"

"I'll call you," she said.

"You don't have my number."

"I had it from the start."

CHAPTER 5

Jordan was drafted during the final stages of the Pacific war, and did his basic training at Fort Dix. What the Pentagon needed in the spring of 1945 were bodies to fill uniforms, hundreds of thousands of men expected to be slaughtered in the invasion of the Japanese homeland. From Fort Dix he was sent to Camp Edwards, Massachusetts, on Cape Cod, to become adept at taking a beach under artillery and machinegun fire while being strafed by Zeroes.

He was 18, fresh out of high school, and wasn't leaving behind a promising career, a wife and kids, or steady girlfriend. Without means for tuition a college education was as real a possibility as a Hollywood screen test or a tryout at Ebbets Field. The arrival of his induction notice took his immediate future out of his hands. But he had an important decision left to make.

Before reporting for his physical on Whitehall Street in lower Manhattan he was advised by his friends on how best to flunk. He could elevate his blood sugar by drinking pure Coca-Cola syrup, and be rejected as a diabetic. He could raise his temperature by sprinkling cayenne pepper in his armpits. He could act insane, or play the spastic, or shit on the floor when told to bend over and spread his cheeks. He could wear a bra and panties under his suit. The army doctors wouldn't be fooled. They recognized who was legitimately unfit for service and who was gold-bricking, but awarded 4-F status for initiative and determination.

Jordan accepted his 1-A gladly, eager to find out how he measured up against the heroes who had defeated Hitler and brought the war to the emperor's backyard. Infantry school added ten pounds of muscle to his frame. He relished learning how to fight, and after Hiroshima and Nagasaki were bombed felt cheated when he was transferred to a military police unit under training in Fort Benning, Georgia. His IQ was wasted on a grunt. He was more valuable to Uncle Sam keeping the peace among GI's in occupied Europe.

Jordan hated the South. It was hot, and there were poisonous snakes, and biting insects, and weeds that made him itch. Outside the base lurked the Klan. His New York accent made him the butt of idiotic jokes. Frequently a stranger's hand would sweep his head, a new barracks mate checking for the horns Jordan was alleged to keep hidden under his crew cut.

Backed up against the base was a dreary strip of bucket-of-blood bars, two-dollar whorehouses, tattoo parlors, pawn shops, a chop suey place run by a tubercular Cantonese known as One Bum Lung, a rooster-fighting pit, back alley craps games, three stores that sold marital aids and Tijuana bibles, a clap clinic, a third-run movie house, 17 churches, a Salvation Army chapel, the USO. Jordan had no buddies in his unit, knew no one in town, and could not make heads or tails of the mushmouth dialect. He was dying of homesickness when he discovered jigtown.

It was still the nineteenth century in the Negro district of Columbus, Georgia, as Jordan saw things, the Emancipation Proclamation a hoax. Jigtown was poorer and more backward than other parts of Columbus. But Jordan had grown up around Negroes, had occasional Negro friends, and understood their take on the language. When a jigtown Negro tried to steer him to a nickel bag of marijuana he might have been back in the schoolyard at P.S. 161.

Jordan was not an idealist. He wore his big army revolver where the toughs wouldn't miss it on his visits to the colored part of town. He went there for the jump jazz and rhythm and blues rather than drag his feet to Harry James and Sinatra on the jukebox at the USO. No one spoke to him at the joints where he was barely tolerated as the only ofay. But he liked the loud humor of the other customers, liked watching them dance and carry on, and trailing after them to a barbecue stand for a big feed.

Negro refugees from southwest Georgia were well-established in Atlantic City. Jordan's favorite place for barbecue was Mae's in the colored district off Missouri Avenue near the Convention Center and the Million Dollar Pier. Jordan didn't pretend that it was healthy food. The meat was not choice cut, and came out of the smoker dripping fat, a pallid vehicle for the spicy-sweet sauce heavy with molasses and God knows what else. If Jordan had advance notice that the sun was about to flame out, he would take all his meals at Mae's until the earth turned to ice. But he was trying to fulfill his life expectancy, or at least to see his thirties, and so he stopped there no more than once a week, or when he was feeling let down and sorry for himself and wanted comfort, or was left hopeless about a girl.

Jordan was starting home with an order of beef on the passenger's seat when a boy with a stack of newspapers came up to his open window. Jordan figured he'd been drawn by the smell, as were a couple of scroungy dogs. He gave the boy a nickel, and slipped a paper under the leaky bag from Mae's in the hope of saving his upholstery. He was stalled at a red light when he raised the bag for a look at the front page.

The Freeman, Atlantic City's Negro weekly, was a broadsheet that had turned Jordan's fingers black the one or two times he'd had a look at it. A headline across eight columns announced:

HOOFER SONGSTRESS VANISHES
A.C. COPS WITHOUT LEADS

He kept one eye on the page until a near collision with a motorcycle. On a quiet, sunlit street he shut the engine, slipped the second section over his lap, and tore open the paper bag.

The first section was hung from the steering wheel for easy reading.

A performer with the Louis Armstrong All-Stars, 21-year-old Etta Lee Wyatt, had disappeared after Saturday's midnight show at the Ruckus Room. The missing woman was described variously as a chanteuse, chorine, song stylist, thrush, brilliant newcomer, showstopper, and the next Lena Horne. Jordan doubted she was many of those things. As the big band era came to a close, Armstrong had folded the 19-piece orchestra he'd fronted since the mid-1930s, and returned to the traditional New Orleans-style combo with which he'd made his name. Atlantic City audiences were not jazzhounds. When the All-Stars came to town Satchmo hired pretty light-skinned girls to dress up the stage.

Etta Lee Wyatt had appeared with Billy Eckstine, Cab Calloway, and the Nicholas Brothers in Atlantic City. Headshots of a moderately attractive girl with an overbite left Jordan underwhelmed. He licked his fingers, and turned the page. A photo spread explained why the big acts sought her for local runs.

In a trifle called *The Zanzibar Review* Etta Lee's specialty number was a seductive hoochy-coochy front and center before a chorus line of darker-skinned, thick-featured girls. The new Lena Horne looked to Jordan like the old Josephine Baker in an apron of bananas and a cantaloupe halter. He cringed, thinking of how he used canteloupes to describe what was under the canteloupes in the picture. Nice canteloupes.

With the All-Stars she shimmied during Satchmo's medley of "St. James Infirmary Blues," "Black and Blue," and "Shine." Band members remembered nothing out of the ordinary at Saturday's late show. When Etta Lee missed the Sunday performances, and failed to call in, the All-Stars' drummer and reed player visited her rooming house off Missouri Avenue. Fannie Potts, the 83-year-old landlady, told them she had last seen her young tenant around 8:30 on the day she vanished.

"She was wearing sandals and a summer shift, and I could see the straps of her bathing suit under her coat collar," the old woman was quoted as saying. "Dearie, I told her, are you looking to come down with the grippe? She told me she had business on the beach. Weren't none of my business what kind. I let her go, for which I'm sorry. She's a lovely child, but God didn't give her the sense to keep warm or safe."

Armstrong's management reported Etta Lee missing to Atlantic City police, who were told by Fannie Potts that the girl had walked off along Missouri Avenue in the direction of Chicken Bone Beach. Detectives concluded that the young dancer left town with a new boyfriend. The article, and the investigation, ended there. An editorial denounced the police for abandoning the case without an inspection of the beach. A Negro gone missing, the paper charged, was not a major priority.

There was more to the editorial, but Jordan dripped brown sauce on the final paragraphs. Eating barbecue in the car wasn't a great idea. Each time he did it he promised would be the last. He pinched a handkerchief from his pants, and blotted his face, his shirt, the seat, the mats and the dashboard. Then he drove the few blocks to the beach. A good reporter followed up on everything the cops did. Without newsmen looking over their shoulder, Jordan believed most police departments were worthless bureaucracies.

Chicken Bone Beach, Atlantic City's colored beach, had acquired its name because Negro bathers packed their lunch hampers with fried chicken on hot summer days. Off-season the name did not ring true. Nothing distinguished the deserted black beach from the white beaches surrounding it on both sides. Other than newspapers propelled by the wind the sand was immaculate. Not a chicken bone in sight to spoil the view.

Ducking into the blowing sand, Jordan went to the water's edge. A mile off shore freighters ploughed toward the port of

New York. He wished he could put out his thumb, and hitch a ride. There was nothing to see here. Etta Lee Wyatt was not playing hide and seek, waiting to be found. He looked back at the boardwalk done up for summer, like a vacant stage set. "Business," Etta Lee's landlady said had brought her boarder to the beach. What business did anyone have here now?

The odds were that Etta Lee was okay. The police might have it right, and she was with a new beau. She was only 21, but parading onstage in humiliating costumes for the amusement of leering strangers grew stale fast. Easy to understand why she would take off without letting anyone try to talk her into a change of heart. Why had she stopped first at the beach? The smaller mystery cast the larger one in an intriguing gloss, a gold mine for a writer if things turned out bad for Etta Lee.

Wet sand pulled at Jordan's heels as he dodged a breaker crawling up the tide line. Chicken Bone Beach, between the Convention Hall and the Ocean One Pier, was the finest beach on the municipal oceanfront. Segregation wasn't official in Atlantic City. This was New Jersey, after all, not the South, and a Negro could go to any beach he pleased. If he used his head, though, he came here. An isolated Negro or two would be tolerated on the white beaches, but Negroes showing up in large numbers on a sweltering August afternoon might be a different story. Maybe that was why the city fathers had given the Negroes the nicest beach—as a bribe to keep them in their place.

Jordan enjoyed these conversations with himself, the arguments that he never lost. But they didn't put him closer to Etta Lee. He stared out to sea, half expecting to spot the girl in her tropical get-up riding the waves. There was only the gray water under grayer skies dissolving into foam at his toes. Soon he began to shiver. He went to his car, and drove back along Missouri Avenue.

Fannie Potts' rooming house was two gloomy stories in a

popular Japanese style that fell out of fashion on the Jersey Shore after the First World War. The once-grand homes in the Negro district had seen better days. Miss Potts' was a foreboding place. Most of a chimney had toppled off the roof. Several windows were glazed with cardboard. Beach grasses sprouting from cracks in the mortar caricatured a haunted house. In Jordan's head as he pulled up to the curb was a list of questions for Fannie Potts, and her possible answers. They were quotable answers, touching recollections good for a second-day lead, which wouldn't advance a story for a detective magazine. If he were writing for a paper, he would storm Fannie Potts' door. But he didn't need anything she was likely to give him. The evidence pointed in another direction.

Jordan checked the *Press* to see how McAvoy was playing Etta Lee's vanishing act. There was nothing—not even a mention that she was gone. Like most mid-size east coast dailies the *Press* gave little ink to Negroes. Sure, Negro criminals preying on whites made for good copy. But if you played up the disappearance of a Negro girl, you would be expected to cover her friends' weddings, and the births of their children, and to make space on the obituary page, too. The readers did not want integration with their morning coffee. A good many might cancel their subscriptions, and take a suburban daily for which Negroes did not exist. If Etta Lee turned up dead, she would not be ignored by the *Press*. McAvoy wasn't heartless. The death of a pretty colored girl with connections to Satchmo Armstrong, everyone's favorite Negro, had the makings of a good story. The *Press* was a progressive paper with a commendable outlook on civil rights, but wasn't prepared to cover the meanderings of a 21-year-old Negro dancer. McAvoy would say that he was saving Etta Lee embarrassment by not playing up her case. *What if he was?* thought Jordan. *Since when was that his job?*

Jordan didn't care who he embarrassed, even if it was himself.

His talk with Fannie Potts would come at another time. A word with the police couldn't be put off. Noticing a speck of beef on the upholstery between his legs, he picked it up with his fingertip. It didn't taste bad. He found more.

Atlantic City police headquarters was located near City Hall and the central fire station in the part of town caption writers called the nerve center. Jordan had an easy relationship with the local cops, who deferred to the troopers in major investigations that invited criticism from the *Press*. For taking a kitten down from a tree, or walking an old lady across a busy intersection, Jordan endorsed the Atlantic City police. The cops didn't care what he said privately about them, as long as he kept it out of the paper.

Captain Eamon Halloran was chief of detectives, a retired Army lifer with six years of service under General MacArthur in the Philippines before the war, and Guadalcanal vet. He was from the old school of policing, and regularly sent men into bad neighborhoods to beat up the hard cases with fists and saps. The *Press* didn't always look the other way. But when Halloran was called to account, he denied that the beatings happened. Since crime in Atlantic City was at low levels, the public supported the roughhouse tactics. The *Press* never called for Halloran's badge, and everyone remained on good terms.

But Halloran wasn't happy to see Jordan coming to his door. Jordan supposed that no cop ever was. He took it as evidence that he did his job well.

"What can I do for you today, Adam?" Halloran's County Mayo brogue was for news conferences, police funerals, and grade school assemblies, and made Jordan feel like a fourth-grader sent to see the principal.

"You can give me a few minutes to hear what I have to tell you."

"Shouldn't it be the other way around?"

"It should," Jordan said. "But we'd both get nothing."

Halloran's lip retracted from his upper teeth. He had perfected his small grin in the Philippines under orders not to let the locals know what he thought of them. "Nothing about what."

"Etta Lee Wyatt."

Halloran had to think. "The shine dancer? I've got something for *you*. Take a load off, I'll fill you in."

Jordan remained on his feet.

"You've got the wrong face on, patronizing when it should be grateful," Halloran said. "You come to see me as you do from time to time, like you have me in your pocket. But my sources are more reliable than yours, they give me information I can *use*. You won't tell me who your sources are. You've promised them confidentiality, you say. I say your sources are voices in your head."

Jordan pulled up a chair. "You first."

"That's polite of you, Adam. You wouldn't be here if you didn't think something terrible hadn't happened to your dancer, something we can make hay with in our separate ways. Sorry to disappoint. I've got two witnesses, not a disembodied voice, but flesh and blood human beings—" He put up two fingers, and waggled them. "They tell me she's fine."

"Who—?"

"First is a trucker who noticed Etta Lee roll up in a pre-war Ford to a motor court outside Trenton. An older gent was at the wheel. For luggage they had several brown paper bags, and a bucket of ice. The Ford was still there when the trucker left in the morning."

"How does he know it's her?"

"He saw her picture in a Negro newspaper," Halloran said.

"How do you know he's right?"

"They may all appear alike to you, but not to this fellow, he's several parts colored himself. The other witness is a cashier in a

Negro restaurant on U.S. 1 near Baltimore. Your wayward entertainer stopped for a bacon, lettuce, and tomato sandwich, hold the mayo, around eleven last night."

"With the older gent?"

"The witness didn't say. We didn't ask. She's Negro herself, Negro through and through. It's a good ID, which makes two independent sightings. Don't tell me we don't know what's going on with the girl."

"Two sightings in opposite directions a hundred miles apart," Jordan said. "If Etta Lee Wyatt was headed north toward Trenton, why did she show up in Baltimore to the south?"

"I'm a policeman, not a guardian angel. She hasn't been harmed, no law's been broken. She's free…uh, free, and twenty-one. She can go anywhere she pleases, even in circles."

Jordan shook his head.

"Who are you to say she can't?"

"She's dead."

"You've mentioned that you want to be a novelist, but haven't gotten anywhere. You're trying out your fictions on me, aren't you, to see how they play?"

"I've given up writing novels. She was killed."

"This is a moving performance, Adam. Have you considered your real talent may be for the stage?"

Jordan said, "I have an idea where to find her."

"How do you explain this sudden helpfulness? I heard you lost your job. Now you're doing mine. Do you want it for yourself? If you can't get the facts straight when they're spelled out for you, what will you do with them?" Halloran glanced out the window at Jordan's Hudson. "You parked in the spot reserved for the *Press*. You're taking a chance you'll be towed away."

"Do you know the Chase case?" Jordan said. "The woman found by state police on the beach at Little Egg Harbor?"

"You have your facts wrong again. It wasn't troopers who found her, it was a reporter."

"I beat them to the scene by a few minutes, yeah," Jordan said.

"You're not telling me you discovered the Wyatt girl's body, too? Even a failed novelist should know that's too great a coincidence."

"I think she ended up the same as Mrs. Chase."

"You don't listen. My witness saw her alive and well last night."

"She left home the last time headed for Chicken Bone Beach. No one goes to the beach this time of year, but Suzie Chase was murdered on one just a few miles away."

"An enterprising newsman, former newsman, would hunt for the Wyatt girl before trying to sell me on his pet theory with nothing to back it up," Halloran said.

"The body could be buried in the sand, and I missed it. It might have been carried away by a wave, and is riding the tide, or lying in a morgue anywhere on the coast."

"Where does someone who can't hold down a reporter's job come off thinking he knows about criminal investigation?"

"I've been reading up on murder, studying it. I learned more than I ever did trailing after your detectives."

"Have you now, Adam? What text do you use?"

Jordan turned toward the window as a patrolman went by with a summons book in his hand. The officer walked around the Hudson, then unlocked a green DeSoto coupe in the adjacent spot, and drove away.

"One woman is dead on the beach and another is missing after visiting a beach off-season, and I'm supposed to believe the cases are unrelated?"

"Your imagination has let you down again," Halloran said. "There is no connection between a colored tramp and the young lady who might have become our next Miss America. Don't take my word for it. Ask your friends with the state police."

"They're deliberately blind, same as you. There's nothing in it for them if they make headway in one of your cases."

"The jazz musicians passing through town are Southern Negroes, many of them, scarcely civilized. On the road, without the restraints that keep them in line at home, they become animalistic. One of them could easily have…picked her up."

Jordan didn't contradict him. The players he brushed shoulders with were braggarts whose favorite riffs (after stories about marathon jam sessions when they achieved ecstatic breakthroughs with their music that tragically went unrecorded) were wild tales of whiskey-guzzling, smoking reefer and occasionally skin-popping heroin, and of the armies of women who ambushed them at every stop.

"Which is not to say," Halloran went on, "that we aren't concerned about the girl. The well-being of each of our citizens, white and colored, is important. If we find the witnesses are mistaken, we'll speak to the band and the employees at the club, and look into her relationships. But first we need evidence she's been harmed."

"Is Satchmo—Louis Armstrong a suspect?"

"I caught his act opening night. A handful of elected officials and police are expected to be on hand when the stars come out. Etta Wyatt was there in the flesh. If you'd seen her, you'd have a better understanding of her popularity with men."

"That doesn't answer the question."

"You have no place to publish the answer."

Jordan nodded. Halloran hadn't asked if he was making note of everything and would use it when he could. The detective chief, who did not like being quoted, wouldn't allow his name in a pulp magazine even if Pelfrey campaigned for him as *Real Detective*'s police officer of the month. "Between you and me."

"He's one of the best-liked figures in America," Halloran said. "You've got to hand it to him, a Negro in the public eye who doesn't have an enemy. It's to the department's credit that we won't let him hide behind his celebrity. The day we have knowledge that a crime was committed he'll be interrogated. He hired Etta Wyatt, he put her onstage. Presumably he knows the kind of girl she is, and where her real value to his troupe lay."

Jordan had mixed feelings about Armstrong. The man was a genius, the greatest trumpet player ever—but his music had been in decline for twenty years. He'd deliberately diminished his art to be assured of steady work, a performer who'd turned himself into a brand name. To younger jazzmen he was an embarrassment who'd sold out musically and on race. "No one Toms like Louis," Billie Holiday said. "Louis Toms from the heart."

Jordan was fourteen, a Gene Autry fan, when he discovered Armstrong's early recordings at a secondhand music shop. He'd worn them out, and never replaced them, but Armstrong remained his idol. Louis Armstrong had made jazz the world's music. More important, he'd made it Adam Jordan's. He deserved better than to be dragged into a seamy missing persons case touching on murder. Jordan wanted to talk to him, to get his take on Etta Lee Wyatt, and to warn him to be careful around a cop who would try to bring him down. And, if they hit it off, to ask for an autograph.

At 8:30 he was nursing a beer in the Ruckus Room on Ventnor Avenue. He saw no one he recognized, few people his own age. Armstrong drew a crowd too square to get a handle on the modern jazz that was Jordan's passion. At the clubs where he went to hear the boppers Jordan was sometimes the only ofay in the house. At the Ruckus Room there were no Negroes. Black audiences, young blacks in particular, had turned their back on Armstrong, whose fans—middle-class, middle-age, frumpy— reminded Jordan of his aunts and uncles. But his aunts and uncles were too hip for the Louis Armstrong of 1953.

The set began with "Back Home Again in Indiana," the same number Armstrong had opened with when Jordan caught him at Roseland during the war. Not a jazz tune, or Tin Pan Alley standard, but a cornball jingle with a rah-rah chorus. What could be less cool? More deliberately unhip? Armstrong was stingy with his playing, a minimalist who blew the notes that were the heart of the song and discarded the rest. Jordan surveyed the house. If he wasn't careful, he'd be clapping and tapping his feet like the squares.

After a slow blues Armstrong waved his dancers out of the wings, three high yellows in satin shorts, halters, and tap shoes. Jordan couldn't help thinking of the Harlem Globetrotters, but with lousy footwork. The girl in the middle was half a step behind her partners. Jordan figured she'd been called in on short notice to pinch hit for Etta Lee Wyatt.

Armstrong announced "West End Blues," skipping over the famous cadenza at the start to get to the melody. His playing was uninspired, while his eyes popped and he grinned like an old lecher at the shimmying girls. Billie Holiday told only part of the story. No one tommed like Louis because Louis was a parody of a tomming Negro, a parody of a parody, the joke turned back on itself so many times that the crowd squirmed until a wink and a nod let them know that it was okay to laugh.

Armstrong was happily married, not known to have a wandering eye. The audience howled as he ogled the dancers, brought his horn to his lips, and lowered it to mop his face with a handkerchief. Jordan didn't think it was funny. The new girl was a klutz. Armstrong, trying to deflect attention to himself, continued to mug while she stumbled. Suddenly he launched into the cadenza, stringing the notes into gorgeous arpeggios fired off like balls of light from a Roman candle, limpid and pure. His sidemen put down their instruments and listened. In his early fifties Armstrong could play as well as ever, a casual genius when an emergency called for it.

The end of the solo was lost in wild clapping. Jordan, snapping his fingers, saw Armstrong frown. If you dig my playing, he seemed to say, don't be coy. Jordan banged his bottle against the table, but Armstrong was reaching for a high note and couldn't be bothered.

The piano took the next solo, then the trombone. The rhythm section kicked in, and when it was the trumpet's turn again Armstrong had lost interest. Thirty years on the road, Jordan figured, gave him the right to be sloppy. The audience fidgeted, drank more, listened less. The All-Stars closed with "Sleepy Time Down South," Armstrong mugging shamelessly for the hell of it. As the crowd drifted to the exits, Jordan followed the musicians backstage.

A bouncer with twin anchors on his forearms got in his way. "Band members only, and their families," he said. "Which are you?"

Jordan turned his pockets inside out for a joint he'd been carrying around since catching Thelonious Monk in Philadelphia. Armstrong was a heavy pot smoker who'd been busted once or twice on minor drug beefs and didn't let a day go by without spending a large part of it stoned. Jordan held out the reefer like a badge. "I'm with Mary Jane," he said, "to see Satchmo."

The bouncer, toying with a lighter, made Jordan feel like an undercover cop in a whorehouse trying to get the goods without taking off his pants. He heard giggling behind a tattered curtain. When finally he was allowed behind it, he looked in on the dancers freshening their makeup in a dressing room the size of a closet. Next door the All-Stars were playing gin rummy for a penny a point as they passed around a short dog bottle. There was a third door in the corridor. Jordan rapped on it, and a familiar voice growled, "Ain't no need to knock."

Louis Armstrong, in white socks, patent leather shoes, boxer shorts, and thick glasses, flashed a grin that came from a lifetime of practice. Jordan accepted it as a meaningless souvenir.

"You doing here, boy?" Armstrong said. "Got two more sets to play."

The skirl of the clarinet came through the wall, the reed man polishing a riff he'd botched earlier. Armstrong peeled off his shirt. He was soft, his big barrel chest swollen from self-indulgence. Jordan was surprised to notice a star of David on a chain around his neck. He folded his trousers over the back of a chair, and sat down careful not to crease them. Jordan was lighting the joint when Armstrong caught his wrist.

"Feeblest reefer I ever seen."

Several hand-rolled cigarettes came out of his trumpet case as fat as White Owl cigars. He lit up, took the first hit for himself, and then the second, handing over a soggy joint with a grin that stretched the thick callus on his lip till Jordan thought it would tear apart.

"Got something you want to tell Pops 'bout his music, or just stopped by to get ripped on his dope?"

Jordan said, "Big fan—"

"I see you are, son. Still didn't say which."

"Don't get me started. I'm effusive, I mean enthusiastic about both subjects."

"Nothin' wrong with 'ffusive," Armstrong said. "It's in Mr. Webster's book."

Jordan's cheeks were hot. He blamed it on the marijuana. He needed to explain that he was trying to cut down on two-dollar words even around people who weren't Southern Negroes. A portable typewriter stood beside its carrying case at the edge of the dressing table. Paper was curled around the platen, and he tried to steal a peek at a couple of paragraphs typed with a red ribbon.

"You a writer?" Armstrong said. "Or natural snoop? Not from the newspaper. Been years since they sent anybody down to talk to me."

"Some of each," Jordan said.

"Here to write 'bout Pops?"

Jordan shook his head.

"Won't be offended, I don't believe you?"

"I might be," Jordan said.

"Won't be offended, I don't give a damn? People writing 'bout me most of this century, but I know more about me'n they do. Keeping a diary longer'n most of 'em been on earth. Sure you don't want to talk 'bout music?"

Jordan started to correct him, but caught himself. Louis Armstrong wanted to talk jazz to him, and he was going to shut him up? Was his brain useless? Maybe there was a story for him, and he could sell it to *Downbeat*, and wouldn't that be a hoot?

"The music got no future," Armstrong said. "New generation making what they call bebop, lay it on them. That Miles Davis, the Mingus boy, want to rile you. Ain't it proof they artists, give you a headache. Few years down the road won't be nobody paying 'ttention to jazz 'cept old folks like you and me, and how many records do we all buy? How many bands we keep on the road? But that ain't what brings you here, so what does?"

"One of your dancers," Jordan said.

Armstrong took the last hit, and stubbed out the roach. "Funning with me, boy? Nobody come by 'bout my dancers, 'less you mean you want one for yourself."

"No, just to talk."

"Ain't what to discuss. I can't keep a girl long enough she learn the steps. They spend a few weeks with the band, go their own way when I move on to the next date. I hire new girls where I find 'em. Want to see good dancing, catch Swan Lake. Like to look at pretty brownskin gals in short pants, you at the right address. Was less bother when I had the orchestra. Folks came to hear us play, didn't need girls shaking their what-have-you to fill seats."

Jordan nodded woozily.

"One in particular you here 'bout? All of them? Two out of the three? What?"

"Just the one."

"Which?"

"She wasn't onstage tonight," Jordan said. "Etta Lee Wyatt."

Armstrong took a fresh joint from the trumpet case, lit up, and looked skeptical when Jordan refused it. Then he turned his back, and Jordan watched in the mirror as he used a toenail clipper to trim the callus on his lip. Armstrong began pruning his lip like it was a hedge, cutting back the mass of dead skin at the edges, and thinning it across the top. The callus was part of his embouchure, the product of decades of contact with the trumpet mouthpiece, an important element contributing to his sound.

"Did you know her well?" Jordan asked him.

"Persistent cuss, ain't you? Not a cop. Cop wouldn't be in the confused state you in. Why an amateur snoop interested in my dancer?"

"You know she went missing."

"Lot of girls missing in action," Armstrong said. "The way it is, that's all."

"This one may be different."

"Ain't two cents' difference 'tween any of 'em. Colored girls in these towns got one kind of future—as a domestic. Band come to play, they want to run off with it, same reason little boys run off with the circus. Look like fun, pay better'n what they got here. They strut their stuff, and we hire the frisky ones, give 'em a paycheck till the excitement wear off and they take a powder. Some of 'em, they sleep 'round, figure *somebody* going to marry 'em, give 'em a comfortable life. Wishful thinking. Jazz-man don't want a girl hanging on him like an anchor. The fellas sleep with 'em, and leave 'em for the next band come through town. Why you making a big deal out of a little deal?"

"Something bad might have happened to her," Jordan said.

"Nothing good happened," Armstrong said. "Never does. You mean by bad?"

"She may have been killed."

"Gonna say why?"

"Another girl was murdered on the beach here several weeks ago. Etta Wyatt was going to the beach when she disappeared."

"Colored girl, the other one?"

Jordan shook his head.

"Ain't no connection, 'cept they girls."

"The other girl was ambitious, out to make a name for herself. I think Etta Lee was, too. They had more in common than you might suspect."

"Ambitious women got one thing in common," Armstrong looked at Jordan to say that it wasn't necessary to spell it out, and seemed to change his mind. "Handful of trouble for any man fool enough to want 'em."

"Who wanted Etta Lee?"

"Seen what she looked like, boy? How she moved? Asking the wrong question."

"What's the right one?"

"Who didn't? Damn—!"

Blood on Armstrong's lip was running into a corner of his mouth. Jordan watched him pluck tissues out of a box, ball them against the wound.

"I'm not looking to dig up dirt on your musicians," Jordan said to him. "But shining a light on a mess is the best disinfectant."

"Be shining a light on yourself, too," Armstrong said. "You want disinfecting, or just the bright light?"

"It's what writers do—"

"Never cleaned up none of mine— Forget it, wasn't you." Armstrong put down the clipper. He sopped up more blood, and examined the tissue before throwing it away. Then he turned around. "Ambitious women, they ruthless. 'Nother word you'll find in Mr. Webster's. Don't look scandalized, you didn't know women use their loveliness in ways got nothing to do with love. Figure it give 'em power over men, when it's the other way 'round. The gals that dance for me, too many of 'em like that, even the ones straight out of church. Etta was worse'n most. Was also my best dancer, only one wouldn't be doing mankind better service on her back. Tried to straighten her out, but she wouldn't listen, 'cept to the lying voice inside her head."

"Who was she involved with?"

"Bad publicity'll kill the All-Stars," Armstrong said. "Promoters believe I'm transporting loose women, they'll ask us to stay 'way. I wouldn't tell you who she was sleeping 'round with, even if I knew 'em all. Ones I do know, trust Pops they didn't harm her. Been messing with showgirls twenty, thirty years. They ain't provoked to murder in all that time, they never will."

"I don't think they were. I'd like to talk to them, and hear what they can tell me about her."

"Weren't even in town when that white woman got herself killed. What more do you need to hear?"

"They might have gotten closer to Etta Wyatt than you know. She could have introduced them to her friends, or to someone who knows someone…"

"Don't come to me with suspicions. Colored band on the road got all the suspicions we can use, hang over us like a, you know, black cloud. Write 'bout suspicions, might as well be shouting out for people to invite us not to come to their city. Got proof, tell the police. Got suspicions, keep 'em under your hat. Son, playing for the public is my whole life. All I ever done. What I do three hundred nights a year. I ain't gonna connive with you to put an end to it. Have to find out what happened on your own. Try bugging folks knew the white girl you *know* was murdered. Be better for everyone, you take that approach. It's the best I got for you."

❊

Pelfrey had been released from the hospital, but wasn't home. Jordan tried him at the office. A woman with a central European accent handed over the phone after asking who he was.

"Your secretary sounds like Dietrich," Jordan said. "Lucky dog."

"Hitler's big sister, you mean," Pelfrey said. "Helga's a visiting nurse who comes by twice a week to see if I'm alive, and to clean out my infections if I am."

"You're getting back to your old self. That's good."

"My old self didn't whistle when he exhaled. His lungs hadn't been nicked by a knife. I hope you're better with the facts than you are sizing people up."

"You're divorced, aren't you?" Jordan said. "Not many close friends. Bet I've got that right."

"What's that got to do with—?"

"Nothing," Jordan said. "Remember the body found on the sand here? There's a new wrinkle that's going to land the case on your cover. Another woman's disappeared on her way to the beach. A dancer with one of the top name acts to come through Atlantic City."

"What name's that?"

"Louis Armstrong."

"Stop right there."

"Don't you need to hear the rest?"

"I know the rest. The missing dancer is colored—"

"Sexy light-skinned girl, twenty-one or so. I can get all the pictures you want. Publicity shots of her and Armstrong together, and alone wearing next to nothing."

"I can't use them."

"That's nuts."

"I can't use *her*," Pelfrey said. "We don't do Negro cases. If somebody kills Armstrong, that's different. Unless the killer is Negro, too, and then we wouldn't touch it with a barge pole."

"You're passing up a terrific story."

"Murdered Negroes don't sell magazines. The public doesn't think they're worth the two bits cover price."

"Enlighten them, why don't you?"

"Get off your high horse, Jordan. *Real Detective* isn't in the business of changing anyone's thinking. Our readers want confirmation that the world is a dangerous place for decent, narrow-minded white men and women like themselves. There's fewer of them for each issue. They're dying off, and we can't replace them because their children would rather watch TV than read. I'm not going to chase them away faster by mocking their ideas. I'd like to live in their world, too, where Negroes kill mostly each other and the occasional white woman who sparks animal urges. I don't know what your politics are. I'm a…at Christmas my conscience sends a check to the NAACP. One place I don't care to see integrated, though, is a police morgue."

"Don't tell me you've never been tempted to use a case like that."

"Don't tell me what not to tell you. What else have you got?"

"A big, fat nothing."

"I have something that might interest you," Pelfrey said.

"Who's the victim?"

"I am," Pelfrey said. "Till I find a new managing editor. Mine just quit. Ever do magazine work?"

"I've sold a few pieces to the Sunday supplements."

"Editing's the other side of the coin. It's being an English teacher for disagreeable semi-literates who can't draw a sober breath when you need to double-check a fact. Pays sixty-five a week with no chance of advancement unless the next crazy bastard with a knife does a better job of killing me."

"What about vacations and holidays?"

"Why are you asking about a vacation? You haven't started yet."

"Benefits?"

"You get advance copies of the magazine every month. Plus all the pencils, paper clips, and typewriter ribbons you can steal. It's a unique opportunity. What do you say?"

"Try me again later," Jordan said. "After I've cut another notch in my belt."

CHAPTER 6

The drumming was primitive and heavy-handed, jazz gone insane. Jordan came awake straining to shut it out. He was in bed, pretty sure it was his own, mid-morning light at the edge of the blinds. What wasn't clear was why someone was at his door so early. Thinking was hard. It was easier to find out who was there and send him away. The ice-cold floor was a crime against his toes. He stopped to look for socks.

"I woke you, huh?" Pix Pixley said.

"What do you think?"

"It depends," the photographer said, "on whether you usually greet visitors with nothing on but blue argyle."

Jordan went for his clothes. Pixley waited in the living room eyeing the typewriter buried under news clippings, the books and manuscripts in erratic piles on the floor. He inspected the furnishings and the paint job, and went to the window to take in the pallid view. "Just as I imagined," he said.

"Why were you imagining my place?"

"It's how I get a read on new people, by conjuring how they live. When I do their portrait, I know what props are essential to the shot."

"Is that why you woke me? To take my picture?"

Pixley shook his head, a little rueful. "No, I want to show you someone else's."

"It couldn't have waited?"

"I couldn't. Why should I?"

Jordan had ready answers. Some were winners, but it was too early to argue. "How'd you know I live here? I don't give out my address, and I'm not in the phone book."

"You are—in the reverse directory. I'd be lost without it," Pixley said, but didn't say why.

He shook a handful of pictures out of an envelope, and laid them flat beside the mess on the floor. Jordan turned a light on a gruesome rotogravure, black-and-white glossies of a young woman—a Negro, he thought at first, but maybe not—her sad, shamed face made grotesque by a beating. It was impossible to tell what she had looked like before. Both eyes were swollen shut. A cheekbone was several times the normal size. The other had been crushed and the pieces displaced, an earthquake under the skin. Jordan flipped over the pictures, and Pixley said, "Looking for a police photographer's stamp?"

"There's no identifying mark."

"They're copies."

"Where'd you get them?"

"You have your contacts. I have mine. For all we know they're the same." Pixley laughed a little boy's mischievous laugh. "You know I won't give them up."

"Okay, who am I looking at?"

"Name's Carlotta Abigail Bianchi, 23-years-old, formerly of Erie, Pennsylvania, most recently of the Bronx, Carla to her friends, Francesca to diners at the Mermaid Room in the Park Sheraton Hotel, where she's a waitress."

"I'd ask who was driving the truck that ran into her," Jordan said, "but a truck wouldn't have done so much damage. Who slugged her?"

"Not a slugger. A switch hitter with lefty power."

Jordan looked at him sharply, and Pixley winked back.

"Hub Chase."

Jordan examined the photos together, and again one by one, trying to put Carla Bianchi together again. Without evidence he'd stipulate that she'd once been good-looking. Suzie Chase's husband didn't seem the type to bust up a plain woman.

"Not that he admits to anything. He says," Pixley said, "her brains were scrambled, he was in the sack with someone else when she got it, a young lady whose reputation he's protecting, stand-up guy that he is."

"What does Francesca say?"

"He came into the nightclub with a bunch of players from the Yankees around one A.M., last Friday. She didn't know him from the batboy, but was ga-ga for pinstripes. Hub was rude, crude, lewd, and drunk as a skunk. He pawed her every time she came to the table, which she didn't object to—they're both agreed on that—till someone pointed out he was a bush lea-guer out on the town with the big club. When he slipped her his number, she gave it back to him. His teammates called it a night at three, but he was still hanging around when she knocked off an hour later. He didn't take it like a gentleman when she turned down his kind offer to escort her home. The rest you see for yourself."

"Why haven't I read about it anyplace?"

"No charges were filed," Pixley said. "Did I mention the Yankees are picking up the tab at the plastic surgeon's, and resodding the Police Athletic League ballfield at Macombs Dam Park?"

"It's not something that stays swept under the rug. Why did—?"

"Why'd someone give me the pictures?"

"Why bring them to me? I cover murders, not near misses."

"I'm trying to help you with a murder."

"I get my help from the dictionary," Jordan said. "*I'm* not a real detective. I'm a writer, that's all I do."

"Close enough. I'll show you more."

Jordan stopped him. "Is Carla Bianchi white?"

"Huh?"

"It's hard to tell from the pictures. Her face is so distorted, she barely looks human."

"What are you getting at?"

"It's the first question a real detective asks before taking a case."

Pixley looked uncomfortably at Jordan, who didn't explain. No one had to know he'd dug into the story of a Negro girl and been rebuked by his editor. Let Pixley think he was the kleagle in the Klan's Atlantic City klavern. As long as he got the facts straight, spelled everyone's name properly.

"I'm surprised you care," Pixley said.

"If she's colored, I can hardly leave it out."

"Why not?" Pixley said. And when Jordan wouldn't give in: "Unless she's passing, she's a white girl. The Mermaid Room wouldn't employ a Negro waitress."

"Better safe than sorry."

Pixley shook three pictures out of a small envelope. They were portraits of a man about 25 years old, full face and profile, blandly handsome despite a crushed flat top. Around his bull neck a placard certified a New York police department photo shoot. He was glaring boozily at the camera, challenging it, thought Jordan, or the whole damn world, an expression teased out of the color portrait of his new Fleer's baseball card. Jordan didn't want to run into him in a dark alley even when he wasn't holding a bat.

The third photo was a negative print. On closer inspection Jordan saw that it was an X-ray of a hand. One thing stood out, a ring on the third finger. Pixley pointed to a hairline crack in the knuckle behind it. "Hub'll be late for spring training."

"Francesca's lucky to be alive."

"Don't try to tell her," Pixley said. "Reconstructive surgery can only do so much. It won't bring back something special she had. She was rara avis, a small-town girl in New York to make it on her looks who actually got somewhere. She had a bit lined up on *Arthur Godfrey's Talent Scouts* on TV that she can kiss goodbye."

"You make it sound like you've seen her."

"I shoot contestants for the Miss America pageant," Pixley said. "A friend of mine in New York—if you must know, he's the source for these photos—he helps models put together their portfolio. He told me he'd never done a girl as fresh and lovely as Francesca. I'm something of an authority on beautiful women, and I've never shot anyone quite like her."

"I'll quote you."

"I'd rather that you help me find buyers. *The Sporting News* and the Erie papers might take a flyer, but they'd barely cover the postage. If Hub is charged with murder, the glossies will throw serious money around."

"If he is, I'll call you."

"Why wait? Today he's just a thug who beat up a pretty girl. God knows there's no market for that. Put a New York Yankee rookie on death row for murdering his beauty queen wife, and we'll make out fine."

"I don't know for certain that he killed her," Jordan said. "I'm not recommending him for the chair on what I have."

"Of course you know. You know, I know, anyone who reads between the lines of the story knows, as well as some who don't. What's stopping you? Does Hub Chase get the opportunity to hurt more women because you don't have the courage of your convictions?"

The little man was giving him hives. Pix was out to make a shameless buck. What noble cause sent Adam Jordan racing to crime scenes, harassing witnesses, and pestering Satchmo Armstrong? Suzie Chase's killer had remained an abstraction while Jordan assumed the role of avenging angel. Pixley, no angel himself, attached a name to that abstraction, and proposed cashing in on the evidence. Jordan felt transparent.

The percolator bubbled, and he smelled Savarin. The civilized thing was to invite Pixley to join him in a cup. But what did they have to talk about when the conversation moved away from brutalized women, psychopathic ballplayers, and corrupt dreams?

"I should go," Pixley said. "I have a shoot, and need to prepare."

"With a bathing beauty?"

"Well, you can't have a banana split without the cherry."

"Next one, give me a call. I wouldn't mind watching over your shoulder."

Pixley looked at him blankly. "Why?"

Jordan went for the papers, but there were no good murders, or arrests for old ones, or developments in cases he was keeping an eye on. He drank more coffee, found a Philadelphia station on the radio, and got back into bed. He couldn't think of anything to think about except for the one thing he was always thinking about even when he was thinking about something else. Aside from the dismal episode with Mollie, he hadn't gotten laid in months. His last date was a vague memory, as was the last woman he'd intentionally made smile. He might give Mollie another try. At least she was someone he'd already slept with, though he couldn't say he'd broken the ice. What was the worst that could happen? She'd come up with a new way to tell him to drop dead?

He was working out an excuse for calling when the radio got his attention. "Hard-hitting, hard-luck Hub Chase, the Newark Bears' outfielder who lost his wife to a savage murderer," had been traded to Philadelphia. Jordan tuned out some static. The Athletics had acquired the Yankees' top minor league prospect for two Double A pitchers, cash, and a bush leaguer to be named later. A steal, Jordan was thinking. No mention was made of Hub's arrest in New York. Lucky for Hub that Francesca hadn't died, or the Yankees might have exiled him to Washington.

Next up was the "tragic death of Charles R. Stolzfus, prominent

Atlantic City developer, and guiding light behind the Miss Jersey Shore Beauty pageant. Just forty-seven years old, and in robust health, Stolzfus succumbed to a massive heart attack in the Regency suite of the New Excelsior Hotel, whose rebirth he had overseen. Survivors include his wife, Pauline, and six children by a previous marriage…"

Jordan recalled Stolzfus, from a Sunday feature that had been spiked by his editors, as a bluff, outsize man who smoked Cohibas and cloaked his massive bulk in custom-tailored three-hundred-dollar suits. Something Jordan had left out of the story: Everyone he spoke to had whispered that the developer was asking for trouble if he didn't slim down. It hadn't done much for his blood pressure when Stolzfus was indicted by an Atlantic City grand jury for accepting payoffs from a mob-controlled contractor at the Excelsior, the largest hotel to go up on the Boardwalk in half a century.

"Stolzfus was a controversial figure who left behind the twelve-story Excelsior as his monument." More like his piggy bank, Jordan said to himself as he went back to figuring out a story to hand to Mollie. But his train of thought was derailed, and plans for getting laid had to be sidetracked.

Wasting time till the afternoon papers arrived wasn't so different from turning blue trying to find out how long he could hold his breath. When the *Evening Bulletin* truck pulled up at the corner store he was waiting on the curb. The driver tossed him a copy, and he gave it a quick read before the Standard News Corp. van came by with the suburban dailies. He lugged them home with a six-pack of Yuengling, charging upstairs when his phone began to ring.

"Adam, hey Adam, how's it hanging?"

"Oh, crap."

"This is how you say hello to your meal ticket?"

It was when the meal ticket was Greenie Greenstein. "What do you want?"

"And a fine good day to you. Matter of fact—"

"No, no, no," Jordan said. Fact and its variants were distinctions of slight concern to Greenstein. "Just tell me why you called."

"I've got something for you."

"I have all the dope I can smoke," Jordan said. "I don't use pills, wouldn't touch a greenie if you paid me."

The puns and double entendres that he purged from his writing he saved for Greenstein, who mistook him for a wit. Greenstein was his most active source for information and marijuana, but with so-so reliability, addled by the green Dexedrine pills that gave him purpose as they ate through his brain.

"I should only have somebody looking out for me like I look out for you. I heard you're on the unemployment line."

"Heard it in the joint?"

"It doesn't matter where. What I'm presenting on a silver platter is the sweetest scandal of this or any other year."

"Thirty seconds," Jordan said.

"An hour wouldn't begin to do it justice, all the ramifications. We'll blow the lid off Atlantic City."

"What is it? An exposé on the high price of bad dope?"

"I'm not comfortable talking on the phone," Greenstein said. "Buy me lunch."

"My inclination to be jerked around isn't what it was. See you later."

"Wait. The story's about Chuckie Stolzfus, how he died."

"I already know how. He had a bum ticker."

"That doesn't explain what made it stop." When Jordan didn't bite: "He was in the arms of a woman other than his wife at the time."

"Why should I care?"

"The woman whose arms they were, ask her."

At the coffee shop in the Columbus Hotel, in a corner where the winter twilight didn't reach, Jordan watched a young couple jab their fingers at a menu like it was a tout sheet. Greenie Greenstein, thinner than Jordan remembered, had assumed an unhealthy patina that underscored his nickname. Often Jordan told him to take better care of himself, but the words entered one ear, gathered speed through the porous brain, and exited the other. The girl sitting across from him was a Negro in a red coat. Jordan went to the booth scuffing his soles. It was bad etiquette to sneak up on a Dexedrine user, whose overworked heart might follow Stolzfus' example.

Greenstein's double-take let Jordan know he wasn't the only one worse for wear. "Cherise," he said, "move your *tuches*."

The girl slid over, and Jordan dropped down on a cushion so warm Cherise might have been running a fever. Greenstein used a napkin to wipe his nose. His eyes were red, and his teeth were mottled. Jordan smelled his breath across the table.

"Being out of a job agrees with you?"

Jordan shrugged. Any other answer would provoke a self-pitying story from Greenstein about tough times, and what Jordan could do to help. "Did you order?"

"Cherise is watching her figure," Greenstein said. "Steak is all she eats. I'm watching it, too. The same for me."

The waitress brought coffee. Greenstein struggled with a sugar packet. Cherise tore it in her teeth, and emptied it in his cup.

"Greenie, do the introductions."

"We need to talk percentages. This is a major scoop. I have to protect myself."

"Excuse my friend," Jordan said to the girl. "I'm Adam Jordan."

"After all the work I've done, I'm coming in as a partner," Greenstein said. "Whatever you get, half goes to me."

Greenstein looked at Cherise, who dumped two more sugars into the cup. He raised it to his lips sloshing coffee in his lap. "Ow," he said. "And a share in the byline."

"Write the story yourself."

Jordan left a quarter on the table. He was sliding out of the booth when Cherise caught his hand, hers as hot as the seat. She said, "I don't care what's goin' on 'tween you two, but I'm sure not doin' the dishes 'cause we don't have money for the check. Put up some cash, then you can go on with your squabblin'."

"I know you from somewhere," Jordan said.

"I never saw you before in my life."

"You look familiar."

"I hear it a lot even from folks who don't think we all the same."

Greenie looked up from sprinkling cold water on his thigh. "You're both right."

"Don't be thinkin' you seen me walkin' the streets. I ain't a party girl either, don't bring men for good times in hotels. You never saw me workin' the Excelsior, 'cause I wasn't there before that night. Never saw me noplace till now."

"My mistake," Jordan said. "Tell me what went on with Stolzfus."

Greenstein slapped his hand against the table. "Clock's running."

"I do modeling." Cherise unfolded a page torn from a glossy magazine, and reinforced along the creases with Scotch Tape, a picture of several generations gathered around a Thanksgiving dinner with all the trimmings. Jordan recognized a composition lifted from the *Saturday Evening Post* except that the family was Negro, *SEPIA* in block letters in an upper corner. A girl snatching a drumstick might have been Cherise at fifteen. "Mr. Stolzfus was a big cheese in the Miss Jersey Shore pageant. Miss Lily White Jersey Shore. But there was things he could do for me."

"Do for you how?"

"He had a finger in plenty pies, some for colored."

"Forty-five seconds," Greenstein said.

"How old are you, Cherise?"

"Twenty-one."

"You look eighteen," Jordan said, "almost."

"Was no big deal, him bein' fat and old. He made me laugh with his jokes, listened to my problems, didn't bother me with none of his. You the type of man I steer clear of, pretty face and all. Nothin' funny about you."

"He doesn't care if you like him," Greenstein said. "All *he* likes are facts. He's married to them, he worships them. Adam Jordan never takes a fact in vain, so help him God. Give him the facts, just the facts, ma'am, like that cop on the TV says."

"Some men," Cherise said, "get to where they got every-thing, but ain't satisfied. Can't be a new toy they lookin' for, they already broke 'em all. Idea comes to 'em *I'm* what they lacking to find the, you know, fountain of youth. But my time's valuable, like Greenie's is to him. It'll cost 'em."

"What did it cost Stolzfus?"

"You don't know?"

"If I'm going to sell your story, you have to spell out every-thing, even if some of it's embarrassing."

"Don't embarrass me the least little," Cherise said. "Rest of his life is what it cost him, poor man. Game we was playing was too much for his heart. I'd show you, but it could happen again."

"She's not kidding," Greenstein said.

"He had his pick of gorgeous girls," Jordan said. "Why you?"

"White girls. He'd been down that road plenty times. Wasn't no fountain at the end."

"This is where the story gets good," Greenstein said.

"Forgot my place," Cherise said to Jordan. "Where was I?"

"Going to the Excelsior with Stolzfus."

"Took the roundabout way," she said. "He promised he'd wine me and dine me. I got dressed for a feed at a fancy restaurant, but then his driver came and brought me around the back of the hotel, put me on a freight elevator. Mr. Stolzfus had these old clothes laid out on the bed like for a handkerchief head, you know, Aunt Jemima. After he called the room service, he asked me to put 'em on."

"What'd I say?" Greenstein said. "He was a freak."

"Been with freakier freaks," Cherise said. "Man like Mr. Stolzfus ain't hard to understand. Crazy for black women. Only use he have for a white girl is to be his wife and give him kids."

Jordan said, "I remember where I saw you."

"Don't know what you been smokin', but how about sharing some?"

"Don't be cute, Cherise," Greenstein said. "I'm cute enough for both of us. Where does he know you from?"

"You so observant," she said to Jordan, "tell him yourself."

"I caught you at the Ruckus Room dancing behind Louis and the All-Stars."

Greenstein slapped the table again. "That's time."

"Did you know Etta Lee Wyatt?" Jordan said. "Or were you called in to replace her when she went missing?"

"Ain't nobody's replacement. I worked the Ruckus before Etta Lee. Still there after she left."

"Shut up, Cherise," Greenstein said. "Let me handle this."

"You were friends with her?"

"Close enough that she told me *her* problems. Whatever you make of that."

"You're giving it away for peanuts like you always do," Greenstein said. "He wants two stories, it's two deals. We've got him over a barrel."

"You heard what Greenie say, I want double."

Greenstein shook his head. "*We* do."

Cherise raised Jordan's arm over her shoulder, slid under it, and snuggled against him. She rubbed her cheek against the back of his hand, then looked into his eyes. "What this strange white man doin' at our table, dear?" she said. "Friend of yours?"

"Give me crap, Cherise," Greenstein said, "I'll double *that*."

"I'm trying to tell you what you want to know," she said to Jordan, "but it hard to concentrate, him makin' threats on my body."

"I'll do worse to your body than threaten it," Greenstein said.

"Gettin' so I can hardly think," she said to Jordan, "he upsettin' me so."

"Damn you, Cherise, quit playing games."

"You should go," Jordan said to him. "Phone me later."

"I'm not leaving till we come to an understanding."

"Understand this," Cherise said. "You don't go missing yourself, I'm callin' for the hotel detective to come see what you hidin' in your pockets."

Greenstein's chair scraped against the floor. "When my steak comes, wrap it in a napkin and bring it to my place, or you'll really be in shit."

The chair tipped over as he stormed off. Cherise slid onto Jordan's lap, then continued out of the booth. She set the chair upright, and sat down again on the other side of the table. "Where were we?" she said. "Oh yeah, talkin' money."

"No," Jordan said, "the subject was Etta Wyatt."

Cherise snapped open her purse. She propped a mirror against a water tumbler, and put on her face. A face that wasn't cheap or naïve. A serious face just this side of hard. Not an easy fit, but the right one. Jordan saw what Stolzfus had seen in her, although not why Stolzfus hadn't made her over the way she was now. Even a man who wasn't crazy only for Negro women would see it.

"Why do you want to know about her?" she said. "Mr. Stolzfus was more entertaining."

"You're as much entertainment as I can use."

"Freakish yourself," she said.

"What do you mean?"

"Like Greenie say—said, you're queer for facts." She snapped her compact shut, and put it away. "I can use a drink. Call the waitress over."

"You don't need me."

"She's ignoring us. I want a whiskey sour, and it'd be nice if you had something yourself. Don't have to look like Christmas comin' twice, like Mr. Stolzfus did when we was together, but try and act like you're enjoyin' a business lunch with your new partner."

He signaled to the waitress, who didn't seem to notice. He waved again, and got the back of her head. Cherise arched an eyebrow, and he called loudly for service, snapped his fingers until the waitress came.

"Did you know Etta Lee before she started dancing with you?"

"You still didn't tell me why you're interested."

"It shouldn't make a difference to you."

"You're wrong about me. Everything makes a difference. Think you can shut me out like that waitress was doing—you've got another think comin'. Etta Lee was killed, wasn't she?"

"You can put me closer to finding out."

"The story's going to make you rich?"

"Down the road, maybe."

"What's in it for me? Crumbs off your plate?"

"I'll give you twenty dollars in advance. There'll be more when I interest an editor, and when the check is in my hands."

"That's a lot of trust you're askin' from someone just met you. Gotta do better than twenty, or Greenie'll find a writer can afford top-notch murder."

Their drinks came. She pulled the cherry out of her whiskey sour, and drank off an inch, came up for air licking her lips. Behind the new face the old one flickered, and he glimpsed others that she'd also abandoned. Then she bit into the cherry like a lascivious little girl, an expression that didn't serve her well. With each fresh look he made less of her. That she was black was the smallest part of it.

"Another?"

"Won't do to get me drunk," she said.

"I'm not trying to."

"Didn't say nothing about not trying."

He reached for his beer. Cherise clinked her glass against it. "Cheers. Mr. Stolzfus dropping dead is still in your price range."

The steaks arrived with a hamburger for Jordan. "How many times were you with him?"

"Enjoy your lunch."

Jordan nudged his plate out of the way. He put his notebook on the table.

"Four times." Cherise cut into her steak. "No, make it three. First time don't count because he acted normal, nothin' he wanted but the satisfaction comes with helpin' a poor colored girl realize her dreams."

"You had no idea about him?"

"Wrong ideas. He was dignified as a judge."

"Did you always have to dress—?"

She nodded. "But not every time like Beulah. Once, he had me in my canteloupes from the Ruckus Room. Thought he was askin' for a command performance, but he just wanted to be the loyal subject of the queen of the islands. Thank God he didn't expect a cannibal. Where I draw the line."

"You're kidding."

"Think I got an imagination like that?"

"Why didn't you tell him to get lost?" Before the words were out he was trying to take them back, but Cherise pounced on them.

"Queen of the South Sea Isles pays better'n snitching for a magazine writer startin' down the road."

He poured his beer, drank it watching her eat.

"He was on the lookout for new girls," she said. "Was one of his old girls that introduced us. Let him have her every way but upside down, but put up her back at dressing like a fool. Was the opposite with me."

"You always saw him at the Excelsior?"

"Steak's a little chewy, but don't taste bad," she said. "Have Greenie's. I'll bring him your burger."

Jordan blocked the plate with his hand.

"You sure?" she said. "Mr. Stolzfus was all the time trying to get me to a vacation house he had. I never went. Knew I was safe at the hotel."

"Why wouldn't you feel safe in the country?"

"Don't you listen? The man was strange. Was gonna have a Halloween party, only it wasn't Halloween, invite all his friends there. People from business, and entertainers, racketeers who owned the clubs. One singer, name's so big it'll cost extra. Some jockeys from the track, ballplayers, you name it."

"Which ballplayers?"

"Not from the Negro league, I'll tell you that."

"Where was his country house? Did he say?"

"Wasn't a *country* house. A beach house. Mr. Stolzfus was crazy for the beach."

"Give me someone who'll back up your story."

"Have to trust me."

"An editor won't," he said. "What about the girl who introduced you to Stolzfus?"

"Can't—"

"I know. She costs more."

"C.O.D."

He looked inside his wallet at close to fifty dollars. Cherise put two fives aside for the check, and slipped the rest in her purse. Thirty-eight dollars was highway robbery for a source. But he was almost ready to sit down at the typewriter. Cherise would never be in his pocket again.

"Gettin' a steal," she said. "Two cases for the price of one. Etta Lee made the introduction. Mr. Stolzfus was her main sugar daddy." She picked up some stringbeans with her fork. "Somethin' the matter? Look like you got a bad taste in your mouth, and can't spit."

"A dead killer won't sell as many magazines as a live one."

"Never no pleasin' you, is there?"

"Was Stolzfus capable of murder?"

"Everybody's capable," she said, "apart from me 'n you, and I ain't sure about you. Mr. Stolzfus in no position to complain you're spreadin' lies about him."

"I still need a second source. Who would he have invited to the beach house?"

"My memory could be better on it."

"You're not getting another red cent."

"The racketeer, I remember *his* name."

"What about the ballplayer?"

"On the tip of my tongue," she said. "It'll come."

"When?"

"By the weekend. At a nicer place 'n this."

CHAPTER 7

Pelfrey wasn't feeling himself (wasn't feeling much of anything, thanks to his pain pills) when he returned to work. Unedited manuscripts were heaped on his desk, a reminder that Lou Segar had quit and not been replaced. Envelopes stuffed with wire service flimsies had toppled off the pile onto his chair. Pelfrey swept them onto the floor, and let himself down, clutched the armrests while the office whirled around him.

Tacked to the wall was the roster of unsolved cases that his reporters were watching, more than 3,000 at last count, crimes of sufficient gore and ingenuity to merit coverage in his magazines, 3,000 victims of horrific death, and for each one a killer avoiding arrest. Pelfrey had a permanent knot in his stomach knowing that an army of murderers walked America's streets. Some day he would retire to write the book that would sum up his career. He wouldn't focus on his most memorable cases, but on a society infested with killers. Already he'd decided on a title: *The Homicidal Maniac Next Door.* He often wondered what 3,000 murderers were up to, what was going through their minds while he worried about them.

At a quarter to nine a gray-haired woman in a gray wool suit came into the office. Pelfrey swallowed another pain pill.

"Are you sure you wouldn't rather be at home," she said, "or back in the hospital? Your color's dreadful."

"I feel better having something to do."

She patted his hand consolingly. Hers was sandpapery, cooler than room temperature, how he thought her body must feel to Dwight Turner, the president of Turner Men's Group, whose secretary Helene Bryer had been before she began sleeping with him thirty years ago, and been named publisher.

"The magazines have been going to hell without you," she said.

"I'm here to…" he stopped to let the room go around again. "To fix them."

Mrs. Bryer smiled thinly as Pelfrey dared her to mention again how sick he looked. If she did, he might be persuaded to go off to recuperate, and she'd be left with no one to get out the magazines, which would die.

"Circulation is down three percent since the June issues," she said. "If Mr. Turner doesn't see a turnaround, we'll have to fold one of the titles."

"We're being eaten alive by TV," Pelfrey said. "People would rather sit on the couch with one eye open than read."

"Our format is stale. Find a fresh approach."

"The facts are the facts. There's nothing I can do about them."

"You can get better writers."

"Good writing intimidates the readers. We'd sell more if we had prettier girls on the cover. The models we're using scare away customers."

"Beautiful girls are expensive," Mrs. Bryer said.

"You're telling me?"

Helene Bryer turned a sharp eye on Pelfrey, but couldn't tell if he was being sarcastic. One reason she kept him in charge of the magazines despite falling readership was his seriousness. If he wanted to be funny, he'd also be out of a job.

"We can't afford them," she said.

"They don't have to be Hollywood starlets, but we can improve on the dogs…uh, Plain Janes we have now. Hire fashion photographers to shoot them in their underwear, and we can forget about declining circulation."

"Unclothed women on the covers of his magazines embarrass Mr. Turner in front of his friends. Besides, if we show too much skin we'll be taken down from news racks in the Bible Belt. Use real news photos. What we sacrifice in sales, we'll save on models and photographers." She had more to say, but Pelfrey's color was worse. "You look awful."

"I never felt better."

She stepped out, and Pelfrey went to the art department. Alejandro de Costa, Turner Publishing's art director, was examining slides of a handsome young couple exchanging marriage vows for the cover of the lead confession title, *Modern Love*. Pelfrey picked up the contact sheet from a *Real Detective* shoot, pictures of a man with a three-day growth holding a filleting knife to the throat of a girl whose eyes bulged with fright, the pop-eyed girl cowering from a hunting rifle, a tire iron, a tree limb, a broken bottle, a two-by-four. Circled with a red crayon was the pair grappling for a .38, the action incidental to the girl's tight red sweater. De Costa would airbrush pimples from her forehead while Pelfrey decided which story in this month's line-up the picture best illustrated, and wrote a cover line.

De Costa put down the slides. The way the art director looked at him, Pelfrey had an idea that he was being sized up to model for a funeral scene as the corpse. He returned to his office, and began blue-penciling a manuscript, a lovers' lane rape-slaying identical to hundreds he'd used before. Often he wondered if the writers weren't sending the same stories every month, running them through the typewriter to change names and locales.

He'd lost track of the time when Mary Glenny told him that she was going home and hoped he felt better tomorrow. Pelfrey muttered goodbye without looking up. Anyone seeing him alone in an empty skyscraper wrestling copy into readable English wouldn't believe it more than Mary or Mrs. Bryer did, but he'd never felt happier.

The heat went off. The elevator operator stuck his head in to say that he'd have to walk down eighteen flights if he didn't leave now. Pelfrey buttoned his cardigan, told the elevator operator he'd see him in the morning.

Pelfrey lived nearby on Third Avenue. The El ran by his windows almost close enough to touch, but it wasn't the noise keeping him away from his apartment, it was the quiet. He'd been alone since his wife announced that she was leaving him, and asked him to be a sport about it. Her lawyer found a B-girl and the photographer who shot Pelfrey and the B-girl together in bed, the B-girl wearing hoop earrings and not much else. The pictures won his wife an uncontested divorce on grounds of adultery. Nine years later Pelfrey was still paying alimony. In his desk were the negatives of the B-girl and himself. When he had the right story he'd use one for the cover of *Real Detective*.

At 9:30 he went home, and thawed dinner. He started on another manuscript, but couldn't get settled. When his wife left she took most of their friends. His closest acquaintances were writers, faceless voices on the phone. The long distance operator put him through to a New Jersey exchange.

"It's Pelfrey," he said. "I've got something to keep an eye on. A couple of little girls, twin sisters—"

"Rita and Rina Pulaski, eleven years old," Jordan said, "vanished while walking home from Grover Cleveland Elementary School in Sea Isle City. Last seen with the school janitor, who's got a county record for exposing himself to children."

"When did we talk about it? My memory's shot. These damn pills—"

"I caught the case from the United Press while you were in the hospital," Jordan said. "What's the time?"

"After ten. Too late to call?"

"No, it's a treat to get away from the typewriter. I've been at it all day."

"Which story are you working on? I forgot that, too."

"It's not for you," Jordan said. "I've been working on and off on a book, mostly off, for years."

"The great American novel?"

"A novel. If I ever finish, I'll find out how great."

"I've been thinking about starting a book myself," Pelfrey said. "That's as far as I get."

Jordan hated to talk about writing, a subject on which everyone but the practitioners was an authority. But a 10 P.M. call from a man he scarcely knew wasn't about literary theory. What did it cost to lend an ear? He liked Pelfrey, and he owed him. And he could make use of a character with no one but a stranger to cling to late at night. "Thinking's the hard part."

"The dick books are shot. I figured I'd hang on till I retire, but I don't see them lasting five years. I'm the last of the Mohicans. There's no future here, not much of a present."

"Get out while the getting's good, why don't you?"

"It's not something to brag about, but—"

He didn't sound like a braggart. What he sounded like was a career criminal copping a plea.

"I love the magazines. Editing them's what I want to do forever. You're just starting out," he said, "but you've got the knack. When we go under, it'll be a terrible waste of talent, yours and mine. In the meantime, we can pray."

"That they don't fold?" Jordan said.

"For big murders to keep them going longer."

Pelfrey replaced the receiver, and felt under the desk for his pencil, which had rolled onto the floor. He almost had it when the phone rang, and he pulled his hand away. "What did you forget?"

"It's a good thing you didn't die."

Was it necessary to point that out? He'd misjudged Jordan, who was as flaky as his other staffers without the excuse of being a souse.

"...so I can have the pleasure of killing you myself."

The connection was too clear for long distance, the voice deeper than Jordan's, and with a rasp. He felt a twinge in every one of his stab wounds. "Who is this?"

"Fifteen years I lost on account of you. You and your damn magazine turned the jury against me. You know who I am."

He was too angry to admit being afraid. If Morris Wing wasn't able to finish him while driving a blade into his body, what could someone on the phone do?

"The line forms on the left," he said.

"Laugh now, comedian. After I'm done with you, nobody'll be laughing but me."

Pelfrey dialed the police, but knew what he'd hear. The NYPD didn't have enough men to watch over everyone. Didn't he know that someone serious about harming him wouldn't announce it? They advised an out-of-town vacation. Or he could bunk in jail till the threat blew over. He put down the phone, and went to set the chain on the door. Then he locked all the windows. The fire escape was a highway between the roof and the alley. Nothing he could do about that. It was high time to quit being every screwball's sitting duck, and get started on his book.

He put aside the manuscript, and typed notes on his run-ins with men who wanted to kill him. He'd never given a thought to writing fiction, but the voice of authenticity might make a novel an easy sell.

The phone rang again. He stared it down before making a grab. "Stuff it, you gutless bastard."

"Edward, how did you know it was me?"

"My mistake," he said.

"Not at all. It sounded like pillow talk."

"I thought you were someone else, Barbara."

"She's a lucky girl, I'm sure," Barbara said. "How are you feeling? I'd have come to the hospital, but I had doubts I was what the doctors ordered."

"They kept me sedated. I'd have tolerated a visit."

"Don't be arch. Who did you think I was?"

"Someone else who wants me dead."

The sniping brought back the last days of their marriage, when it was a question of who would move out first.

"Are you receiving combat pay? Is that why you remain loyal to the magazine?"

"How many times have we had this conversation?"

"Dozens?" she said. "Hundreds? But I was your wife when we started, and you assumed I was trying to get under your skin. I'm your ex now. If you can't believe your former spouse, where is the foundation for trust?"

"Why did you call?"

"The check—"

Pelfrey shook a pain pill out of the vial, and swallowed it dry. "I brought it to the post office two days ahead of time."

"You're a dear. It's already on deposit."

"If it isn't late, what's the problem?"

"It's small."

"It's right on the number, the same amount you receive every month."

"Don't I know?" she said. "A dollar doesn't go as far as when we were divorcing. The same amount is less than it used to be."

"Take it up with a judge. I've been fair with you. You're asking for too much."

"Of course I am. Would you respect me if I settled for less? Living as you do, you don't even respect the money. It's fitting and proper that you take better care of me."

"Everything I have will be yours one day."

"That's what you *say*—"

"But don't get your hopes up that that day will come soon, no matter who is sneaking past the parole board. I intend to have a long and healthy life, and to run through my last dollar living it."

"How very selfish of you."

"Good night, Barbara. It's always a delight to hear your voice."

"Watch your back, Edward," Barbara said.

❖

Toward the end of the week Jordan called New York to find out how Pelfrey was feeling. He dialed collect, lowered the window against a squall as he waited for the girl to accept the charges.

"Mary," he said, "let me talk to your boss."

"This isn't Mary. I'm Amy Lund. And I'm here alone."

"I don't know you. Where's everybody?"

"At the cemetery."

Jordan lit a Lucky, and sealed the windows. How come everybody picked the rottenest days to visit a cemetery? "Why?"

"For the funeral," Amy said. "I'm a temp. They didn't tell me much, only that somebody tried to kill Mr. Pelfrey, and he died."

"He'd been stabbed," Jordan said, "but he was getting better. It looked like he was going to make it."

"They didn't take chances this time. They shot him."

"Who did?"

"No one knows. Mary says we'll probably run it as an unsolved."

By the grace of Ed Pelfrey he'd fielded a gig that was the next best thing to what he loved to do, and he blamed Pelfrey—poor bastard—for blowing it. An editor with ideas of his own would be brought in to run the magazines, and he had a feeling it wouldn't work out for him. No reason to think that way—just the feeling. Joe Btfspik from *Li'l Abner*, who went around under a permanent black cloud, had nothing on him.

He wanted a woman to talk to, at least to talk, but didn't know any who'd give him the right time. Maybe one. Good-looking enough in her way, though not his type. All wrong for him, in fact. When did he ever let that stop him?

A man picked up on the first ring. "Cherise there?" Jordan said to him.

"What time you need her? For how long?"

"Who am I talking to?"

"Who're *you*? Where you want her?"

A hand slapped the mouthpiece at the other end of the line.

A woman asked, "That for me? Give me the damn phone."
Then Cherise, out of sorts, but keeping her anger in check,
said, "Yeah?"

"It's Adam Jordan."

"Who?" she said. "Oh. Oh, you."

"It's nobody, go on, get out," she whispered. Then for Jordan
again: "I didn't expect to hear from you so soon. Got to give me
time."

"Who was that?"

"My pimp," she said. "That what you thinking? Sorry to disappoint, but he's my nephew. 'Scuse his juvenile humor. You
don't feel a fool for askin'?"

For calling. And for the notion that this coarse girl could
help to smooth his crash landing. "Did you find out anything?"

"Some. I ain't Dick Tracy."

Coarse—not to mention a wiseass. And his only link to Etta
Wyatt. Smooth never went down easy with him anyway.

"Still there?" she said. "I should have more by the weekend."

"I need it this afternoon."

"Promised me a feed at a high-class restaurant," she said.
"Lunch don't count."

"Teplitsky's puts out a great buffet."

"Was thinking along the lines of the Ship 'N Shore at Tarrantino's."

"I'll have to rob a bank."

"Be quick about it," she said. "See you at Mississippi and
Atlantic at eight."

The intersection was in the colored district a few blocks from
Etta Wyatt's boarding house. He was there on the dot, running
his engine beside a pump. On the sidewalk women paraded
coatless in winter's chill. A teenager in a red dress mouthing
"Wanna date?" rapped on his window. She pressed her lips to
the glass leaving a hot coral bow around a wet spot where she

rolled her tongue. Why meet here unless Cherise wanted him to think the worst of her? He was up in the air about whether he did.

The teenager ran away. An unmarked cop car took her place alongside his door, the detectives watching her go, then focusing on Jordan through the smudge in the glass. Jordan knew the man riding shotgun from accidents where they'd been first on the scene. There was a delayed instant of recognition, an accusatory look before the cop nudged his partner, and the car took off through a red light.

Spike heels clattering like castanets, Cherise jaywalked across Mississippi, stopping traffic. Her skirt wasn't especially short or tight, her neckline scooped just low enough to make things interesting. A faux fur coat and a wig with a twisted bun achieved an effect of semi-respectability. Jordan reached over and unlocked the passenger door. Cherise powdered her nose, she tapped her toe. He got out, held the door, shut it behind her. Cherise tuned the radio to the rhythm-and-blues station, and whisked her hand against the leathery upholstery before rendering her verdict. "Nice car," she said.

"I got it for a song."

"Threw you a compliment. Suppose to say how pretty I look."

He'd said it to himself. What more did she need?

"I didn't recognize you."

"Spotted *you* a mile away," she said. "I get all done up, and you, look at you, like you come from touting losers at the track. Would've hurt to put on a clean shirt?"

Whatever was bugging her, why take it out on him? How many other women from this part of town would have steak and lobster tonight in Atlantic City's best restaurant? He rummaged in the glove compartment for a tie, and threaded it under his collar. Cherise batted his hands away. With a strangler's determination she crafted a fat knot and cinched it tight, then smoothed the wrinkles against his chest.

"Live around here?" He pulled away from the curb, tromping on the brake as a couple of young women in low-cut tops ran across the street after a gang of GIs.

"I had business to tend to."

It annoyed her that he didn't ask what the business was. "Booking agent needed to talk to me about a job in Philadelphia," she said.

"That's good."

"The producer wants a private audition at his place. That's bad."

The conversation stopped cold. The little they had in common didn't include an ice-breaker. Etta's disappearance, Francesca's beating, Pelfrey's fresh grave pressed on Jordan with the accumulated weight of all his other cases. Violent crime also exacted a toll on its chroniclers. If he found newspaper work again, he'd try for an assignment on the sports page, build his life around games.

Tarrantino's scripted in neon outshone the moon, two signs— front and back—strung between the stacks of an old Cape May-Lewes ferry tricked out with a paddle wheel like a Mississippi riverboat. As he walked Cherise on board some of the diners looked up like they'd discovered a roach in their soup. The hostess came without menus or a smile to say that reservations were required, and every table was booked solid into the spring. Jordan provided the smile. After a smoky fire several months ago he'd used the hostess' picture with a thousand-word story, plugging the osso bucco. She brought them to Siberia, near the kitchen door. Cherise didn't make a stink about it.

"Greenie took me one time to Merrill's in Chelsea Heights," she said. "Shylock friend of his was holding their note, and swore they'd give us the royal treatment. They refused service, but not on account of me. Didn't want Greenie's like on the premises."

"I've never seen him embarrassed."

"Makes two of us," she said. "Told me it was me they wouldn't serve."

As an ice-breaker it ranked between a missing woman and a murder.

A waitress dropped off menus. Cherise caught her wrist, and had her recite the specials. "Gettin' off cheap," she said to Jordan.

"What did you learn?"

"Not a goddamn thing," she said. "Figured I could play you for a meal. Don't want to watch me eat, settle the bill before you leave."

He ordered for both of them, lit a Lucky.

Cherise patted his hand. "You sweet, know it?"

"Compared to what?"

"Don't be sulking. Truth is, I got plenty for you. Had to be sure you in control of your 'motions, you don't hear what you like."

"What don't I want to hear?"

"Hold your horses." She shook a cigarette out of the pack, tapped the end against the back of her hand. "Us two, me and Etta, have the same booking agent. Slipped my mind till I was at his office. Her picture's next to mine on the wall, 'long with his other clients, big stars, too. Be glad you weren't there when I brought up her name."

She put a cigarette between her lips, leaned close, and touched the tip to Jordan's, blew smoke past his cheek.

"Was his opinion Etta was a rising talent. Could sing and dance, tell jokes that'd make you run home to change your pants. Even play soprano sax passable well, and some clarinet."

"Where do I find him?"

"Uh-uh. He can make things hard for me. Has a lawyer's license, but more money comes in from entertainers he books into the clubs, and providing girls for private parties."

"You mean prostitutes."

The smoke went into his face. "I worked some of those parties.

Etta brought me to one where I met Mr. Stolzfus. Nobody said nothing about turning tricks. I was there to dress up the room, to *look* available. Anything else, I was on my own. Our agent was gonna supply the girls for Mr. Stolzfus' party that didn't happen."

"Is he a Negro?"

"He'll let you think he is."

"I don't get you."

"Ain't read his birth certificate. Wouldn't be the first white person I know passing for black."

Jordan placed his notebook on the table, uncapped his pen.

"Never knew nobody like that?" She stopped to let him get something down on paper, but started talking again as doodles filled the margins of the page. "Ain't making it up. There's white folks'll do anything to make a dollar off of Negroes—even be one. Some get to feeling that's who they are, heaven knows why. It'd be unkind to tell 'em to go back to what they were before."

"He didn't send Etta to private parties to crack jokes."

"Etta knew the ropes, and was okay with it. Was nobody she wouldn't go to bed with if she thought it'd help her career."

"What about someone who couldn't do anything for her?" Jordan said. "Did he stand a chance?"

"She didn't let herself be in love, that's what you're getting at. Never took her eye off the ball."

"Speaking of which," Jordan said, "last time we talked you mentioned a baseball player. His name was on the tip of your tongue."

"Must've swallowed it."

"Hub Chase," he said. "Sound familiar?"

She shook her head. "Don't mean I never ran across him. Not everybody at the parties'd give out their right name."

"His wife was murdered a few weeks before Etta disappeared. She was also young and ambitious."

"What was *her* name?"

"Susannah. Suzie Chase."

"Miss Monmouth County? Miss Phillie Cheesesteak the year before? Redhead with a build like that Jane Russell?"

"You know her?"

"Knew who she was. Gorgeous girl like her, if you're in the business of being beautiful in Atlantic City, you heard of Suzie Chase."

"Did you see her at any of the parties?"

"Her husband was on the guest list, remember?"

"They were living apart."

"Wouldn't be the first gent with a beautiful wife looking for something not so beautiful. Same goes for the beautiful wife."

"What's in it for her?"

"Find the right man, she could put those parties—put Miss Phillie Cheesesteak behind her."

"I can't prove it, but I think her death is connected to Etta's disappearance."

"Be a special story, huh, two beauties for the price of one?"

"Without Suzie's killer, Etta isn't worth anything, even if I found out what happened to her."

"How's that?"

"No one who reads my magazine gives a damn when a Negro girl is murdered."

Her toe barked his shin as she uncrossed her legs. He gave her a moment to make a stink, but what she said was, "Don't I know?"

"Not that I'm close to cracking either case."

"Nothing more I can do for you."

"Let me talk to your agent."

She shook her head. "He's an important man. Ain't got time for jawing with a lowly magazine writer."

"Getting important people to let down their hair is what lowly writers do."

"Ain't got no hair," she said. "Shaves his head clean."

"Give me his name."

She stubbed out her cigarette, looking past his shoulder. "Here come our drinks."

Jordan didn't turn around, afraid that when he looked back she'd be gone.

"Try Beach," she said.

"*What?*"

"Sound like you long-lost friends."

"I don't know what you're talking about."

"Didn't think so, 'less you knew him before he was colored," she said. "Beach, that's his name."

"What's his first name?"

"He lost it along with being white, and everything goes with it. Beach is all. Just Mr. Beach."

CHAPTER 8

"Please hold for Mrs. Bryer."

The crackle of long distance introduced a woman whose measured delivery nearly concealed a Bronx twang. "Mr. Jordan, this is Helene Bryer." An imperious woman, dry and menopausal, though Jordan was damned how he knew so much about her from just six words.

"I'm president of Turner Publications. Ed Pelfrey spoke highly of you."

"He was very kind," Jordan said. "I'm going to miss him, really am. What can I do for you?"

"Since his death the magazines have been more or less running themselves." A second of open air left Jordan to consider that Mrs. Bryer was attempting a cordial tone rather than fighting a weak connection. "No obvious candidate to replace him has emerged. To be brief, I've called to offer you the position of editor-in-chief of *Real Detective*."

"I don't know the first thing about magazine editing."

"Expectations will be modest at first." The dry voice with overtones of umbrage, Helene Bryer informing him that he'd let Pelfrey down. "It's not a great leap from writing. All editors have made it."

"It's not for me," Jordan said.

"Ed didn't mention that you were closed-minded. You haven't heard what we're paying and the generous benefits that go with it."

"I'm a reporter. I'd rather make errors than correct them."

"Feel free to make all the errors that you like," Mrs. Bryer said, "and then to catch each one."

"As the new man on the staff, I'm the least qualified."

"On the contrary, it's your strongest qualification. The others are hacks telling stories the same way they've been doing it since the Coolidge administration, which for many of them is the last time they drew a sober breath. You haven't picked up their bad habits—not on the printed page. I've read some of your pieces. You're the best of the bunch by far."

"I'm flattered," Jordan said. "It doesn't change my thinking."

"I have no one else, please believe me. If you turn me down, I'll be forced to fold the magazines. Forty writers, dozens of stringers and photographers, an art director and an editorial assistant will be out of work. You're being unconscionably selfish in not accepting my offer. Also short-sighted. The job pays ninety-five hundred. If that's not enough, assign yourself all the freelance work you can handle, and take home a good deal more."

Jordan said, "Crap."

"Not at all. It's an opportunity that may not come your way again. You'd be foolish to turn it down."

"That's what I was trying to say. When do I start?"

He was up half the night, unhappy about letting a woman he didn't know sell him a bill of goods over the phone, deciding on a graceful way to back out. Drifting off to sleep, he pictured himself in a green eyeshade prodding tortured copy into brilliant prose while a receptionist with Jane Russell's curves poured coffee. An apartment in a swank midtown tower came into focus, high-ceilinged rooms done up in Danish Modern with spectacular river views. All that was missing was Adam Jordan, who was squandering his talent in a city where the major celebrities were beauty contestants and a high-diving horse.

In the morning he told his landlord that he'd be gone by the weekend. Cherise called an hour later while he was pushing his sofa out the door.

"Can't wait to have grandkids, so I can tell 'em about the time I had the Ship 'N Shore at Tarrantino's," she said.

"Hold off on a family till you try the cheesecake at Lindy's in New York."

"Want to return the favor first. I told Mr. Beach about you. He set aside time to talk."

"He knows what I'm after?"

"Save your questions," she said. "Find him at 373 Mississippi Avenue, fifth floor. Be there at 4:45, he'll squeeze you in."

"Squeeze me between what?"

"First thing to ask."

The tile minarets of the RKO Alcazaba dominated the 300 block of Mississippi, which it shared with a Chinese wet wash at 371 and a Negro barber shop at 375. Under the marquee Jordan watched serpentine lights hop to a spastic rhythm around strips of peeling paint. The girl in the ticket booth was doing her nails with one eye on a paperback novel. The Alcazaba was fine for summer napping in air-cooled comfort, but television left little reason to stay open the rest of the year.

Gilt filigree in the tilework hid the outline of a door. Behind it a red Exit sign floated in the caramel-flavored darkness. Jordan was starting upstairs when he was frozen by the screech of tires, the amplified prelude to a crash that rocked the building. He squeezed the banister till Lou Costello's frightened yawp drew laughs from the spare audience on the other side of the wall.

A dentist's pebbled glass door filtered the fifth-story light. More spilled over an orthodontist's transom, puddling in an alcove where a guitar, bass, and piano offended Jordan with a leaden rhythm-and-blues riff.

Alone in an office Jordan saw a man drumming his hands on

a bare desk. A beret had a tenuous hold of his slick scalp. He had no sideburns or facial hair aside from a single eyebrow that did the work of two. At the final beat he reached over to a turntable and flipped the record. Jordan recognized the new side from the intro—Big Mama Thornton's hit, "Hound Dog."

"You don't care for Negro music?" the man said.

"What makes you say that?"

"It's all over your face."

"I wouldn't call it a Negro record, Mr. Beach. 'Hound Dog' was written by a couple of Jewish boys in Los Angeles."

Beach looked at him gravely. Since when was a Los Angeles Jew disqualified from being Negro?

"It's a lousy tune," Jordan said, "and the lyric is moronic. Big Mama's hardly Bessie Smith. Oh yeah, and her band stinks."

"Ofays don't know shit about music," Beach said.

Jordan let go of the notion that he would straighten out this strange man on a number of subjects besides music.

"I'm here to talk to you about something more important."

"Nothing is, man."

"Yeah. Yeah, you're right. About Etta Lee Wyatt, though—"

"A so-so voice, but you should see the way she moves."

"What do you think happened to her?"

"Girls like Etta come and go. A pretty dancer-singer with a second-rate sound is an A-number-one candidate to vanish."

"No one vanishes," Jordan said.

"Don't they?"

"They leave a body behind."

Beach shut his eyes, concentrating on the record. Jordan listened along with him. The ponderous beat was an anchor against the breezy sophistication of swing, and the modern jazz that came from it. It seemed presumptuous to tell a stranger, especially a Negro, a white one in particular, that his taste in black music was retrograde and crude.

"When was the last time you saw her?"

"I don't recall. We spoke right before she took a powder."
Beach's eyes remained closed, his head bobbing. "I needed a
young brownskin gal for a party that was right up her alley."

"Where?"

"Newark? Beach Haven? I'd have to check."

"Was the customer white or colored?"

One eye opened, fixed on Jordan. "Colored wouldn't have
use for a black girl. Couldn't afford white if I trucked 'em in.
The customer put in a call for two chicks, personable and clean,
affectionate with gentlemen and with each other, if you get my
meaning. I sent Etta with an older gal that's been with me for
years."

"What went on there?"

"You'd have to ask the other girl." Beach nudged the beret
back on his head. Jordan noticed a jagged scar in the shiny
smooth skin. "And she knows better than to talk to strangers."

"I thought you were a theatrical booker," Jordan said.

"All my girls are theatrical. Nothing real about them."

Beach opened his other eye, pulled back his cuff, and examined the time with a glance for Jordan that said only a fool would
waste a precious commodity. "TV, Vegas, the new music, they're
destroying the variety business. Nobody twists my girls' arms,
forces 'em to do this, that, the other thing the customer wants
'em for. They need to eat while I find 'em stage work, there are
compromises they have to make. My customers are successful
people, not perverts, names you'd know from the papers, but
not the headlines. Are they a little kinky when it comes to
women? Who ain't? They want black women for whatever
floats their boat? Who don't?"

"What happened at that party? You know a damn sight more
than you're letting on."

"Cherise said you were smart," Beach said. "Shows how much
she knows men. One of my best earners goes missing, my other
girls are afraid to go out on jobs, and you think I'm covering

up? Find out who messed with Etta, and I'll deal with him. Then you got a story."

"Ever talk to Etta again?"

"She called when she got home. I can't sleep till I know my girls are all right. I'm a father to 'em."

"And?"

"I didn't hear nothing I didn't hear a million times before. She made a new fan, who was gonna take it on himself to promote her career, didn't want nothing but the pleasure of seeing her a star—the colored Dinah Shore, the Negro Patti Page, the sepia singing rage. The situation in this country's changing. America don't need to be short-changed on talent like hers."

"She didn't laugh in his face?"

"She reads men like Cherise does, figures there's nobody don't come wrapped around her little finger. If trouble finds her, she'll send the devil packing, that's how fucking cute she is."

"Any idea about the fan?"

"A nothing," Beach said. "A hanger-on."

"How do you know?"

Beach spoke like a white man with a few Negro affectations, but Jordan had never heard anyone of either race laugh with his mirthless howl.

"It wasn't the customer. He had the cancelled check to remind him she was bought and paid for. The guests knew why she was there, didn't have to hand her a line. Who's that leave? A barman, a bouncer, the cabbie that took her home? Might even've just been Etta wanting me scared I'd lose her if I didn't give her personal attention."

"The customer probably can tell us."

"Drag him into it, I'll lose him for a customer. My other customers'll drop me 'cause I ain't discreet. My girls'll be reduced to peddling their ass on the street, 'stead of being the center of attention at high-class smokers where Sir Fucking Galahad wants to rescue 'em from the tragic life they're leading in my employ, and all on account of you bothering the wrong people with questions."

"You'll have to give up his name to the cops."

"Go home, get outta here," Beach said. "Police don't know nothing from nothing about a colored girl that might be dead. Anybody hurt Etta, he did it with a get outta jail free card in his pocket."

"Your girls know they're on their own if things get out of hand?"

"Ain't the case at all. They got *me* looking out for 'em."

"The way you looked out for Etta? Looking the other way?"

"What're you getting at?"

"You have a sweet racket pimping colored girls to weirdos, freaks, voyeurs, God knows who else. One goes missing—that's the cost of doing business. They should teach your profit model at Wharton. Unlimited inventory with free replacement in case of theft, damage, depreciation, or death."

"Take a look at a map of the United States, you'll see Atlantic City's below the Mason-Dixon line," Beach said. "Nobody cares about those girls like I do." He put another record on the turntable, Tiny Bradshaw's "Train Kept A-Rollin'."

"Ever see your girls in action, Beach? Sorry, I forgot, the customer wouldn't invite a black man." Rage flooding the shaved head darkened it, and left Jordan with the idea that for Beach anger delineated race. "I've been to parties like those. One of the regulars was a girl built like a young Lana Turner, but with needle tracks up and down her arms, who'd show up with a German Shepherd to entertain. Her pimp was also a humanitarian. He'd slip booties on the Shepherd's paws so the animal didn't claw the girl's back when it got excited."

"That vileness amuses you," Beach said. "Who's the real freak?"

"I did an exposé that embarrassed the state police into shutting the parties down. That much I could do. The girl was white."

Beach turned up the volume. Jordan was talking to himself, and to Tiny Bradshaw.

The curtains billowed as a door opened. Before Jordan could turn around he was hoisted out of his chair with an arm bent behind his back, and his head pressed down, concentrating his vision on the tan-and-white uppers of gunboat-size wingtips. Pain came with the understanding that the arm would be wrenched out of its socket if he struggled. The pain lessened, and he had a notion of taking a swipe at his abductor, but realized that he was being baited into something that wouldn't end well. He let himself be prodded out of the office, didn't lock his knees till he was staring down a long flight of stairs.

He had a solid grip on the banister when he was released with a kick in the pants. Over his shoulder he watched a man in a chalk-stripe suit walk toward Beach's office past a woman holding the hand of a boy about ten.

"Don't be afraid, mister," the boy said. "Go back, it'll make you feel better."

"What?"

The boy put a finger to his mouth, and lifted his upper lip. An incisor was missing from the top row of teeth.

"They give you gas," the boy said. "It doesn't hurt even a little."

Jordan went down the stairs clutching the handrail. He called Cherise from the corner.

"You saw Mr. Beach?" she said.

"I just left."

"Get anything out of him you can use?"

"If I was a blackmailer…"

"You don't sound right."

He didn't. Not to himself. He sounded like he'd had a whiff of the gas, and the pain hadn't gone away.

"Meet me at the Excelsior," he said.

"That dump? I got a better place. Be at my corner in ten minutes."

She was there first, wearing furry earmuffs and tight dunga-
rees with the cuffs turned up. It was the first time he'd seen her
in pants, and he came up on her slowly, giving her the once-
over while she frowned.

"Field clothes," she said.

"I don't get you."

"I'm from South Carolina originally, on the coast, worked
rice till we come north when I was thirteen. Everybody went
around in jeans 'cause we couldn't afford better. Makes me
laugh, seeing white girls here fuss over 'em like they from Mr.
Dior. Don't need you droolin' all over yourself to know how I
look in 'em, but they ain't my idea of high fashion."

"Where are we going?"

"Ain't far." She tucked her arm inside his. "Where you parked?"

An elderly white couple stepping out of a cab had a disgusted
look for them. A colored woman averted her head.

"Know what they're thinking, do you?" Cherise said.

"I can imagine."

"You'd be wrong. It's worse than I'm your good-time gal.
They think we're in love."

Someone had left a religious tract under the Hornet's wiper
blade. Jordan sailed it toward a trash can as Cherise let herself
into the front seat. "Drive to Massachusetts Avenue," she said.
"Take it all the way back to Clam Creek."

Jordan turned the car north, then west, away from the boardwalk. "How did you get Beach to see me?"

"Said you were a big cheese on your newspaper. You'd write
nice things about him, and he wouldn't get in trouble over Etta."

"He told me what a solid citizen he is for a whoremaster."

"Gonna clear his name anyway?"

"He isn't charged with anything."

"Get him charged, can't you dear? Then clear it."

"What's in it for you?"

"Something in it for everyone," she said.

"Don't do me any favors."

"Got no cause to talk to me like that," she said. "Ain't my fault you couldn't get what you want out of him. You're a reporter. I figured you can squeeze truth from a stone."

A light changed to red. They were through the intersection before Jordan brought the car to a stop.

"Pay some mind to your driving," Cherise said.

They rode in silence to Clam Creek, a tidal inlet edged by boat yards and marine repair shops. The smell of cooking oil, not fresh, blew from a cedar shack in the shell lot.

"The fried scallops," Cherise said. "That's all I got to say to you now."

They ordered from the take-out window, sat down at a picnic table on a grit beach. The wind swirled sand into the food, and chased them back into the car.

"There's a pier on the next street with a view," Cherise said. "Park there, and we won't have to look at each other."

Jordan's first date in Atlantic City had brought him to nearby Absecon Inlet to watch the submarine races before pulling him into the back seat. Cherise had nothing else on her agenda but scallops.

He balanced a bottle of Pepsi against his crotch as he backed out of the lot. After investigating a couple of dead ends they found a concrete dock that was home to a fleet of rustbucket trawlers. The Hornet spun its wheels in a sandy windrow, and stalled. Jordan re-started the engine, and the heavy car bounced onto the pier past a small ice house.

"You're not paying attention again," Cherise said. "Slow down."

Jordan hit the brakes. The pedal went to the floor, and he pumped it with the same result. Then he wrenched the emergency brake. The car slowed, but not by much. Cherise pressed her foot against the mat. That didn't help either.

An old man crabbing at the end of the pier stared down the speeding Hornet, then dropped a rotten chicken breast and jumped out of the way. Jordan slammed the transmission into reverse. The wheels locked to the tune of shrieking gears, and the rear end drifted. He steered into the skid, and the car fish-tailed, straightened, crashed through a railing, and snagged on a piling with the front wheels dangling over the water. Jordan took a deep breath. Before he could let it out, the car nosed into the sea.

Flung against the steering wheel, he bit his tongue. A crack zigzagged across the windshield from a starburst where Cherise struck it with her jaw. The car dipped under the chop, came level, and bobbed up like a rubber duck in a tub, thin streams entering through the dashboard vents. Looking out at water lapping against the window, Jordan remembered the salesman boasting of what reliable vehicles Hudsons were. But he hadn't thought to ask if they were seaworthy. He tasted blood in his mouth, which wasn't the worst thing. Then the front end began to sink, which was.

"Do something," Cherise said.

Jordan swallowed blood, open to all suggestions.

The car went belly up. It settled hard on the bottom, and Cherise moaned as she was thrown against the roof.

They had air. No need to panic, Jordan told himself, and kept repeating it until his door refused to open. His hand was on the window crank when Cherise caught him.

"Roll yours, too," he said, "so you're not pushing against the ocean."

"Don't go without me."

"You plan on staying?"

"I heard worse ideas." She winced as she rubbed her chin. Blood ran up her arm, and she took time to decide whether to become hysterical. "I can't swim."

Jordan cracked open the window, eased himself down to the roof. Cherise began to mutter. He thought she was cursing, but decided it was a prayer. The door still wouldn't move. He cranked the window all the way down, shivering in blackness as icy water rushed over him. Then he tried the door again, heaved his shoulder against it, lay back and kicked.

"The frame's bent," he said. "It's stuck."

Cherise gobbled up air, gorged on it.

Jordan slipped off his shoes. He put his head out the window, squeezed his shoulders through, and swam free. Fifteen feet above, or a little less, sunlight dissolved against the surface of the bay.

Using the driveshaft, the transmission, the oil pan, he pulled himself over the undercarriage. Cherise hadn't opened her door. The window remained sealed. He tugged at the handle, and the door swung easily.

She tackled him as he reached inside. He was in a no-holds-barred wrestling match that scorched his lungs and made him regret each of the tens of thousands of Luckys he'd lit since the first one when he was twelve. He got an arm around her throat (a submission hold; wasn't that what the pro wrestlers called it?) and was adjusting his grip when he lost her. Clinging to his legs, she anchored him to the bottom while he calculated his responsibility to keep her alive.

He kicked her away, and exhausted himself going after her. When she'd almost quit struggling he took her again. Scissoring his legs, he started for the surface, marking time until he switched to a frog kick that brought him into the sun and the frigid salt air he couldn't get enough of.

A wave caught him in a trough that funneled the horizon. On the back side was the dock. He paddled with one hand, the other inching Cherise's face out of the water. The old man tossed a line, nearly skulling him with the crab pot. He kicked as the old man reeled him in, but the cold took his remaining strength, and it was all he could do to hang on.

Cherise was wracked by a fit of coughing that threatened to sink them. The old man shouted something in Spanish that

Jordan didn't understand, pointing to rungs at the side of the dock. Jordan let the tide carry him, and the old man went down to the water, and took Cherise. Climbing after them, Jordan saw her on her side with her eyes rolled back, not breathing. Her skin was ashy. The old man drew a cross over his heart.

Jordan zipped open her jacket, pressed the heel of his hand below her ribs, and tried to force life back into her body. All he knew about artificial respiration was what it looked like in the movies. Water belched from her mouth with every push. More spilled from her nose. Still she wasn't drained.

He pushed, released, pushed again, assumed the rhythm of breaths that refused to come. The old man sighed, rolled the lids over Cherise's eyes, and put his hand on Jordan's arm. Jordan didn't let up. An eye fluttered—he thought it did—and he pushed harder, then spread her lips apart and blew air into her lungs while he pinched her nose. Cherise gagged. She shoved him away, and the old man cradled her head through another coughing bout. "You broke my ribs," she said when she could talk.

"That's the thanks I get for nearly killing myself saving you?"

"You'd've slowed down like I told you, we wouldn't've gone in the water in the first place."

Her eyes shut. Jordan collapsed beside her, and would have frozen, he thought, if a couple in a forest green Nash hadn't stopped to see what the commotion was about. The couple loaded them into the back seat wrapped in blankets, and ran the engine with the heater on high. The man said, "Hospital's not far. I can bring you, if you want."

"I don't need a hospital," Cherise said, "just a bowl of hot soup, and to lie under a hundred covers near my radiator."

"What about you?" the man said to Jordan.

Jordan shook his head. He couldn't get his teeth to stop chattering.

Cherise told them she lived off Missouri Avenue. She rolled against Jordan as the Nash backed onto the street, and arranged him on top of her. The couple looked at them disapprovingly, and at the puddle accumulating on the seat. After ten minutes Cherise rolled down the window a couple of inches. Jordan was going to ask why she hadn't done that at the bottom of the bay, but didn't want an argument.

"Where am I going?" the man said at Missouri Avenue.

"I'll walk from here," Cherise said. "Bring him home." She opened her door, closed it as the wind hit her. "Take a left at the second light, please."

Seeing the couple look anxiously around the neighborhood, Jordan knew what they were thinking: Con artists—desperate actors—had lured them to this squalid place to rob them. He got out after her.

Cherise lived on a street of row houses blackened by fire. In twilight's soft glow her apartment was an icy dump. The furniture was secondhand, second or third. Green paint flaking off the walls was filled in in a lighter shade. The radiators made hissing sounds for appearances' sake. Jordan ran the kitchen bathtub as hot as he could stand it, and then soaked until he stopped shivering.

Cherise came out of the bedroom in a chenille bathrobe. She watched him dry himself until he noticed her, and held the towel across his middle.

"Think I ain't seen a naked man before? What you got's too shocking for my innocent eyes?"

She tossed him a robe, a yellow shorty, and hung his wet things on the clothespin dryer above the tub.

"Want soup?" she said. "We got Campbell's concentrated."

She put up a pot of chicken soup, and they sat at a scarred table waiting for it to simmer. "You drive like a crazy man. Don't expect me to thank you for saving my life, and all. You didn't, I'd haunt you to your dying day."

"I wasn't driving fast."

"Want to tell me what we were doing at the bottom of the ocean?"

"The brakes failed."

"That beautiful new car? Puh-lease."

"Someone cut the hydraulic lines."

"Who hates you enough to do that?"

"No one."

"See what I mean about your driving?"

"Someone's afraid of me."

"Same question again: Who?" she said. "Also: Why?"

"Your friend Beach."

"Ain't my friend."

"Now you tell me."

"You didn't ask," she said. "He ain't my enemy either. Could be yours. I'll find out next time I see him. He ain't a killer, though."

"Up to now," Jordan said.

"We're still alive, far as I can tell. Mr. Beach, he's efficient, hates mistakes. He wanted us dead, we wouldn't be waiting on soup, discussing what a two-face son-of-a-gun he is."

"I'm going to file an accident report," Jordan said. "The cops will fish out the car, and do an inspection. Want to bet they find the brakes were tampered with?"

"What you got I want now you don't have the car?"

She poured soup while Jordan tried to think of a snappy comeback.

"Did you go to parties with Etta?"

"Beach paid me."

"To have sex with the men there?"

"What do you take me for? To have it with Etta."

"I see."

"Seeing what you want to see, like those men. Was pretend sex is all. Didn't do nothing I'm ashamed of, didn't take money to sleep with men. Colored girl's like a tiger, far as they're concerned, never petted one before, but figure it's a maneater and they better treat her with respect." She blew on her soup, tried it, and spilled it back in the bowl. "Some other girls were plain whoring, and robbing the house while the party was going on."

"Etta?"

"She loved to show off her loot. Favorite thing was a new camera, makes its own pictures without bringing the film to the drugstore. And a jewel wristwatch wasn't safe around her. She'd pawn it for the least little thing she could get."

"Did Beach know?"

"Ain't nothing Beach don't know."

"It couldn't have made him happy that she was stealing from his customers. He might have decided to teach his girls a lesson."

"Don't need lessons in anything," she said. "He *sent* us to steal. Kept two thirds for himself, and kicked back the rest. What didn't make him happy was a girl who held out."

"Why didn't you tell me before?"

"Wouldn't have had the pleasure of your company going off the dock."

"Everything points back to Beach as a suspect."

"You think too much," Cherise said. "Eat your soup."

"I'm exhausted, I want to go home."

"How'll you get there?"

"Without a car? There's a bus—"

"Without clothes," she said. "Yours are soaking wet."

"What do you have that I can borrow?"

"How about a navy blue fall dress from the Monkey Ward catalogue. Chic number that'll show off your curves."

"Do you have pants and a shirt?"

"Fresh out of those in your size, dear. Same for shoes and a coat. Walk out in my duds, and you'll have a pack of johns on your back before you go two blocks."

Jordan finished his soup, and then he went into the living room and stretched out on the couch.

"It's a backbreaker," Cherise said. "Promise not to snore, you can bunk with me."

"I'm fine where I am."

"What are you afraid of?" she said. "Maneater?"

"I snore like a bear."

"I'm being neighborly, and you acting like I'm trying to have my way with you. I'm the one should be looking over her shoulder, bringing a strange man and all into my house. You could be bad as that killer you say you're looking for. You could even be him."

"I'm too tired to kill anybody tonight," he said. "Can we go to sleep?"

"It's up to you. I'm just a helpless woman."

Her bed was a little wider than his old army cot, with a deeper furrow. The springs protested every twitch as they settled in. His arm was squeezed between their bodies, and he made room by resting it on her hip. When she rolled against him the covers fell away.

She was taut and lean with broad shoulders and angular hips, yet the overall impression was of softness. Her breasts were large, a shade lighter than the rest of her. A scar curling across her abdomen was too blunt to have been made by a scalpel. She made a slow play for the light, let him catch her hand as it landed on the switch.

"Seen enough?" she said.

"Not really, no."

"Ever been to bed before with a—"

"A colored girl?"

"Any kind of girl. Ain't that much to look at after you seen it once."

He put his lips to hers to stop the chatter, curious if she

kissed like other girls. He'd never been with a Negro girl, an Oriental, a redhead. Had never slept with girls from west of the Susquehanna River, north of New London, Connecticut, or foreigners aside from the Austrian whores he'd screwed by the truckload, a degraded species who'd taught him nothing about women, nothing he wanted to know.

The springs groaned as he slid over Cherise. She kissed him, and he decided it was for encouragement. Her ankles curled around his, and as he came inside she sighed, and thrust herself against him. Her arms locked behind his back in a death grip.

He stopped thinking, ideas not as compelling as the sobbing sounds Cherise made which he influenced with the motion of his hips. The springs whined, shrieked, struck a violent rhythm, and for a moment he was afraid the bed would shake apart, and he held back. Then he didn't and neither (unless she knew the same tricks as the Austrian whores) did Cherise.

When he was reaching for his Luckys she pulled him back. "Ain't done with you yet. I mean for tonight. Got no use for you right now," she said as she let him go. "Give me a smoke, too? Gotta have one."

He lit up for her, and she said, "You a good deal of fun, know it?"

He wanted to ask if it was something she told all her men. He was a reporter who asked the tough questions, and it carried over into his private life. But he kept his mouth shut.

After a couple of puffs she stubbed out the cigarette, and squirmed against him. He thought she was trying to maneuver him on top till she said, "I'm gonna close my eyes now."

"Yeah, that's a good idea." Trying not to sound disappointed.

"Only for a little bit. I'm exhausted, too," she said. "I don't usually have nightmares, but if you hear me breathing hard, and bunching up the covers, wake me before I start screaming. Know what I'm frightened about?"

"Being trapped in a car at the bottom of the sea."

"Uh-uh," she said, but didn't explain. "You my boyfriend now, huh, in a manner of speaking?"

"Yeah, I guess I am."

"Can I be your girlfriend more than a month?"

He kissed her, grateful for the darkness. Listening to her drop off, he tried to figure how to tell her he'd be living in New York by the weekend.

The mechanic, whose name was George C. Brutus, said, "Back up, Bud. Insurance regs." His elbow caught Jordan across the chest, moving him away from the lift as the air compressor began to hum, and the Hudson rose off the floor.

Several gallons of water rushed out of the passenger compartment while a grease monkey broomed them into a drain in the floor. The antenna was bowed against the ceiling when the lift stopped climbing, and Brutus ducked under the front end with a portable light.

He rattled the steering mechanism, reached behind the manifold, and felt left and right. A worm of ash fell on his shoe as he tilted the beam at the undercarriage, played it from bumper to bumper.

"Hydraulic lines are intact," he said. "I can take your wheels off, and examine the brakes, you want, but I won't find anything out of order. Somebody's out to commit murder, making it look like an accident, they don't jack up the wheels and remove the brake drums. They do what you thought happened, they slice through the lines and let the brake fluid run out. But you can see that isn't the case here."

"What is?" Jordan said.

"You were driving a Hudson," Brutus said. "Biggest hunk of junk on the American road. Dreadful cars put together with spit and baling wire. Management's trying to save a buck here and there, and thought they could get by with cardboard brakes. Fifty-three Hornet is a rolling deathtrap."

"There's no chance someone tampered with it?"

"I wouldn't say that. You got an enemy who knows his way around a drive train, he could've done something to the accelerator. I'll look there, it'll make you feel better, but nobody cut your brake lines."

"I'll take your word."

"You sound disappointed," Brutus said. "You'd be happier knowing someone's trying to kill you?"

Jordan shaded his eyes as the light swung across his face.

"If I was out to kill you, I wouldn't leave evidence. I'd mess with your suspension. That's my job, being a mechanic, not the other," Brutus said. "It's more trouble, not everybody could do it."

Brutus was at the front end, fiddling with the wheels when Jordan opened his eyes.

"Here's what I mean. Your ball joints are shot. It's a good thing you went in the drink, made a soft landing. You had this baby at sixty on the open highway, you'd've thrown a wheel, and really been in trouble."

"My lucky day," Jordan said. "Did someone play with them?"

Brutus clicked off the light. "You garage this car, or leave it in the street?"

"The street," Jordan said.

"I'd keep my next one in the garage, I was you."

"You need a few minutes, or just having a good time," Cherise said, "don't stop on account of me. I got nothing I'd rather be doing."

"I was about to say the same thing," Jordan said.

Cherise parked her heels on his hips, encouraged him with growls and whispers, the bed creeping away from the wall until sharp raps on the heat riser froze him. "Mrs. Williams downstairs in 4D is telling us she had enough love," Cherise said, "enough of ours."

In forty-five seconds Jordan was on his back with the pillow bent behind his head, looking at the posters on the wall through Lucky smoke.

"That one there's from my first time in front of an audience," Cherise said. "The Nat King Cole trio, Moms Mabley, and Sandman Sims at the Alhambra Theater in Philadelphia. I danced in a sandbox with Sandman, who's a sweetheart."

"How old were you?" Jordan said.

"Fourteen. Told 'em I was sixteen, which was still too young to work. They gave me four dollars each performance off the books, and I blew it all on alligator boots caught my eye in Wanamaker's window. Wore 'em home in a foot of snow, and ruined 'em."

"You were in all these shows?"

"Some," she said. "Some I didn't get closer to the stage than the second balcony."

She reached under the bed for an album bound in leather. On the first page he saw her in a shot with Sims looking so young he wouldn't have recognized her, the Sandman posing in his sandbox while she hogged center stage.

"Loved seeing my picture in the papers," she said. "Only thing, I was afraid my mom would see it, too, and lock me in the house at night, make sure I was up early for school."

Several pages devoted to Lena Horne and the Nicholas Brothers had nothing about Cherise. They were her heroes, and she was in awe of them. Page after page showed her in cheesy jungle reviews wearing next to nothing in photos credited to the *Freeman*. There were also publicity shots from beauty contests. It wasn't easy for Jordan to pick her out of a long line of black girls in swimsuits. She never looked the same twice. She hadn't figured out how to stand out from the crowd, and was experimenting with her look. In a cluster of pictures she was posed on the Steel Pier with other girls in Negro League flannels. The photos were credited "Pix."

"Know Pixley?" Jordan said.

"Do I know what?"

"Pixley. The photographer on this shoot."

"Don't think so. Wish I did."

"Why?"

"Gonna get anywhere on the beauty circuit, I need better pictures than from a scrapbook. A portfolio's expensive, a good one is. He a friend of yours? Give me the friend-of-a-friend special rate?"

"We're working together on some crime stories, but I wouldn't call Pix my friend. We don't have the first thing in common."

"Oh, you talking about *Pix*?" she said. "Sure I know him. All the girls do. Small, little fellow, a sissy who don't even try and hide it. We crazy about him, and he crazy for black women... crazy to take our picture. Like to tell us we all African princesses. Funny guy."

"How do you mean?"

"All the time cracking jokes. Barrel of laughs. Know how to put a girl at ease in front of the camera. Some of the girls, church girls, never been with a man, and Pix such a card they don't cover up when he come in the dressing room, they half out of their clothes."

Jordan looked closely at the pictures of the girls with bats and gloves. "I knew he had a knack with ice cream and corpses, but—"

"What?"

"I didn't know he was this good with beautiful women. I'll tell him to give you the full treatment."

"Gonna want something in return."

"He isn't going to want it from you," Jordan said.

Cherise laughed lasciviously. "What *you* got he wants, Honey?"

"As a matter of fact," Jordan said, "he's looking to do a lot of work for my magazine."

"*Your* magazine?"

"They offered the editor's job, and I went for it."

"Congratulations. How can you be the editor of a magazine in New York when you're living in Atlantic City?"

"I can't. I'm moving."

"When?"

"Over the weekend."

She yanked the album away from him. "Forgot to mention it?"

"I was going to," Jordan said, "when I found the right time."

"How about after we had our clothes off, and you were laying on top of me. Had my attention then."

"You make it difficult—"

"Didn't make nothing difficult," she said. "I remember being agreeable. Anything you were up for, I was game. You didn't think I'd mind never seeing you again?"

"Very difficult."

"Heard every riff on that tune: Baby, I meant to tell you, I'm going away for good…Sweetie, I got a wife…got kids…got a girlfriend in a family way…We were only having fun, why you being so serious…We were lucky to have each other for one night. Every damn riff, all come down to the same thing—liars out to get what you want."

Jordan tried to look injured, but couldn't pull it off.

"Didn't suppose I'd see you down on one knee begging me to become Mrs. Jordan, or even your main squeeze. Was okay if you used me, so long as you kept on with it. Never thought you'd give me the bum's rush before you could say Jack Robinson, not you."

"I'll be back often," Jordan said. "We'll see plenty of each other."

"What you're saying, you'll come look up your old friends, and when you got nothing left to do, you'll show me a nice time here in bed. My, my, my, ain't I the lucky gal being showered in kindness by Prince Charming?"

"You'll visit me in New York."

"Yeah, sure."

"I mean it. Hop on the train whenever you're in the mood." He reached for his wallet, but pulled his hand back. He'd hurt her enough without trying to slip her cash before running out.

"Don't have your number," she said.

"As soon as I have one, I'll call."

"Ain't holding my breath."

"It's up to you."

She shook her head. "When it comes to white men, nothing is."

CHAPTER 9

"Jerry Gannon's calling from West Hollywood with a story he says is going to shake the world," Mary Glenny said. "Will you accept the charges?"

Jordan picked up the phone. He signaled Mary to hang up, but she kept the receiver to her ear.

"Hello, this is Adam Jordan."

"Where's Pelfrey?" Gannon said. "I deal direct with Pelfrey."

"Pelfrey died," Jordan said. "I'm the new editor."

"I hadn't heard," said Gannon, a fast talker with a mid-Atlantic drawl. "Give my condolences—"

"What have you got?"

"You're not big on sentiment, are you?" Gannon said.

"We're talking on Mrs. Bryer's nickel."

"All right. Couple days ago, the body of a blonde wearing gold earrings and nothing else was found in a cabin near Tujunga in the San Gabriel Mountains north of here. Dawn Gayle-with-a-Y Twining, 22, originally from Prairie du Chien, Wisconsin, was working as a cocktail waitress at the Ambassador Hotel while she tried to land a contract at one of the picture studios. She'd had a line or two in a few oaters on Poverty Row. Couldn't act a lick, but a kisser that lit up the screen."

"How did she die?"

"She'd been invited to a party in the mountains. Not much of a guest list. Just her and a man. That type of party. They got to boozing, smoking Mary Jane—"

"How do we know?"

"Empty Jack Daniels bottles all over the cabin."

"About the dope."

"Cops found half-smoked reefer cigarettes."

Jordan glanced out the window. Aside from the view (there was no view; the office looked out on the back of taller buildings) this was how he'd imagined magazine work in New York. His first week at *Real Detective* he was being offered a story more exciting than any he could expect to have in Atlantic City.

"Normal sex would have been a problem for her," Gannon said. "A physical irregularity prevented her from having intercourse with a man. The cops think the couple got stoned, and they got drunk, and when they were in the sack she wouldn't or couldn't screw him, and he clubbed her with his fists and a bottle of Jack."

"Who's the suspect?"

"Paul Lyle Hartnett, 33, a telephone lineman who was stringing wire near the cabin."

"Good detective work?"

"None whatsoever," Gannon said. "They had him twelve hours later."

"You know what Pelfrey would say," Jordan said. "That hasn't changed."

"Harnett was framed," Gannon said. "Local cops, sheriff's deputies, and a gal from the DA's office told me the charges will be dropped and reinstated against the real killer. It'll be the biggest scandal to hit Hollywood since Fatty Arbuckle."

"Why?" Jordan said.

"The real killer," Gannon said, "is Clark Gable."

Jordan looked at Mary Glenny, who smiled pertly.

"The word around town," Gannon said, "is Gable hasn't been right since his wife was killed in that plane crash during the war. The King of Hollywood can have any woman, but he's never found the one he liked? That add up to you? There's rumors he's not all man. He's got into trouble before that's been hushed up. MGM isn't about to have its biggest star sent up the river without a fight. But there's no covering up his involvement in murder. Too many people saw him at the cabin. Act fast, and you can have the exclusive."

"Why come to us?" Jordan said. "The glossies can pay a hundred times more than we can."

"They're afraid," Gannon said. "No one wants to go up against MGM. *Life*, *Look*, *The Saturday Evening Post*, *Colliers*, even *Reader's Digest* told me that if they break the story they'll be dead in Hollywood. Not just at Metro, but with all the influential press agents."

"We don't go to print on rumor. Our legal department wants to see the evidence."

"It's not going to be a problem," Gannon said. "But I need an advance. I've got witnesses to grease, and I need to spread money around the courthouse and police station for transcripts, official reports, and pictures. This isn't a shoeshine boy getting shot down in the crossfire from zoot-suiters. It's the most important story *Real Detective* will ever put into print. It doesn't come cheap."

"You know we don't give advances."

"For Clark Gable you do," Gannon said, "or I'll go to the competition. Are you ready to be the laughingstock who passed up a scoop on the brightest star in the movies nailed in a hideous sex killing?"

"How much do you need?"

"Two hundred should cover it," Gannon said. "You have an hour before I call *Front Page Detective*. The clock is ticking."

Jordan hung up, and said to Mary Glenny, "Is Gannon in his right mind?"

"Oh, absolutely. He was a top-notch police reporter with the *L.A. Examiner* forever. Mr. Pelfrey couldn't wait to get his hands on his copy. He's fast, and very clean. He doesn't require much editing."

"I mean—?"

"Is there truth in anything he says?"

"I mean why's he coming to me with fiction?"

"Jerry Gannon is a drunk, a bigamist, a degenerate horse-player. Any money left over from the track goes to shylocks and hookers. Mr. Pelfrey stopped taking his calls after he did a story on a rash of fatal bank robberies in Beverly Hills that had Shirley Temple driving the getaway car. He knows Mr. Pelfrey died. He figures he can put one over on the new editor before the new editor gets wise."

"If he'd said Errol Flynn, he might have had me," Jordan said. "How many of our staffers are like that?"

"More than there were before an outsider was brought in to run the magazines."

This wasn't Atlantic City where no one ever tried to hoax the boss. No, that wasn't entirely accurate. A reporter with a shameless disregard for journalistic ethics had fobbed off an account of a speech by Congressman Theodore Garabedian at a time Garabedian's corpse was growing cold. When you got down to it magazine journalism as practiced in New York wasn't very different from newspapering in Atlantic City.

Jordan felt like a fraud. On his desk was the current *Real Detective* with *ART COPY* scribbled on the cover in red crayon. He didn't know what an art copy was, or what to do with one. Mary would tell him if he asked. But he could turn to her just so many times before she decided that he was helpless without her, and he knew where that would lead. How the hell was he going to put out four titles a month while avoiding sharks like Jerry Gannon when he didn't know the first thing about magazines?

That didn't stop him from making plans. He wanted to go to press on heavier paper with thicker cover stock that would give the feel of quality publications. More photos would open the cramped layouts that had been standard since the 1930s. He was full of ideas, but Mrs. Bryer wouldn't hear them. She had courted him aggressively. Now she avoided him. It drove him crazy that he could make the magazines better and no one cared.

Mary poked her head in. "Manny Rothstein is here to see you," she said. "He's a homicide detective."

Jordan shook hands with a man half a head shorter than Mary, who was chatting with her like an old friend.

"Which murder do you need to talk about?" Jordan said to him.

Rothstein moved an unlit cigar from one corner of his mouth to the other. "Yours."

"You're ahead of yourself."

"Not by much," Rothstein said. "We still don't know who killed Pelfrey. If he's holding a grudge against the magazine, you're the obvious target. Is there anyone, anyone in particular, who'd want the new editor of *Real Detective* dead?"

Jordan gestured toward a card file on Mary's desk. "Take your pick."

"What's this?"

"An index of ten thousand killers," Jordan said. "Not one was happy to see his name in print."

Rothstein slid open the A's, fanned the yellowing cards. He looked around the office, and Jordan saw his gaze caught by red spatters near a ceiling fixture.

"The investigators who worked the initial attack on Pelfrey weren't surprised he was killed," Rothstein said. "They warned him to keep his eyes open. My advice for you is to do the same."

"A lot of good it did Pelfrey," Jordan said.

"Let's see how it works for you."

In the afternoon Jordan held interviews for managing and associate editor. The applicants were not promising. Choice talent went to the glossies. A 37-year old copy boy at the *World Telegram & Sun* was explaining an eight-year gap in his employment record when Mary called Jordan away. "Sam Orr's on the line from Virginia Beach."

"Who's Sam Orr?"

"Our man in the Tidewater. He's got a story he promises is going to set you back on your heels."

"Like Jerry Gannon's?"

"Sam's one hundred percent trustworthy. He's just—you'll find out."

Jordan took the call at Mary's desk. Orr said, "Hello, you the new fellow? I'm Sam…" A coastal twang thickened by an early cocktail hour made it hard for Jordan to understand him.

"Best damn case ever," he seemed to be saying, "and I was writing for dick books when Pelfrey was a pup."

Jordan said, "I've got someone waiting—"

"Don't rush me, you'll confound the facts. Ever try the banana puddin' at Mackie's by the shore? Hardly lived till you had it after a plate of single-fried oysters."

Jordan watched the 37-year old copy boy pick up several magazines and study the girls on the cover. "What about the murder?"

"Get this: Friday night, after the kitchen shut down, and the staff was sent home, fellow put an ice pick in the owner's ear, and scooted out of Mackie's with close to six hundred dollars."

"Hell of a way to do a robbery," Jordan said.

"Gonna let me tell it?" Orr said. "Or tryin' to improve it before I even set it down in black and white."

"Go ahead," Jordan said.

"Thank you. Mackie Parsons crawled outside onto the sidewalk, where one of his busboys found him. Before he expired he said the man that killed him was—" Sam Orr stopped. Jordan heard a match strike, and Orr taking in smoke, and the smoke expelled in a phlegmy cough. "Buster Clarence Calvert, 28, of Nassawadox, that's a fishing village on the Delmarva Peninsula.

Calvert worked as a liquor distributor makin' occasional rounds by Parsons, whose wife, I should point out, he was occasionally tossing it to."

"What made him think he could get away with it?"

"There you go again," Orr said, "tellin' it your way. Calvert was deep in the hole to various bookies for large amounts. If he could pick up some quick cash, and knock off his major love rival in the bargain, he'd be hittin' the daily double. Thing is, he needed thousands. Six-hundred was about enough to put distance between himself and his troubles. Hello—?"

"I'm listening," Jordan said as the copy boy opened the current *Fascinating Detective*.

"After the murder Calvert made a beeline for the Back Bay Wildlife Refuge, which is generally deserted on account of all the mosquitoes and biting bugs. No one was there to see him strip off his duds, put on a new suit and shoes, and leave the old clothes with his watch and wallet on the sand. Nice Bulova watch. Couple days later, the chief of police received a handwritten letter from Calvert apologizing for killing Parsons. His conscience was eating at him so bad, he made up his mind to throw himself in the ocean. By the time the chief had the letter he'd be dead. Still with me?"

"Still," Jordan said.

"From the refuge Calvert drove to Chesapeake, and checked into the Dunroaming Motel on Route 17 under the name Bill Black, and proceeded to lose most of the six hundred in a rigged poker game. He liked to look on the bright side, though. The bookies, the cops didn't know he was alive. He didn't have a care till he sent out for burgers and the papers, and the deliveryman ran out without waitin' for a tip."

Jordan glanced again at the copy boy, who was having a second look at the cover girls.

"Ever know a deliveryman not to stick around to have his palm greased? Gave Calvert the willies, like a black cat cut across his path. It got worse when he looked at the papers. His kisser was splashed over all the front pages above the caption: *Wanted For Murder*. Took the lead right out of his pencil. He called the cops on himself."

"What gave him away?" Jordan said.

"Was an ivory-billed woodpecker. You didn't hear about one peckin' holes in the Back Bay Wildlife Refuge last week? Nobody's seen an ivorybill in thirty, forty years. The birdwatchers poured in from as far off as Florida. One of them stumbled on Calvert's clothes so soon after he left them there that the cops had them before his letter reached the chief, even before the postmark was stamped on the envelope. Calvert ain't explained yet why he'd leave his clothes on the shore and walk into town buck naked to drop his letter in the mailbox, and then walk back to the beach to throw himself in the ocean. The indictment came down this morning. They're still looking for the bird."

"Give me five thousand words, and all the photos you can scrape up."

"Have to do without artwork. I burned all my picture contacts."

"I need photos," Jordan said.

"You want the story, or don't you?"

Jordan said that he did, and hung up. "Orr's got an early load on," he said to Mary.

"He's one of our most productive writers," she said, "but Mr. Pelfrey wouldn't accept his calls after the cocktail hour."

Jordan went back to his desk. "How do you like the magazines?"

The copy boy, Arnold Glass, said, "They're written by idiots for bigger idiots."

"Do you also have an opinion about our covers?"

"Not really. I wouldn't give these girls a tumble."

"Managing editor pays seventy a week. Associate pays sixty."

"You're offering a job? Knowing what I think?"

"Everyone's too smart for the pulps," Jordan said, "till they get serious about them. You have an idea about women. The rest you'll learn. Tell me where you were those eight years."

Mary went home at five o'clock. Jordan closed the door, and pulled a story from the manuscript pile. It was badly typed. The pages were coffee-stained, and required so much editing that he was rewriting word for word between the lines. The byline read *Sam Orr*. He rolled the paper into his typewriter, and started over on page one.

At eight he called Pixley at the loft. "Do you have connections in Tidewater, Virginia?"

"What do you need?"

"One of the locals knocked off a restaurateur whose wife he was screwing. I need shots of him, the victim, the restaurant, the motel in Chesapeake where he hid out, and a wildlife preserve in Virginia Beach, where the killer staged his suicide."

"How utterly fascinating! I adore an intriguing mystery," Pixley said. "Don't leave out a single detail."

"Not that intriguing. After the killing, the murderer left his clothes at the preserve, and disappeared himself. His stuff was found before he put his suicide note in the mail, and the cops had him before he caught a deep breath."

"He had the right idea. He didn't take it far enough," Pixley said.

Everyone was an authority on murder. Everyone, from Jordan's experience, but the practitioners.

"What you should do if you ever find yourself in his situation, you should leave a corpse in your clothes, someone who looks just like you," Pixley said. "Cops are stupid. Lazy, too. They hate digging deeper into a case than they absolutely have to. You'd get away scot-free."

"When I need to get away with murder, I'll call you first," Jordan said. "Meantime, can you find pictures?"

"There's no need to get huffy. I'm merely trying to be helpful."

"Be helpful with the pictures."

"They won't be a problem," Pixley said. "Give me names."

Someone brushed against the door, rattled the knob trying to get in. Jordan decided it was a murderer. He was looking for something to defend himself with when he heard the cleaning cart roll along the corridor. Aside from the custodians he was alone on the seventeenth floor. He didn't have to stay late. He was his own boss now. But he had nothing—no one—waiting at home.

There wasn't a shortage of women in New York. He was put off by the ritual of cutting one out of the herd, and playing the charmer to clear the way to bed. It was easy to get around that. Just snap his fingers and he'd have Cherise to help kill the long nights. But where would he park her in the morning? What better reason had he needed to quit Atlantic City than that he'd taken up with a colored prostitute?

Not exactly a prostitute. Yet their relationship boiled down to one thing. If the situation with women didn't improve, he'd wire her money for a train ticket. He'd saved her life. She'd practically be doing the same for him. It was just the one thing. Cherise wouldn't have it any other way.

Alejandro de Costa had been in Hollywood in its golden era thirty years ago. The morning after two Charlie Chaplin shorts were projected onto the whitewashed wall of the church in San Tomas, the Andean village where he was born, he'd left for the United States. It took three years to reach California, where he changed his name from Saul Hernandez, and found work standing in for the movies' biggest names. In *Son of the Sheik* his broad shoulders filled the screen as Vilma Banky cowered before the chieftain of the desert brigands. Not until the close-ups did he retire to a camp chair to watch the great Valentino kiss the gorgeous girls who were so tantalizingly near yet out of his reach.

De Costa, at 20, believed he was star material. He was tall and handsome, but thick around the middle, and the camera added ten pounds to what was there. He photographed miserably. Every casting agent told him so. He continued to scrape by posing for the famous screen lovers as he learned the business of making motion pictures. By 1925 he had graduated to best boy, then to assistant director, second unit director, and to uncredited director of a jungle serial. He filmed two westerns under his own name, and a half-million dollar sand-and-sandals extravaganza that was released as Cecil B. DeMille's, which was okay with de Costa because the same girls he had warmed up for the famous lovers were fighting to have him in their dressing rooms.

As a director and film editor de Costa saved many big-budget productions from ruin. His modest star was rising when talkies came along. Splendorous epics shot through the eye of a visual artist were old hat. Audiences craved sound. They wanted music, and to hear Garbo speak. De Costa had no better understanding of those things than did any of a thousand other faceless names in Hollywood, and so he drifted east. Since 1933 de Costa had been the art director for Turner Publications. He introduced himself to Jordan in his eighteenth floor studio where models were auditioned for *Real Detective* cover shoots.

"Any interesting possibilities for the June books?" he said.

Jordan had shootings, knifings, and several girls strangled, a Brownie raped and then shoved off the roof of a four-story tenement, two college coeds incinerated in a sorority house arson fire, a housewife dead after acid was thrown in her face. An Apache girl, a 16-year-old prostitute, had been dropped down a well. Another hooker's arms and legs had been sawed off by a client.

"Nothing out of the ordinary," Jordan said. "Let's try something new."

"There's nothing new in murder."

De Costa seemed to be mocking him, but it was hard to read the art director's part-Indian features, an expression that would serve well for a sociopath's. The Apache girl had been killed by a white man, but readers wouldn't know that till they read the story. De Costa was a natural for a cover. Jordan would hold the piece, make the suggestion when he knew de Costa better.

"What would you say to a cover that isn't tied to a story?"

"The readers will object," de Costa said. "They expect guns and ropes, a look of fear in the victim's eye."

"The older ones do, but they're dying off," Jordan said. "With sexier girls showing more skin, we'll make new subscribers."

"Mrs. Bryer won't approve the additional expense."

"I'll kick in out of my own pocket if it means the magazines hang on longer. How about you?"

"You are asking me to pay for beautiful women? It isn't something I've had to do for a long time." De Costa glanced toward the door, but didn't rush Jordan to it. "Let me see what is available in the fifty to seventy-five dollar range. Anything less, and we can do as well bringing in shopgirls from Ohrbach's."

Outside the studio young women were lined up on a bench smoking furiously. Jordan wasn't bowled over by their ordinary good looks.

"These are thirty-five dollar girls," de Costa said.

"Thirty-five an hour seems like a lot."

"Thirty-five for as long as we need them in front of the camera. And for some, who are ambitious, anything else we may want them for."

Why be beautiful if the payoff was the cover of *Real Detective*? Jordan wanted to see the seventy-five dollar girls, and what a hundred dollar girl looked like, and girls who earned more. He wanted to know how the price was decided, and if they were worth the money. Most of all he wanted to know where to meet them.

"I contacted some of the better agencies," de Costa told him after the weekend. "They weren't enthusiastic, but the models want their face everywhere."

A different crowd had taken over the bench. Not the most beautiful girls Jordan had seen in New York (those were concentrated around Washington Square, and in the quaint Greenwich Village streets west of the park); they were all of a type, fine porcelain by way of the Midwest, a breed apart from the earthy downtown women who turned his head.

Katrin, with a stagey European accent, unzipped her portfolio, and spread pictures over de Costa's desk.

"Fashion shots don't tell me how you'd photograph menaced by a strangler." He handed her a dressing robe. "Put this on, if you don't mind."

A shower curtain was suspended in front of a photographer's white backdrop. When Katrin came out of the changing room, de Costa bunched it over her shoulder, exposing her face. "Take off the robe, please. Try to look as if you had just heard someone come in."

He turned up the lights, and the curtain seemed to melt away. The lush shape behind it caught Jordan by surprise.

The lights went off. "Thank you for coming."

"What's wrong with her?" Jordan said.

"Next girl, try looking at her expression," de Costa said. "Readers want to believe the victims of murder are not very different from their wives, sisters, daughters, and therefore must have done something to deserve their fate. Katrin is like no one they've known. The trouble with these models is they are more at home in Tiffany's than dodging a homicidal maniac."

He called for another girl, who left her portfolio with him as she hurried to the changing room. Jordan was following her inside when de Costa pulled him back.

"If you want her, I have her number. You can't go in."

Jordan shook him off, and opened the door. The girl was in her bra and panties when he coughed into his fist. She whirled around holding her dress against her body, and then she let it down. "What are you doing here?" she asked.

"I have the same question for you, Mollie."

"A girl's got to eat."

"I don't think the next Miss America's coming from the cover of *Real Detective*."

"That's a silly dream I've given up, and good riddance. I've been in New York four weeks, and doing nicely for myself, thank you. And you? You still haven't told me."

"I'm the editor."

"You mean I get to cash in on our friendship—we are friends, aren't we, Adam, something like that—to land my first cover?"

"I have one vote," he said. "The other belongs to Mr. de Costa."

"I can count on yours, though?"

"Wow him, why don't you, and make it unanimous."

De Costa was waiting when Jordan stepped outside. "You can't watch the girls undress. She could have screamed rape, and held us up for a lot of money."

"My mistake," Jordan said.

Mollie came out in the robe, and de Costa showed her where to stand. As he draped the curtain over her shoulder, she said, "I have an idea for the shoot."

De Costa adjusted the curtain, and stepped back. "I'm sure you do."

"Would it hurt to listen?"

"Don't move now."

"I had my hair done for the audition. No one told me I'd be posing in the shower. Can we wet it like I really am taking a shower? It will look more real."

"Your hair is nice the way it is."

"No one's hair looks nice in the shower."

She made her case to Jordan, who filled a glass from the studio sink, and was sprinkling her when she tilted his wrist over her head. "What do you think?" she said as she smoothed her hair against her scalp.

De Costa grunted. She shrugged the robe off her shoulders as she undid the sash, surprising Jordan as it fell around her feet. De Costa looked hard, but showed no expression while Mollie's confidence melted, a woman naked in every way.

De Costa gave her a second look through the viewfinder of a Nikon. "You've been startled," he said, "and are trying to locate the source of a disturbing sound."

Her head canted toward the camera. At the ideal angle her eyes narrowed, and she retreated into herself.

De Costa fired off a handful of shots, then removed the camera from the tripod. "Let me see you cognizant of danger, but not panicky, prepared for anything."

Expression flickered across her face, and was extinguished at de Costa's command to clear the slate for their next experiment. Jordan knew the edgy look he wanted from the shooting on Park Place, when Mollie had walked past the dead body on the floor. De Costa would refine it into something glamorous, keeping readers in mind that they were paying for a detective magazine.

De Costa changed lenses and came close, barking commands. Jordan saw tears on Mollie's cheeks. De Costa ordered her to stop crying, mocked her, browbeat her while he captured each drop. Then he unloaded the camera, and gave her a towel to dry her face, brewed a cup of tea for her, and thanked the other girls for their time.

"That was a terrific impersonation of quiet fear," Jordan said when she was dressed.

"What impersonation? I was scared to death I wouldn't get the job. Thank you, Adam."

"I had nothing to do with it. You were great."

"Thanks anyway."

He walked her out of the office, and they waited for the elevator on the empty bench. "Are you living in the city?" he said.

"I have a place with a roommate in Brooklyn by the Botanical Gardens."

"Give me the address."

"It's far, almost an hour on the IRT."

He had his pen out. "…also your number."

"They're on the release Mr. de Costa had me sign," she said. "But nothing's changed since Atlantic City. I'm grateful to you for giving me a chance, but I don't want to get involved with you again."

"Were we involved?"

"If you have to ask, what was I doing in your bed?" She carried her portfolio to the elevator, and pressed the button.

"Turner Pub puts out a lot of magazines, and I'm making new contacts in the industry every day. I can do a lot to help your career."

"I'm not a prostitute. I won't sell myself even for the cover of *Life*."

"Not even for *Life*?"

"We'll discuss it when you're in a position to do that for me."

"I'm trying to make up for what happened."

The car came. She stepped inside dodging a kiss. "By trying to make it happen again?"

The doors slid shut. Jordan pulled his head back just in time.

The closets were filled with cartons he'd never get around to unpacking. He ransacked them till he had his novel, and put it beside the typewriter. He was off to a solid start with the magazines. A good time to push his luck in other directions.

Including Mollie's. Till he needed her for another shoot he'd make excuses to call. Even apologize, if he didn't think she'd see through him.

The phone rang as he was getting into bed. No one called after midnight unless it was murder. Maybe Mollie was surprising him again. A huge surprise. His number was unlisted.

"Hello?"

"Who's this?" a woman said.

If it was Mollie, she'd caught a bad cold on the ride to Brooklyn.

"What do you want?"

"It's you, after all," the woman said. "You didn't sound like yourself, but now you do. Must be the long distance."

"Brooklyn is hardly—Cherise?"

"Who'd you think, dearie?"

"Someone from the magazine," he said. "What's new?"

"What could be, stuck here like I am? I wouldn't know you were alive, only a card came with your number."

"You can't believe how busy I am. I haven't had time to unpack."

"Couldn't take ten minutes to call?"

"*You* called," he said. "What's the difference?"

"I'm paying. Long distance ain't cheap, you know."

"Hang up. I'll call right back."

"Ain't getting away that easy," she said. "This one's on me."

His old life had no business intruding on the new, Mollie—though he also knew her from Atlantic City, had known her before Cherise—being part of the new. He wasn't bothered by flaws in that logic. The rules of logic were superseded by the rules of Adam Jordan every time.

"Still there?" she said.

"Where were we?"

"You were telling me how happy you are, hearing my voice, and can't wait to have me for a visit."

"It's going to be a while. Like I said, I'm not settled."

"I told Greenie I was gonna stay with you in New York. He laughed in my face, said you were selling me a bridge there."

"Greenie doesn't know what he's talking about."

"What I told him," she said. "Why you making so I gotta say he was right?"

"Just a little longer."

"I understand," she said. "Next week? Next week's good for me, too."

"Longer than that."

"Understand everything."

"I'm rushing four magazines to the printer. They take all my time."

"Take as much as you need," she said. "I gotta go now. Oh, I almost forgot. They found Etta dead late last night."

He listened to the dial tone while the words sunk in, and then he called back Atlantic City.

"Pix Pixley's."

It was a woman, breathy and inviting. Just the way she sounded, she belonged on the bench outside de Costa's studio. Even if she wasn't anything much, he wondered what she was doing with Pixley.

"Put him on, please."

"This is Mr. Pixley's answering service."

"It's an emergency."

"I'm sure, but he can't be reached."

"Okay, tell him to send me the latest on Etta Wyatt, and pictures of her corpse, and everything that goes with it. Got that?"

"If you say so, sir."

"And have him send along some of you."

An interoffice envelope was on his desk when he got in. The flap was sealed with layers of heavy tape. Inside was a contact sheet, thirty-six miniature portraits of Mollie playing peek-a-boo behind the curtain. The best were marked with a crayon pencil for de Costa's crop. Jordan hated to see the pictures cut. He could sell millions of magazines using Mollie in the raw, and collect his bonus in federal prison. Only the nudist and sunbather's newsletters sold under the counter in Times Square had the nerve to take on the postal inspectors.

He was at the breakfast cart when Mary called out, "Mr. Pixley on the line."

"Accept the charges."

"It isn't a long-distance call."

Jordan hurried back to his desk via a trail of confectioner's sugar. "How are you?"

"Not bad, you?"

"Trying to get used to an office job. Why didn't you tell me you were in town?"

"I just checked in. Heard about Etta Wyatt?"

"Yeah. Yeah, I did," Jordan said. "What's available?"

"First let me tell you what brings me to New York."

"First tell me about Etta."

"She can wait."

"I can't," Jordan said.

Pixley's giggle touched a raw nerve. "She turned up under a chicken coop in Poultrina."

"Where?"

"Take County Road 413 north into the Pine Barrens. Poultrina is the wide spot in the road, a socialist farm community founded by Russian immigrants that went belly up after the war. The hen house was being razed to make way for a drive-in movie when a bulldozer scraped up the body of a colored girl in a sleeping bag. They brought a sideman from the Basie orchestra to make the ID. Dr. Melvin says she died around the time she was reported missing."

"Died of what?"

"Homicide detectives don't confide in lowly shutterbugs. But

I've got shots of her up close, what's left, and ligature marks are visible around her throat. I've also got the farm, the dozer jockey, the cops. If there's ever an arrest, we're covered."

"Any new leads?"

"The cops couldn't care less. I may have something, though," Pixley said. "I may even have photos on that case out of Virginia Beach. But let Etta rest in peace for a while. My first solo exhibit opens Saturday in Greenwich Village."

Jordan wasn't ready to change the subject. It wasn't up to him.

"It's a round-up of my best work."

"Plenty of ice cream?"

"See for yourself. The gallery is counting on a big turnout. Can I expect you to be there? Bring a friend."

"How do I say no?"

Jordan lit another Lucky and stamped it out after a couple of puffs. He was starting inside when he heard his name, made a big deal of looking at his watch as Mollie came across the street.

"I was beginning to think you'd stood me up."

"It crossed my mind," she said. "But I was afraid where the pictures might turn up."

Jordan put an envelope in her hand. She shook out a contact sheet. "One shot's missing," she said.

"The June cover. Very demure. What will you do with these?"

"Destroy them? Use them for Christmas cards? Sell them to sailors?" She dropped the envelope in her bag. "It's up to me now. I'd be crazy to let you have them."

Jordan nodded, and lit up again. Then he gave her the negatives, and they went inside together.

A group show had brought out a mob to the first floor exhibit space. Jordan poked his head in, and gazed noncommittally at

color field canvases. Upstairs, Chablis and stale cheese drew
freeloaders to view Pixley's photos. Jordan liked the stark German
racing cars from his commercial work. Liked them better than
the cute children he'd seen first at the photographer's studio,
but not as much as the charred teeth and bone fragments, all
that remained of Bess Pomeroy, 26, found in a charcoal pit in
the Barrens, which ran with her story in *Real Detective*.

Men posed heroically on a beach could have stepped out of a
Charles Atlas ad, if Charles Atlas had stepped out of his leopard-
skin trunks.

"Where's your friend?" Mollie said. "I want to meet him. If I
didn't know you like I do, I could get the wrong idea."

She inspected male nudes till Jordan said, "There's Pix." A
blond man chatting with a woman in a double-breasted suit
pricked up his ears, and called them over.

"Adam Jordan, shake hands with Rhoda Sloane," Pixley said.
"Rhoda's the photography editor for *New Journal of the Arts*."

Rhoda squinted at Jordan as she transferred a glass to her
left hand.

"Adam's my *other* editor," Pixley said to her.

"We must have crossed paths before," she said to Jordan, "but
I'm sure I don't recognize you. Who did you say you write for?"

"*Real Detective*."

Rhoda laughed, spilling wine on herself. Jordan said, "Pix, Miss
Sloane, this is Mollie Gordon, former Miss Delaware Valley, the
next Miss New Jersey, future Miss America, and *Real Detective*'s
reigning cover girl. You made a new fan today, Pix."

Mollie extended her hand. Pixley didn't seem to know whether
to shake it or take a picture. "What do you think of my stuff?"

"Some's not bad," Jordan said. "But I'm no authority on art
photography."

"Don't let him rain on your parade," Mollie said. "Everything's terrific, especially the boys on the beach."

"Are you an authority?"

"I've also taken my clothes off for men with a camera. What does that make me?"

"The ultimate authority. Oh, absolutely. Would you model for me?"

"Do you do women, too, Mr. Pixley? I wouldn't like being your first."

Rhoda went for water to wash out her stain as Jordan took Pixley aside. "You said you'd learned something about Etta's death—"

"There's Thom Whiteside from the *Trib*, the most important tush I've got to kiss. I'll talk to you later."

He was angling toward a man in a corduroy jacket when Jordan saw him pulled into a corner by a teenager with a camera around his neck.

"What do you really think?" Jordan said to Mollie.

"He's a sweet little fairy. Since I'm not an authority in that area, I'll reserve judgment."

"You know how to play to his ego."

"I meant most of it. He lets his camera fall in love with his model. If he could do that with a woman, I'd be happy to put myself in his hands."

"Does a photographer have to love you to make you look good?"

"Looking good is for second runner-up. Looking great, that's what makes a beauty queen. I need a great portfolio."

"I'd take him up on his offer."

"De Costa loves me. Can't you put in a good word with him?"

"De Costa doesn't lift a finger without something in return. He doesn't love anyone but himself."

A peroxide blond with a thin moustache, a short, slender man, came up on Pixley from behind with a peck on the cheek. The photographer nudged him away, and Jordan heard, "You're embarrassing yourself, Marcel. Embarrassing both of us."

"Would Pix do it for nothing?" Mollie said.

"It wouldn't be for nothing. Nothing is."

Pixley was by himself now, counting the house beside the picture of a little girl with her back to a lion cage holding tight to a balloon on a string. The big cat was pressing against the bars, huge, dripping jaws wide apart as the child erupted in tears. Jordan went over, leaving Mollie alone with the nudes. "You were lucky to be there just when the lion roared," he said.

"I don't have luck," Pixley said. "I make it. The lion is yawning. When her grandmother was distracted I told the tot that the cage had come open, and the beast was going to jump out and eat her up. I also snapped her from behind running away, two adorable shots of her peeing down her legs."

"The poor kid'll have nightmares till she's a grandma herself."

"What of it? I made her immortal. We all sacrifice for the sake of art. There are no free passes," Pixley said. "Look at the crowd. This is the greatest day of my life."

"Make it great for both of us," Jordan said. "What did you find out about Etta?"

"It could come to nothing. Or it could break the case wide open. It was staring hundreds of thousands of people in the face. But no one knew what to make of it, but me. Assuming it isn't simply a coincidence—"

"Are you going to tell me or play Hamlet?"

"It's not Shakespearean. The egg farm where Etta was killed—"

"Where she was found. We don't know where she died."

"*That* egg farm," Pixley said. "Hub Chase was born there."

"How do you know?"

"*The Sporting News* named him to their pre-season all-star rookie team with a nice write-up. A three-hundred hitter in two seasons of triple-A ball with good power and speed on the basepaths. Six-foot, two hundred pounds, throws right, bats left, hometown Poultrina, New Jersey."

"You remind me of myself," Jordan said, "when I was ten."

He hadn't meant it the way it came out. But then what did he mean? Pixley never showed an angry side. Jordan wasn't even sure he'd recognize the signs. But on the greatest day of the photographer's life this wasn't the best moment.

"I'm a big baseball fan," Pixley said, "always have been."

"Does the *Sporting News* know where to find him?"

"He's at spring training with the A's in West Palm Beach. They break camp next week."

"I—uh-huh." Someone off the street in a beat-up leather jacket was homing in on Mollie. "You'll set up a shoot in the meantime with my friend?"

"That has to wait, too. My best equipment is locked in my studio."

"She'll be disappointed."

"I know a thing or two about beautiful women," Pixley said. "They don't carry a grudge in front of the camera."

"I told her you'd have her looking stunning." The man in the leather jacket had his own opinions about Pixley's work. Mollie was nodding agreeably while he expounded on them. "Gotta get back to her," Jordan said. "Call me before you leave town."

"I'll give her the full treatment," Pixley said after him. "She won't be able to complain about a thing."

The cheese and wine were gone with most of the crowd when a girl dressed all in black walked in. She was nineteen or twenty with a serious expression, and an expensive camera around her neck, an Exakta Varex with a Pentaprism viewfinder favored by pros who could afford one.

A lap around the gallery ended at a portrait of stoop laborers bringing in the melon harvest at a Vineland truck farm. She put her nose close, then stepped back with her fingers squared in front of her eyes. Pixley made her for a rich kid, the arty type hungry for Bohemian life in the Village. An NYU coed, if he wasn't mistaken, with a major in the social sciences. There wasn't much he couldn't tell about some women from a single look.

Mrs. Coopersmith, the gallery owner, came by to answer her questions. "Seventy-five dollars, yes, and signed by the photographer. That's him over there by the window. We close in ten minutes."

"Mr. Pixley," the girl said to him. "I'm Gail Aubrey, a big fan of your work."

She brushed a tendril curl behind her ear. A pretty girl on the wrong side of the camera.

"My first fan," Pixley said. "I'll always remember the name. You never forget your first."

Gail Aubrey's cheeks, which were peaches and cream, went heavy on the peaches. If he had her in his viewfinder (a primitive contraption next to her Pentaprism), he'd shoot her with Kodachrome. Pixley hated the garishness of color. But Gail Aubrey's lovely complexion would be squandered in shades of gray.

"Your subjects look into the camera without knowing it's there," she said. "How do you consistently achieve that effect?"

"You misunderstand my intent. They know it's there. They're playing to it."

Gail nodded uneasily. Something else Pixley knew instantly about most women: Which of their insecurities to exploit first.

"It's the photographer they're not cognizant of. That's the secret. They forget all about me till I have what I want from them. What excellent equipment you have."

She patted the Exakta against her breast. "Greenwich Village is chockablock with interesting faces. I can't walk to the store without shooting off a roll of film. Walker Evans is my favorite photographer. What's your opinion of him?"

Evans' sharecroppers, the smudged aristocracy of Southern poverty, depressed him. Shooting a coroner's slab for *Real Detective* was more uplifting.

"We're all in his debt. Walker is looking over my shoulder every time I set up a picture."

"That's how I feel, too," Gail said.

Such a good-looking girl. He pictured her in sharp resolution on black sand, creamy skin against volcanic ash. A beach far from the yellow grit of the Jersey Shore. Black sand and black sheets.

She was a junior at NYU, an anthropology major, and anthropology bored her. What she wanted to do was to take pictures. He asked to see her camera, and fired off three shots before she could get herself together. A quick finger on the trigger was indispensible. He told her it was the first thing she had to learn.

"I can't wait to see how they come out," she said.

"They're not art, just something to remember you by besides your name." He gave her his address on a matchbook. "Send me the one you think is second best."

"Oh, they'll be art," she said. "I know your time is valuable, but I'd love to hear what you think of my recent pictures. I live nearby, right off Washington Square."

"How can I say no? My hotel is on the way."

She brought him to a fifth-floor walkup. The kitchen had been converted into a darkroom. Her photos were what he expected. A naïve eye for Bowery bums and the Italian pushcart vendors on Bleecker Street portrayed them excruciatingly as exotics.

"Be brutal," she said.

"I can't. You're definitely on the right track. I'm going to keep one or two to show Mrs. Coopersmith."

"You're a dear."

"May I take your picture again?" he said. "Something more revealing of you?"

"I study photography at night at the Artists' League. My instructor says a camera is a knife that cuts through our subjects' defenses."

"I couldn't put it better myself," Pixley said. "If you'll change into something less prim, we can cut through some of yours."

"I'm in your hands."

"I'll go easy," he said, with a smile. "My knife is dull."

Any other man she'd met twenty minutes ago trying to talk her out of her clothes Pixley knew she wouldn't be so eager to please. What did she have to fear from a harmless pixie? Something else he could predict about women was a quick yes when he asked them to undress in the interest of art. It was nothing to brag about. He wanted them thinking hard before they answered, to have second thoughts.

The bedroom door remained open while Gail pulled her sweater over her head. Pixley watched her try on a filmy blouse, then take it off, unhook her brassiere, and slip into the blouse again with nothing underneath. She grinned when she saw him peeking. A peasant skirt completed the outfit.

"Is this what you had in mind?"

"Even better," he said.

"How do you want me?"

"I'll leave it up to you."

She sat on the couch with her legs crossed under her while he fiddled with the flash attachment. When he continued to ignore her, she ran her fingers through her hair, and let the stiffness out of her spine. The flashbulb went off immediately.

"I wasn't ready," she said.

"That's the point."

"What should we try now?"

"It's still up to you."

She moistened her lips, parted them slightly, slitted her eyes. "How's this?"

"Ridiculous," he said, and got the picture he wanted when she went into a pout.

"You don't miss a beat, do you?"

He popped out the burned flashbulb, replaced it, and advanced the film. "What? I didn't hear."

She repeated herself leaning into the camera, exaggerating the words. "I said you don't—"

He pressed the shutter again. "You don't have to shout," he said. "I can't afford to miss anything, because it won't be there again. What else have you got for me?"

She tossed her head, spread her arms across the back of the couch, showing off her breasts inside the thin blouse. In the glare of flashbulbs Gail Aubrey wasn't the proper young lady he'd encountered strolling through his show. He opened her top button, got the picture, and was hiking her skirt around her hips when she caught his wrist. "Uh-uh."

"If you don't like the shot, I'll destroy it."

"I said no."

"You're being childish, Gail. Your instructor would be the first to say so."

"He didn't tell us to make our subjects do things that make them feel cheap."

"So much for cutting through defenses."

"That's enough."

He pressed the shutter.

Gail covered herself, though it hardly seemed necessary. He was less than a man, pathetic once you got past the fey charm. Many big names in photography were misanthropic, she saw it in their work. Pix Pixley's art was humanitarian, but she couldn't say that about him as a person. She was buttoning up when he shoved her onto the couch. Had she ever misjudged anyone so badly? He was a maniac who would do anything for a picture.

"I want you out of here," she said, "or I'm calling the police."

He dropped beside her, bent his arm across her face, and

pushed her onto her back. His other hand slid under her skirt. She heard stitches pop, and saw her panties in shreds on the floor.

He was all over her now. A finger crooked inside her blouse, and buttons scattered across the room. What was happening would almost be comical if it was happening to someone else. An elf was tearing off her clothes, and she was helpless to stop him. In this crazy part of the city you had to choose your friends carefully. A girl wasn't safe even with a fairy.

He twisted onto his side, and zipped open his fly. Gail looked away into the face of a demented little boy. If she lived to be a hundred she wouldn't be able to make sense of him. This wasn't the time to try. She pulled his hair, slapped his ears. A knee slicing between hers made space for the other, pried her legs wide, opened her, announced her vulnerability before he forced himself inside wriggling and grunting, his heart hammering against her dead one, tearing her apart. She dug her nails into the sweaty back of his neck. She felt herself blacking out, and prayed that she would while she concentrated her hate on him, cursed the rotten chain of events that had brought them together going back to the day she was born.

"You vile piece of shit," she said when he was done with her.

"Flattery will get you nowhere."

"How could you…?"

"You said it yourself, Gail. I never miss a beat."

She'd be lucky not to end up pregnant or diseased, but would always have sorrow. What more could he do to her? "I'll see to it you're put away forever," she said.

"Who'll believe I'm capable—that the terrible thing you're accusing me of ever crossed my mind? They'll say you're delusional." His voice was up an octave, and had taken on a lisp. "I'll tell them they've got you wrong—you're a blackmailer."

She clutched the blouse around her shoulders.

"If you go to the police, pictures telling a different story will be sent to the newspapers, to your parents, and to the administrators of your school."

She felt tears welling, but wouldn't let them come. They were a part of herself she was able to keep him from having.

"I hope you die," she said.

CHAPTER 10

Jordan hopped the rail, jogged down the third base line past empty box seats. It was a gray afternoon threatening rain, and the weather was keeping the fans at home.

In the visitors' dugout a few teammates looked around the old ballpark as groundskeepers spread a heavy tarpaulin over the infield. The last game of the exhibition season had brought them to Brooklyn. For many it was their first visit to Ebbets Field. At the end of the bench a player in a satin windbreaker was studying a comic book. A pink bubble exploded on his lips, and he scraped the gum back inside his mouth and blew another as Jordan sat down next to him.

"Hub? Adam Jordan with the *Atlantic City Press*. I'm putting together a story on American League rookies with a strong shot at sticking in the majors. As the A's top prospect, what's it been like for you breaking camp with the big ballclub?"

"After three years kicking around the bushes? Figure it out yourself."

"I didn't come all the way to Brooklyn to answer my own questions."

"It's like this," Hub Chase said. "Everything's first class in the bigs. The meal money, the hotels, the twat can't be beat. Even on a second division team going nowhere."

"What you're saying," Jordan said, "is you're looking forward to a great season, and bringing the fans out to Shibe Park so the A's can stay in Philadelphia where they belong."

"You don't need me." Hub turned the page. "Lemme read."

"After the year you had in Newark, my readers want to know why the Yankees let you go."

"Why do they think?" Hub spit out his gum. He was a big man with powerful arms and shoulders, wide across the chest. A pink wad landed in the coaches' box alongside third base. "On account of that lying cunt at the Park Sheraton that said I roughed her up."

He reached under the bench for a first baseman's mitt. Jordan recognized a real scoop. If the A's planned to use Hub at first, it was something to pass on to a sports desk. Hub slipped the glove on his left hand, pounded it with his fist.

"What's your side?"

"I ain't allowed to talk about it. The lawyers warned me if I open my yap I'll be sent down to Class D ball."

"Are the Yanks paying her off to make her go way like they always did for the Babe?"

Hub ground a baseball into the pocket. "Like I said, figure it out for yourself."

"You'll be getting in some work at first base?"

"Can't talk about that either. Manager's orders. Anything else I can help you with?"

"I'm thinking about calling you the Hard-Luck Kid," Jordan said. "How does that sound?"

"I don't get it."

"You've got legal troubles, and then you're traded right after your wife is killed. That's got to be rough."

"Couldn't've come at a better time," Hub said. "She was my *ex*-wife. I don't got to pay alimony no more."

"Can I quote you?"

"It's a free country. You do, though, I'll deny we ever talked. The A's've got lawyers, too. They'll sue your ass, yours and the *Press*."

Jordan screwed the cap off his pen, opened his notebook. "I'm trying to make you look good, Hub, but I need help. Isn't there something to say about her that would put you in a better light?"

"She was another cunt that got what she deserved." He swiped Jordan's hand off the page. "Suzie was born with a swelled head. It got bigger every time she stood in the mirror, and didn't get no smaller when she started winning beauty contests. She thought being Miss America was a bigger deal than being Mrs. Number Twenty-Four on the New York Yankees. People told her I was dragging her down, and she fell for it."

"What people?"

Hub removed his hand from Jordan's. "Put down she left me for assholes that promised they could do things for her. One or two, maybe they had the right connections. One thing all of them could do was fuck her. Fucking those assholes, she didn't think twice about it if she thought they could make her Miss America."

"You don't want to say that," Jordan said. "It'll look like you might have had an interest in hurting her."

"You want the story or not? She was fucking everybody from the beauty contests, and she was fucking their friends, and she was fucking the friends of their friends, whoever said they could give her a jump on the competition. Goes to show what a sucker I was. I married her for it, and she was giving it away for free."

"Men lie about beautiful women," Jordan said.

Hub Chase lifted his thigh, and placed the comic book carefully underneath. "In that life she was in, all the lies get told to the girls. A contest organizer, a judge fucks my wife, next thing everybody's lining up to fuck her, too. The same people that want to fuck a beauty contestant, they like rubbing shoulders with a ballplayer. They'd say Hub, come to the house, and have your pick of the most beautiful women in the world, Miss Delaware Bay, Miss 4-H Clubs, they're yours for the taking. I'd go to a party, and there'd be twenty knockout girls there. Anybody could have the one that caught his eye, and the one they all wanted, the one everybody was dragging in the bedroom, was my wife." He put his hand outside the dugout, and felt for rain. "Shitty day," he said. "Start writing. I want the fans to know what Suzie was."

Jordan didn't need notes. The story would stay in his head without being allowed to cloud his judgment. In playing the sympathy card Hub might be keeping to the facts. But *Real Detective* was filled with sympathetic figures who'd murdered out of righteous indignation.

"Let's get away from that," Jordan said. "Tell me about yourself."

"Didn't I already?"

"I'm looking for a local angle. You grew up near Atlantic City, right?"

"It wasn't near nothing. It was on an egg farm out in the boondocks. My family—I shouldn't say it, it'll turn the fans against me—they were commies from the old country. There were fifteen families on the farm, reds like my folks, didn't have nothin', but smarter'n Rockefeller. They knew the U.S. was heading to hell. My parents, they were gonna lead the revolution to save it."

"Where are they today?"

"Retired to Sarasota. They opened a restaurant to get rid of some of the birds that didn't lay. The Red Hen. It was the first time they had two nickels to rub together. Never went back to the farm."

"Where was it?"

"A place you never heard of, it don't exist no more."

"Try me."

"Poultrina." The name came with a smile, the handsome smile from Hub's baseball card. "Mean anything to you?"

Jordan shook his head. "I thought I'd been everywhere in Jersey."

"You probably were," Hub said. "Poultrina's nowheresville.

The only time I got asked about it before, it was Suzie asking. I mentioned I was raised in the Barrens, and she drug me out to the car, had to see where. I couldn't find it in the dark, it was that long since I was there. After going around in circles, we came to a bunch of old falling-down shacks, nobody around. We didn't stay two minutes before she said, 'Take me home.' When I asked why we had to drive thirty miles for nothing, she said, ' 'Cause I want to know everything about the man I'm married to.' "

"Did she?"

"She knew a thing or two, I'll give her that," Hub said. "Not so much outside of bed."

"What did she really want there?"

"It ain't for the sports."

"You told the cops?"

"Had to."

"You don't want it coming from them."

Hub shook his head, but then he said, "When I was throwing out her stuff after she got killed, I found some pictures, nude shots where she was tied up with ropes, and a gag over her mouth, and a blindfold, and handcuffs. They looked like they were shot at the farm. I figure she needed an outdoors place where she could take off her clothes without drawing a crowd. She should've gone to the Boardwalk. Everybody and his brother already knew what she had."

"The cops took them?"

"Like a look? I bet you would. I burned them for her. There's no hard feelings between me and Suzie."

"Been back to the farm?" Jordan said.

"What for?"

"Know a colored girl name of Etta Lee Wyatt?"

"She an Annie?"

"A what?"

"Baseball Annie. You know, with hot pants for the players."

"She was on the black beauty circuit," Jordan said, "and entertained at private parties around Atlantic City. Never ran into her?"

"I was plenty entertained without her, whoever she is. What's she got to do with me?"

"She was murdered last month. Her body was found in Poultrina."

"Some coincidence, huh? Hey, look, the fucking sun's coming out." He scraped mud from his spikes with a beer can opener. "I gotta get loose."

Sparks sizzled at his heels as he clattered to the field. Jordan got up to go, poked his head out into cold rain.

Using cuticle scissors Jordan cut away a cluster of gray hairs over his ear. The last time he shaved they weren't there. He didn't mind having them, but would reserve judgment until they grew in again. Tonight was not the time to experiment with a new look.

He buttoned up his twenty-dollar shirt, tried on a striped tie, a solid, polka dots, then opened the collar button. He wasn't crazy about the shirt, but had to go with it. After the stink he'd made about getting it back, Mollie would expect to see it.

Inside the pocket were two $7.50 tickets, third row center orchestra, for *Kismet* at the Ziegfield Theater. He wouldn't stuff himself at the restaurant, or else he'd be snoring by the second act. A Monk jam session at the Village Vanguard was where he'd rather be, but he'd be on firmer ice with Mollie on Broadway. Tonight wasn't for experiments of any kind.

The bell rang while he hunted for more gray. He couldn't think who it was unless a killer had picked the worst time to settle a score. Tiptoeing to the door, he put his eye to the peep.

"Open up, Adam Jordan, I know you in!"

Too bad it wasn't a killer. With a killer he might stand a chance. He threw the bolt, unhooked the chain. Cherise scuffed her feet on the mat, and came in clutching a cardboard valise.

"My, my, my, don't we look pretty," she said. "Stepping out?"

"I didn't know you were coming. You should have called."

"*You* should've," she said, "but no mind, here I am. Owe me for the train."

"How long are you staying?"

"Long as you want me." She put down her bag, and kissed him. "After that, we'll see."

A frightening thought: Because he'd saved her life she was his responsibility forever.

"I'll find you a hotel."

"Ain't here to sleep anyplace but with you."

"I have a date tonight with another woman."

"Glad to hear it ain't with a man," Cherise said. "I didn't expect you wouldn't find somebody. I ain't been sitting alone by the radio since you left either. But you invited me, and now you treating me like I brung bed bugs. Want to be with your new sweetie, that's okay long as you don't forget who's waiting up for you."

"It isn't okay."

"Wouldn't have it no other way," she said. "Where you taking her?"

"To a Broadway show."

"Fancy restaurant, too?" She picked a loose thread from his collar. "Hot damn, I'm gonna have a swell time in New York."

Coming out of the subway he spotted Mollie across from the *Times* Tower looking up at the big clock above the news zipper.

"Sorry," he said, "a friend came by."

"I didn't know you had friends here."

"Neither did I. Toffenetti's is up the block. Let's hurry."

"We don't have time," she said. "The play starts in forty minutes."

His appetite was shot anyway. It began to come back when the theater lights dimmed, and the orchestra struck up the overture. The square music left him cold, but Mollie tapped her foot to every tune, and didn't let a single cornball joke get by without a laugh. They were last up the aisle when the curtain came down.

"Hungry?" he said.

"Starved. Aren't you?"

There was a half-hour wait for a table at Toffenetti's. They went to Sardi's, and were seated immediately. Scanning the menu, Jordan calculated that he would break the bank tonight without much chance of a payoff.

Mollie gushed about the show while he nodded agreeably and tried to figure a way to land her in bed. Assuming a killer hadn't broken in and taken care of Cherise, he didn't stand a chance. Mollie was moved by his stricken expression. On top of a steady intake of Manhattans it was causing her to look searchingly into his eyes.

"How do you like Brooklyn?" he said.

"I sleep there. I try not to strangle my roommate, and spend every waking minute in Manhattan. What about your place?"

"What about it?"

"It's convenient?"

"Oh yeah, right by the office," he said. "Five minutes from everywhere."

She arched one eye. Jordan was undecided if it was involuntary.

"Do you share it?" she said.

"For the time being."

There was a hotel on every block in Times Square. But most were pricey, and even the fleabags would turn away a couple without luggage. Jordan lit a Lucky. "How's the work coming?"

"The girl-about-town look is in big demand," Mollie said, "but all I have to show the clients is the session I did for you. They think I'm a fugitive from the vice squad. I may just go back to New Jersey."

"Pixley will be glad to help."

"I can't take advantage of a casual remark he probably doesn't remember."

"You'll be doing him a kindness. He's crazy to be around beautiful women. When he isn't taking pictures I don't think he leaves the darkroom."

"I'm not too proud to accept a favor from a friend of a friend," she said. "That's principled compared to what most of the girls do to get ahead."

He let it go by. Sometimes it was smart, being thick. He had to get home. On second thought it would be tragic if a killer beat him to Cherise.

A gritty wind blowing out of the park propelled them toward the subway arm in arm.

"Come back and see my place," she said. "My roommate will find you fascinating."

"Another time."

"I know," she said. "It's an hour on the subway for nothing."

Somebody had to say it. He kissed her goodnight pressing a nickel in her hand for the fare.

The apartment was dead quiet. Cherise must have nodded off with the lights on. Coming inside on his toes, he found her sitting up in bed with *Real Detectives* scattered around.

"This is the magazine you work for?"

"What do you think of it?"

"Don't want no part of your nightmares."

He kicked off his shoes, unbuckled his pants.

"Gonna lay your body next to mine," she said, "need a shower."

"It's close to midnight," he said. "I'm tired."

"Then it's the couch for you. Can't sleep in bed with me."

"What makes you think I want to?"

"Wouldn't be home before morning less you did."

He got out of his clothes. When she wouldn't make room, he took away her magazine. She looked up and said, "You the yummiest thing. Any gal'd want to have you tonight."

"Who's standing in your way?"

"I don't take sloppy hand-me-downs."

"Nothing hap—"

"Don't want to hear about it." She pointed into the bathroom. "Shower's that way."

A knot in his stomach that he hadn't known was there unraveled as hot water played against his skin. Cherise was reading when he came back, and made him wait before she slid over.

"Can't trust a soul," she said. "Everybody has it in 'em to be a murderer. I'm damn scared. Hold me good." She reached over him for the light. "Lucky fellow. How many men sleep with two gals the same night, one white, the other black? Something to tell your grandkids."

"I don't think that's what grandparents talk to their grandchildren about," Jordan said.

"Yours didn't?" she said.

And cracked up because he thought she meant it.

"What makes you think my other girl's white?"

She stopped laughing. "Aw, shut up, you."

Footsteps on the landing brought him awake in the middle of the night. Churchill said that outside the Soviet Union when you heard someone at your door at four in the morning you could rest easy because it was only the milkman. It was reassuring to know he wasn't going to be hauled off to Siberia. That didn't mean he was happy to be up.

He flipped onto his side, his back, the other side as the knot in his stomach tightened. No mystery what caused it. Cherise's legs were tangled in his, and she was purring.

Sex was the biggest part of what they had. Before, it was everything, and he slept like a baby. He didn't know when things had changed. Cherise was still the same, crabby and demanding, seeing the world from the other side of the telescope. If he didn't get her out of his life, she'd wreck his chance with Mollie, who might be dull, but was right for him. Christ, he sounded like his mother. Maybe he'd get off a note to the advice-to-the-lovelorn columnist at the *Mirror*, let her know he had to choose between Miss America and a colored whore at the edge of a double murder case, and find out what a reasonable man in Adam Jordan's shoes would do.

He dozed for half an hour, twenty minutes after that. By a quarter past six he was up for good. He smoked a cigarette, lit another, got out of bed and into his suit, drank a glass of juice listening to the news. He poked Cherise, and she stopped snoring long enough for him to tell her he was leaving for work. At nine, when he called from the office, she asked why he'd sneaked out. She planned to kill the afternoon seeing the sights.

An hour later he tried Pixley in Atlantic City. "When'd you get back?" he said.

"After you left the gallery I ran into a young fan who asked for pointers. I gave her what I thought she needed, and caught the train. All in all New York was an enjoyable, profitable experience."

"I have another one for you," Jordan said.

"Who's the victim?"

"I am, if you won't help."

"I'm so tired of murder," Pixley said. "Tell me more."

"A friend of mine's got show business ambitions. She's not bad-looking, has talent, but she's spinning her wheels."

"Par for the course."

"Correct me if I'm wrong. The big talent agencies, the bookers, the producers want to see pictures before they bring in a girl for an audition."

"Unless it's a cattle call," Pixley said, "she can't do without a good portfolio and professional portraits."

"Give her the full treatment," Jordan said. "On me."

"Oh, I know who we're talking about," Pixley said, "the delightful girl you brought to my opening. Mollie, isn't that her name? I'll be happy to shoot her for you."

"Right name. Wrong girl. I'm sending Cherise."

"Who's she?"

"A friend from Missouri Avenue."

"A *Negro* girl?"

"Is that going to be a problem?"

"For *me*, Adam? I can't imagine what problem you mean. I've always wanted to capture a young black woman in my viewfinder. When can I have her?"

Cherise blocked the way into the kitchen when Jordan returned to the apartment after work. "What are you doing in there?" he said.

"Keep out. I'm busy."

He reached around her into the refrigerator for a Knickerbocker. "Where'd you go today?"

"Saw the A&P on Third Avenue, the butcher on Fifty-sixth Street, the greengrocer on Second and Sixty-first."

It wasn't the most shocking discovery that she knew her way around a hot oven. But until he heard her lecture at Princeton it would be hard to top. She was sending a message about her intentions that was as ominous as an announcement that she was pregnant—something else it might be a good idea to start worrying about.

"I didn't send for a cook."

"Didn't send for me at all."

"There's only about a million restaurants in New York."

"We'll get to 'em all in time," she said. "This is something I want to do for you."

He'd planned to surprise her with the photo shoot, put her

on the train back to Atlantic City before she knew what hit her. Now he'd have to tell her flatly that he didn't want to play house.

"What did you do at work?" she said.

"The usual."

"More dead bodies?"

"Uh-huh. Have you thought about what you'll do when you're home?"

"I just got here."

"You have to keep your eye on the ball all the time, Cherise."

"Like you?"

"Damn right."

"Thinking 'bout who's gonna turn up murdered tomorrow?"

"Something else, too," he said. "I told a photographer about you. He wants to see you in his studio."

"How'm I gonna pay you back for everything? There's not enough hours in the night."

"He expects you tomorrow afternoon."

"Don't worry about me missing my beauty nap," she said. "I don't mind sleeping in."

"You'll nap on the train. The studio is in Atlantic City."

"I see." She raised the lid on a pot, turned a spoon disinterestedly.

"He'll have you looking like a movie star."

"When I'm feeling like one of your corpses?"

And how did you put a happy face on that? "A chance like this doesn't come along every day."

"Nobody asked you to plan my life, thanks just the same. Wasn't moving in permanent," she said. "That don't mean there wouldn't be good times till things fall apart the way they do. Being comfortable around someone's like drinking cream that you got to lap it all up, every drop, before it goes sour. It ain't that I don't 'ppreciate what you done. Been given worse for a goin'-away present—black eyes, a kick in the pants, a ride to the police station one time I lost my head. Thanks for everything, and for nothing." She turned down the heat. "Getting rid of me to be with your other girl?"

After saving her life how did he tell her he was afraid?

"Bad timing, Cherise, that's all."

"Don't make me laugh."

Fat chance.

CHAPTER 11

Tom Flynn, over a liquid lunch at Mulcahy's on East Forty-third, said it was his first time in New York since V-J Day.

"I was thirty-seven years, ten months, six days old when Selective Service called my number. My old man and old lady hadn't waited till the wedding, they'd have saved me the worst two years of my life at Fort Hancock on Sandy Hook."

Jordan rubbed his eyes. An hour of Flynn had put him into a mild coma. If he had to listen to war stories, it would be lights out.

"I was on a sixteen-inch gun crew watching for Jerry subs trying to sneak into the harbor, but we never practiced with live ammo. The sound those guns made would've thrown the city into a panic. If we had to shoot, we'd've taken out Coney Island."

Jordan signaled the waiter. Flynn talked faster. "You haven't asked what brings me to see you. I need work."

"You left the *Bulletin*?"

"It left me."

"What about your girlfriend, the stockholder?"

"The stockholder's daughter," Flynn said. "She left first. She said she was saving herself for Eddie Fisher. What I've got in mind, I used to cover Philadelphia for Pelfrey. I'd like to try my hand full time, move into South Jersey, too, since you're here."

"There aren't enough good killings to make it pay."

"Business picked up after you left."

The waiter brought the check. Jordan put money on the table. Flynn's hands remained in his lap.

"Sunday morning, a party boat out of Margate hauled in a

body off Absecon Light. It took the coroner's office two days to decide it was a woman's. She'd been strangled before she went in the water. Dr. Melvin found rope burns on her throat, and across her shoulders, and she was wearing handcuffs on her wrists and ankles. He said—you know Doc Melvin?"

Jordan put down two more singles.

"Sex games, he said. Football's *my* game," Flynn said. "Baseball a little less so since DiMaggio hung 'em up. If Doc Melvin says she was playing games, who'm I to say it was something else? I figure it's right up your alley."

He pulled clips from his jacket, and arranged them between the wet spots around his glass.

"Name's Anita Paulette Coburn, 21, originally from Bethlehem, Pennsylvania, late of Kentucky Avenue, Atlantic City, an aspiring model, and whatever else pretty young girls who are up for those games aspire to."

"How do we know?"

"From the parents," Flynn said. "They'd reported her missing after being contacted by a roommate, and supplied dental records for the ID. She was something of a wild child who ran away from home a dozen times before she was fifteen, when the Coburns said the hell with it and had her declared an emancipated minor. She'd been to Hollywood to try to break into pictures, and New York, and Miami, where she was picked up for loitering for immoral purposes. Mrs. Coburn said she had dreams of being Miss America."

"Who doesn't?"

Flynn sucked ice out of his glass, and chewed it. "Not me."

"Give me more."

"You were a newspaperman," Flynn said. "I don't have to tell you the best part of the story often doesn't make it into the paper. According to the autopsy, when they examined the corpse they found two dollars with it."

"She was floating in the ocean. How—?"

"Doc Melvin told me it wasn't the largest jackpot he's removed from a corpse."

Jordan wanted to view Anita Coburn's remains, to smell the awful smells, talk to her grieving parents, and write her story himself, to present her murder to his readers as what it was rather than a processed commodity, twenty-five cents for a dozen in every issue.

"The cops linked her to the other girls?" he said.

"What other?"

"Mrs. Chase. Etta Wyatt. The killings follow a pattern."

"I don't know those names."

"They got him for just one?"

"Got who?"

"You tell me," Jordan said.

"I don't know what you're talking about."

"Have you looked inside the magazines recently? We don't use unsolved cases. That hasn't changed since Pelfrey."

Flynn ground the ice between his teeth. "I didn't think anybody cared much who killed them. I thought it was about sex games, two bucks stuffed inside a two-dollar whore."

Out of politeness Jordan wouldn't ask if Flynn was like that himself, which of his interests beyond football and baseball had soured his relationship with the stockholder's daughter.

"Read a couple of stories, Tom. It won't kill you. Learn our style, write a piece on spec, and then we'll see."

"Sure," Flynn said, "that's what I'll do. Meanwhile, can you spot me twenty till I'm back on my feet?"

In a new stack of flimsies Jordan found a squib on the "apparent sex-slaying of Anita Coburn, the former Miss Lehigh Valley, and Miss Silver Queen Corn, who stole judges' hearts with a virtuoso turn on the six-string ukulele. The doomed beauty had been slated to make her professional debut on a variety card at the Alcazaba Theater in Atlantic City." Jordan would be hard-pressed to explain why a gruesome killing made him homesick, but suddenly he was starved for a Boardwalk corn dog.

On Friday at five he made a dash to the west side ferry. By ten he was carrying his bag from the train station at the Atlantic City Convention Center with no place to go. Was there an emptier feeling than to return alone to a city you'd stopped calling home?

A cabbie had a deal at the Bonacker Hotel: Beachfront room with continental breakfast, private bath, and a girl for fifteen dollars. Jordan checked in to the Columbus, and hurried out again to stretch his legs. He kept to the Boardwalk till he was back at the Convention Center, then went away from the ocean along Mississippi Avenue. The early show was breaking at the Alcazaba, and he stood back from the mob pouring onto the sidewalk. Television was driving a stake through Hollywood's vitals, but you wouldn't know it from the stampede under the serpentine lights.

For a dollar they'd seen two movies, and a stage show— Dewey "Pigmeat" Markham, Honi Coles, jugglers, and a ventriloquist with an ebony dummy. Anita Coburn was slated for the bottom of the bill. Edged in black her photo had a place of honor inside the glass showcase.

Jordan ducked under the marquee for a closer look. Anita, in a silver bathing suit, glanced back over her shoulder mimicking the famous Betty Grable pin-up from the war. Anita Coburn did not have Betty Grable's great legs. What she did have were mounds of blonde hair, and a heavy-lidded smile, the come-hither look mocked by a ukulele dandled against her thigh. A girl who knew how to take a terrific picture. The studio name in the lower left corner was obscured by the black border. Jordan's breath was misting the glass when a heavy hand spun him around, and he was face to face with the goon who'd tossed him from Beach's office. The hand on the goon's elbow belonged to his boss.

"Like her?" Beach said. He sent his man to the curb where a black Packard Patrician was idling with another thick-necked lug at the wheel. "What are you doing here?"

"Thought I'd catch a show."

"No refunds," Beach said. "The beauty queen's been canceled."

"Who killed her?"

"Let's think about it. Thirty years ago, Houdini headlined a magic show at the Alcazaba. He was hogtied, locked in cuffs and chains, wrapped in a strait jacket for good measure, and lowered head first into a tank of water. In five minutes he was free. Of course, he was the world's greatest escape artist."

Under the flashing lights Jordan saw Beach as alternately black and white, never both, neither for long. "Anita Coburn didn't tie herself up and jump in the ocean."

"It doesn't take a magician to know what crosses a man's mind the moment he sees a girl like her." Beach tapped the glass over her picture with a ruby ring. "Most of us are too civilized to act on it. Take Narvin for instance."

"Who?"

Beach turned his head toward the car. "Put him in the company of an attractive young lady, he becomes protective. He treats her like the Queen of Sheba. Another friend—I won't mention his name but you'd recognize it from the sports pages—goes to the other extreme. When he's taken with a woman, he can't keep his fists to himself."

"It's a peculiar way of showing affection."

Beach shrugged. "There are men that show their feelings with ropes and handcuffs. They don't always stop there."

"Friends of yours, too?"

A scowl flashing in the crazy light was briefly a smile.

"Every murderer I read about in the papers has a neighbor who says, '...but he was a churchgoer, a scoutmaster, salt of the earth. He was kind to his mother, and loved animals. Who'd've suspected—?' I could be best friends with murderers, but how would I know? What do I know about anyone?"

The quotes were accurate, but often culled from the files. The personable killer down the block was a comfortable character for citizens who didn't like being told that they lived among friendless monsters whose only human contact came in stalking their victims.

"Why was a white girl playing the Alcazaba?"

"I've got a bit of Narvin in me," Beach said. "I'm also protective of the fair sex."

"Why did you need her there, Beach? To keep her on hand till you sold her to friends you don't really know? How much do you get for a white beauty queen?"

"I've given you all the help you're going to get."

"You gave me crap."

"Giving ofays crap is what I do." The smile was a frown again, and didn't change.

Jordan got in his way as he started back to the car. "No good—"

Heavy hands took Jordan from behind, and lifted him off the ground with his arms pinned against his sides. He didn't resist. Interviews with Beach routinely ended with a kick in the pants. Beach was at the curb when Jordan was slammed to his knees. The heavy hands arranged a hammerlock, and the crowd parted as Jordan was frog-marched to the Packard. No one interfered. It was Friday night at the Alcazaba, and the real entertainment played out on the street.

Narvin pulled him inside the back seat, squeezed him over the transmission hump to make room for Beach at the door. The third man took the wheel again, cutting into traffic ahead of an ambulance.

"If anyone wants out now," Beach said, "scram. Kidnapping is a capital crime."

"You sayin' if it goes wrong, we all end up dead?" Narvin said.

"It could happen."

"Who's dead if it goes right?"

They couldn't stop laughing. Jordan's guts tightened. Some joke.

"You couldn't leave well enough alone," Beach said.

A woman pushing a stroller made eye contact with the driver before entering a pedestrian crossing. Spotting Jordan, she paused for a second look. The big car ran a stop sign nearly clipping her heels.

"I'm talking to you." Beach turned Jordan's chin. "The girl died. So what? Girls die all the time. Some of them I don't even know. The life she had, I'd be surprised anybody's aware of the difference."

"Nothing was well enough."

"Enough for me," Beach said. "All I am is a ten percenter introducing girls to men who use them for what they're for. If there's breakage, how am I to blame? They're adult girls, they understand the risks. A good many go in for the rough stuff. Hell, they demand it. I'll be damned if I let a writer, a fucking nobody, take food out of my family's mouth by connecting me to terrible things I got nothing to do with."

"Anita Coburn would be alive today if you weren't so helpful."

"You got a one-track mind," Beach said. Jordan shook his head, tried to as Beach steadied his chin. "One-track to a dead end."

"Where are we going?"

"We ain't started yet, and I'm sick of you already. Turn on the radio." Beach poked the driver. "We won't have to hear him."

A white man playing Negro as unconvincingly as Beach spouted jive through the dashboard speaker. Symphony Sid was America's most important jazz disc jockey, broadcasting from a socialist radio station in New York. After a hep cat intro he cut to a free-wheeling Art Blakey drum solo. "Who needs this crap?" Beach said.

The driver spun the dial. Beach said, "Hold it," for Professor Longhair pounding a tinny piano. Awful noise, thought Jordan,

New Orleans piano for people who didn't know New Orleans or the piano. Then he had another thought: You're being taken for a ride in the worst sense of the word, and you're griping about the background music? What's wrong with you?

Beach pushed the beret back on his head as his foot marked an awkward rhythm against Jordan's. "That's more like it."

They went over the inlet past Absecon Light, and headed up the coast on empty nighttime roads. The rotten egg smell hanging over the salt marshes made Jordan gag. After a while the breeze shifted, bringing fresh air off the ocean, but Jordan's guts didn't stop churning. Miles ahead the Brigantine Light cut the fog. A returning fisherman's boat played hide and seek in the reeds.

"There yet?" Narvin said. "Why we wastin' the night goin' nowhere?"

"Sit back," Beach said. "Enjoy the scenery."

A marsh hawk swooped across the hood. Before it veered into blackness Jordan noticed a squirming packet of fur in its talons. The Packard was cruising at an even 50 when Jordan felt a bump. His right leg stiffened as the driver slammed the brakes.

"What's that?" Beach said. "Squash a bunny?"

"I lost the road."

Highbeams spiraling in fog were refocused over a frayed tangle of swamp grass. The hood ornament pointed the fastest way into a ditch. The driver cut the wheel sharply, throwing Jordan into Beach's lap. The big car shimmied, straightened, gained speed again, and lost it fighting for traction. Beach shoved Jordan away as they ground to a halt.

"You put a scratch in this baby, and it's comin' outta your pay," Beach said. "Try rockin' her."

The motor growled. The wheels churned soft sand, and the Packard settled deep in the ruts.

Beach hurried out. Two feet from the car he was invisible.

The flame from a match congealed into the orange tip of a cigarette. Jordan watched it through the back window as Beach kicked the tires. "Good and stuck," he said into Narvin's window.

"I can take care of him here."

"Wanna be sittin' with his dead corpse when the sun comes up?"

Jordan couldn't see Narvin's face. It didn't stop him from picturing it breaking into a smile.

"How 'bout we bury him?"

"Feel like diggin' a grave tonight?"

"Let him dig it himself. He the one gonna be usin' it."

Narvin showed a gun. Jordan slid out of the car and marched into the reeds. Knotted roots clutched at his ankles, pulled his shoes from his heels. In a patch of sand with little vegetation Beach stopped him. "What you lookin' for? A pretty view? You ain't a little boy been brought to play on the shore. Get to work."

"Ain't gonna get it done without a shovel," Narvin said.

"Go on now," Beach said, "get down and start diggin' with your paws like the dog you are."

Jordan fashioned a filthy look for them. It was the bright side of being out on a night when no one could see in front of his face.

Narvin kicked him behind his knees. "You heard…"

Jordan scooped sand. The wind blew it back. A shallow trench grew large under his hands. He steepened the sides till they collapsed.

A story came to mind, a Greek myth about a man in a situation something like the one he was in who couldn't dig his way out of a hole because the walls kept caving in. Jordan had felt sorry for the Greek because he couldn't stop the hole from filling in, but would have been happy to trade places with him now.

Narvin rested his foot on Jordan's back as a four-sided depression took shape around them. The wind shifted, helping to clear the sand away.

"Fella workin' up a sweat for nothin'," Narvin said to Beach. "He can stop where he at, and you and me, we'll build a little castle over him. Nobody gonna see him from the road anyhow."

"He's just funnin' with you," Beach said to Jordan. "Do a good job here, you'll come back to the car and dig it out before we shoot you. How's that sound?"

What it sounded like was the most he could expect. He pushed sand back into the hole while they laughed.

A jagged shell cut his hand. The sand was damp now, and the digging came easy, which was no favor. Narvin dipped his toe in the center of the hole, measuring the depth.

"Watchin' him's wearin' me out," Beach said. "I'll wait in the car."

A root tangled around Jordan's arm. Tough and fibrous, it was the closest thing to a weapon he was going to find. He moved more sand, but couldn't pull it loose. It shredded while he worked it from side to side.

"Not too deep y'all," Narvin said.

"Beach says different."

"Who you think he gonna tell fill in your grave when you lyin' in it? You? Stop where you at."

If this was his final resting place, at least till the next big storm washed his body out to sea, he wanted plenty of room. He kept digging. It was a long shot, but if he made it big enough he might get Narvin to trade places with him.

"Stand by the front," Narvin said. "When I shoot you, try and fall back on your ass. I don't want blood on my new threads layin' out your body, okay?"

Narvin laughed again. Jordan had to admit it was funny. But not that funny. He smoothed the bottom of the hole, and then he stood up.

Narvin pointed the gun where he wanted him. Oh yeah, he was a bundle of laughs. Jordan hit his mark, and emptied a fistful of sand in Narvin's face.

Narvin spit, but didn't blink. "What the fuck?" he said. Jordan tossed the second handful in his eyes, brought up his toe into the big man's crotch.

The gun going off beside his head wasn't louder than Narvin's howls. Jordan swiped for it, deflecting the barrel away from his ear. Narvin clouted him with his free hand. Jordan hit back with an uppercut, a glancing blow connecting with more stubble than chin, and pulled Narvin into the grave. Using the big man for a footstool, he jumped out.

The second shot was another miss. Narvin, shouting "You a dead motherfucker," was last to know. Jordan heard Beach call out to ask if he'd been killed yet. Narvin said, "No, motherfucker gettin' 'way," and Beach, too angry to sound colored, said, "Idiot, can't you do anything right?"

The voices became indistinct as Jordan ran. Clearer were the tide lapping against the mud, the buzz of insects, a night-hawk's metallic cry. He had little idea where he was going. On his left was the water. The road was to his right. At his back were two men determined to kill him. A third could almost be anywhere. He ran blindly. Later there might be time to find his bearings.

Lacking structures and trees, the tidal flats were cut haphazardly by shallow drainages. Where the grass grew thick Jordan could have been running over a wet sponge. The going was slower still in the dry sand. Thank God for a moonless night and adrenaline.

Narvin, not far behind, said, "Stop where you at, mother-fucker." While Jordan had been thinking, Narvin had been running fast. Jordan ran harder. Where had thinking ever gotten him?

Near the water the grass thinned, and the damp sand allowed him to open his stride. His lungs burned as they sucked air through the residue left by millions of Luckys. Coming down in a hole his knee buckled, but the crack he heard was from dry brush, not cartilage. He was running easily when he stumbled into cold water.

He was up to his hips in a ditch that returned the tide to the sea, ankle-deep in a soft bottom with the consistency of quicksand. The first rule for anyone caught in quicksand, as he'd learned as a nine-year-old at the Saturday serials, was not to struggle. A gunshot kicking into the bank suggested the rule didn't apply here, and he exhausted himself slogging to dry ground. He wished the wet, sandy shoes pinching his feet on Narvin, who was splashing through the ditch with a string of "Dead motherfucker" and "Worthless motherfucker" on his lips.

Narvin had fired off four bullets, and was down to two. Unless his gun was an eight- or nine-shooter. Or he had extra bullets, or a second gun. Did Beach have a gun, too? Jordan stopped thinking about it. It was the best idea he had.

A splintered hulk half-buried in the sand tripped him up. Barrel-shaped, bigger than a rowboat, it was probably a round-bottom skiff. Gasping wind, he listened for Narvin. No motherfuckers from the big man chugging like a steam boiler about to blow.

Jordan was too tired to move. What he had strength for was to squeeze between the broken timbers and hold still. A brilliant idea—unless Narvin had it, too, and put a bullet through the wood. He forced himself back on his feet. Just an idea.

One foot followed the other, then did it again. His second wind would kick in soon, and he'd leave Narvin in the dust. He pushed himself on drunken legs. The wind parted the mist, and a yellow eye reflecting moonglow brought him up short. Had Narvin circled around? Had Beach freed the Packard, and cut him off? He said, "Boo," and a doe bolted for the road.

Narvin shot again. The sand kicked up where the deer had been, and Jordan ran after it. What kept Narvin in the chase? What had Beach promised for the scalp of Adam Jordan? And for coming back without it? Another bullet exploded some clam shells into fragments that stung his ankles. Number six.

"C'mere," Narvin said. "Only playin' with you."

Jordan pumped his legs, alarmed at how little ground they covered.

"Quit tryin' to get 'way, an' you can rest long as you want."

The gun hit him between the shoulders. He looked back as Narvin shortened the gap. He was still waiting for his second wind. Maybe he'd missed it.

They were eight feet apart. Four. Three, Narvin clawing at his back. Jordan dipped his right shoulder. Narvin veered right as Jordan cut to the left.

"Motherfucker stop."

Narvin was on his heels again before they'd covered thirty feet. He snagged Jordan's collar, gathered cloth, tightening his grip, was reeling him in when Jordan broke free.

"Gonna wish you *was* dead."

A surge of adrenaline gave Jordan a short lead. Narvin put his head down, and matched him stride for stride. Again Jordan lowered his right shoulder. Narvin, guessing left, fell behind as Jordan broke right.

The boiler hissed and sputtered. If Narvin didn't smoke, Jordan was counting on other bad habits taking a toll on his stamina. Seven feet separated them. Four again. Less. Then Jordan was ten feet ahead, fifteen.

He was out of adrenaline. There wouldn't be more. But when he stole a look the big man wasn't moving. Narvin's chest heaved as he lifted a foot and put it down in almost the same place. Then he bent over with his hands on his knees, and puked his guts.

Jordan managed not to. He couldn't run, so he walked. Narvin jogged after him, stopping to heave again.

"Why you makin' this hard?"

"What will you do if you catch me?" Jordan said.

"It'll be quick. What else you want?"

Jordan could walk, or he could talk. He didn't have breath for both. He moved off dragging his feet, and when he turned around the next time Narvin hadn't budged. Wouldn't be budging any time soon.

Jordan stopped to rest. Crouching, he fell over in the sand. Narvin coughed, and said, "When I get my hands on you, gonna wish you was never born."

Jordan had been wishing something like that since he was put in Beach's car. But not now. Narvin wasn't going to lay a finger on him tonight. Jordan flattened his palm under his lips, prepared to blow him a kiss. Why make it personal? He picked himself up, and quietly walked away, moving easily as his second wind kicked in.

CHAPTER 12

Mollie put down her bag, watched the couples traipse around the floor. They were out of step with the music, a waltz, and with each other, limber young women with frozen smiles partnered by stiff-kneed men. Atlantic City made its name on girls playing to the fantasies of old men, the sweet, public face of blood sport. Similar rules applied in a dance studio.

The pop tune pouring over the transom one floor up was more to her liking. She freshened her makeup to a Rodgers and Hammerstein ballad. Pix Pixley came to the door wearing a light meter around his neck. A rigid smile patterned after those downstairs made her feel she was being laughed at behind her back. The same rules for a game turned on its head.

He put his cheek against hers, and kissed the air. All men, she believed, wanted to have her. Even the air-kissers, who put up a shy front, but whose fevered skin gave them away. Pixley was different, clammy cool.

He moved her bag inside. "You just got in?"

"I took a cab straight from the train station."

"Do you have a place to stay? I've got tons of room."

"My old roommate will be glad to have me back," she said, "for the weekend. You're kind to ask."

"No trouble. If you change your mind—"

In front of a backdrop representing a desert landscape a man as short and slight as Pixley lay on his back in bright light resting a spear against his thigh. Make that a javelin, she told herself. Aside from leather sandals he was nude, not the least self-conscious. He was around twenty, with short bleached blond hair, and the physique of a prepubescent boy. The sharp point of the javelin was aimed at a camera on a tripod.

"Marcel and I," Pixley said, "are doing a spread for *Today's Sun Worshiper*."

Marcel tilted his head to imaginary high noon, a heroic pose with the javelin raised above his ear.

"Lower your stick, Marcel," Pixley said. "You might puncture someone." He turned to Mollie. "I'm so happy to see you again. If we had to count on Adam Jordan to arrange a session, we'd be waiting forever. He's one of those fellows—yours truly excepted—who make promises they have no intention of keeping. Sometimes I don't know why we have anything to do with them."

Marcel laughed, and shook his spear.

"Not you, dear," Pixley said to him. "I know *precisely* why."

"When can you find time for me?" Mollie said.

"When are you going back to New York?"

"Maybe never."

"Poor girl, you must be delirious. Are you certain you wouldn't rather stay with me?"

She glanced at Marcel, who seemed ready to let fly with the javelin. "You're busy. I don't want to be in the way. I'll call in the morning."

"You traveled all this way just for me?"

"Well, one or two other things."

"I won't ask who *they* are," Pixley said. "I do hope you'll stay a while. I have friends, influential people, who would love to meet you."

"Can they do anything for me?"

"It depends on what you do for them…" Pixley balanced his chin on the back of his hand, and smiled. "…when they see your look."

She was at the door when he said, "Oh, Mollie?" A flash went off as she turned around, and she rushed her hand in front of her face. "You shouldn't," she said. "I look dreadful."

"You couldn't."

He watched her down the stairs, then went back inside and squared Marcel in the viewfinder.

"Who's *that*?" Marcel said.

"Hold still." He got the shot. "A new friend."

Marcel thought it was hilarious. Pixley snapped him laughing.

"I didn't know you had girlfriends."

"There's plenty you don't know about me, Marcel."

"Fill me in."

"If you don't quit annoying me, I'm going to shove that pig-sticker where it hurts. Oh, but that much you already knew."

Marcel's nostrils flared. Pix took more shots. "Good," he said, "just what the doctor ordered. A few more, and you can put on your pants. You did bring pants?"

"Very funny."

"Is it? What we'll do next time, you'll come back Tuesday in a middie blouse and bell bottoms. I have some ideas for *This Man's Navy*."

Pixley rolled up the backdrop, sat down with a magazine while Marcel dressed.

"What are you reading?"

Pixley showed him the cover.

"*Real Detective*? You can't be interested in that trash."

"It so happens I do a lot of work for them."

"I get it. You like looking at the pictures."

"You don't get anything, Marcel. You should pick up a detective magazine, you might learn something. Can you read? You've never mentioned it." He didn't wait long for a comeback before supplying one himself. "Frowning will put lines in your face."

Marcel smiled.

"Better," Pixley said. "Actually, it's the articles I enjoy most. Every issue is a sort of handbook full of practical information."

"For detectives?"

"Yes, for them, too."

"Good day, it's two o'clock. Two P.M."

"What the hell if it is? You woke me," Jordan said. "Who are you?"

"Your wake-up call, sir."

"Oh," Jordan said. "Uh, thank you." He let the receiver down three times before it found the cradle.

He felt as if he'd been put through the wringer, and decided that he had. His legs ached from the long run over sand. A painful bruise on his shoulder was a mystery with a hundred solutions. He stepped into the shower, brushed his teeth, got dressed. His foot didn't fit inside his shoe. He checked for swelling, filled an ashtray with sand.

It had been 6:30 when he'd gotten in after catching a ride with a *Press* delivery truck. When he mentioned that he used to work for the paper himself, the driver launched into a damning tirade against management, capitalist exploiters, the ruling class, and the hoity-toity sons of bitches in the new Packard sedan racing from Brigantine who cut him off.

It was too late for breakfast from the coffee shop. There was a television in the room. What he wanted to do was to get under the covers and spend the day watching it. He slouched against the headboard keeping his feet on the floor. If he pulled them into bed, he'd go out like a light. He reached for the phone again, asked the switchboard for an outside line.

"PixleyPix!"

"It's Adam Jordan."

"You have a terrible connection, or a hangover. Where are you?"

Jordan guzzled tepid water from a tumbler on the nightstand. "The Columbus Hotel."

"That dump? When did you arrive?"

"Yesterday."

"How long are you staying?"

"Let me ask the questions," Jordan said. "What do you know about Anita Coburn?"

"The girl they fished out of the ocean? I meant to call."

"Why didn't you?"

"I was waiting till the police had more than a corpse and a few sordid facts."

"What have you got?"

"Nothing they don't."

"You must have heard something."

"Heard it from whom?"

"I'm asking the—"

"You listen now. I'm a commercial photographer. Not a newshound. When your boss snaps his fingers do you come up with information the cops don't have?"

"It's most of the job," Jordan said. "Look in your files for photos of Miss Coburn."

"My files are in my head," Pixley said. "And, sorry, there's not a thing there."

Jordan gave it a bigger laugh than it deserved. Pixley was right. He had no business badgering him. The mild joke was Pixley saying no offense. Not yet.

"She wasn't a nobody," Jordan said. "She'd won a raft of beauty contests, and was on the card at the Alcazaba with her uke."

"Girls like her are a dime a dozen," Pixley said. "Some, you don't need a dime."

Talk about offensive. "Can you get the photos?"

"I don't see the rush when you don't have a killer, but I'll do what I can. By the way, your friend, what's her name, I haven't heard from her."

"Mollie?"

"Not her. The colored girl. Does she still want to sit for me?"

"Cherise doesn't have regular habits," Jordan said. "I'll tell her you're waiting."

"Not forever."

Two o'clock on a Saturday afternoon in a cheap hotel, and Jordan didn't know what to do with himself. Would it hurt to turn on the TV? He was paying for it, wasn't he?

A man in a safari suit holding a leopard cub in his lap was talking to a woman with a transparent smile. The cub was full of energy, all claws and teeth, and the woman was keeping her distance. Jordan put his heels up on the mattress a second before a test pattern replaced the picture. He picked up the phone again, asked for long distance.

"I'm sick of murder," he said. "Talk to me about something else."

"I'm sick of it, too. Who is this?"

"It's not a great time for games, Mollie."

"If you say so. Which murder?"

"This *is* President 9-9297?"

"You have the right number. The wrong girl."

A honeyed drawl bolstered a plausible case that he'd been pursuing the wrong roommate.

"I'm Gina."

"Is Mollie there?"

"Not till Wednesday, or Thursday. She went to Atlantic City. You still haven't told me about the murder."

"Leave a message that Adam Jordan called."

"Why do I know the name?"

"I edit *Real Detective*. She did some work for me."

"Say, you wouldn't be in the market for a fresh face? I've been thinking of going into modeling myself. Modeling, or taking up Speedwriting."

"Let's discuss it another time," Jordan said.

"You're no fun," Gina said. "Someone who is is bringing Mollie to a party tonight. She couldn't wait to tell me."

"Someone?"

"A name I *don't* know. First she's going out to buy new lingerie. Why do you suppose?"

A picture that wouldn't stop jumping bumped the test pattern. The leopard was gone. The same woman was in a kitchen beating eggs in a bowl.

"Did she say who these everybodies are?"

"How do I know *you* are who you say you are?"

"You don't mind talking about her underwear," Jordan said, "you can tell me who'll be at the party."

"I don't like the way you talk, mister," Gina said, and hung up.

The woman on TV slid a pan into an oven, and took out a perfect cake. Jordan was thinking that if he wanted to see a fake, he'd tune in the channel with professional wrestlers. He switched off the TV, dialed a local number.

"Greenie, it's Adam Jordan."

"How's it hanging?"

"Comme ci, comme ca."

Jordan had two distinct images of his reaction, the half-smile the crack deserved, and the hangdog frown that was Greenstein's walking-around expression.

"You called because you feel bad about the money you owe me?"

"Enlighten me, why don't you?"

"There's my fee for helping with the Stolzfus case. And for putting you together with Cherise."

"You charge for introductions now?"

"I charge for everything."

"You're not embarrassed?"

"Often I am," Greenstein said. "But not around you. Think of me as Cherise's business manager. I hear you and her are hot and heavy."

"Not that hot," Jordan said. "I'm looking for a party."

"First pay up."

"Do this for me, and you can write your own check."

"Scout's honor?"

"We're not Boy Scouts, Greenie."

"What kind of party are you in the market for? Another Negro girl, or something a little more exotic?"

"A party," Jordan said. "Not a woman. A *party*."

"You're looking for a good time, I can move you up in class from Cherise."

"When did I ever want a good time?" Jordan said. "Where's tonight's party?"

"This is Atlantic City. There's parties all over town."

"A party like the one where Chuckie Stolzfus picked up Cherise."

"It wasn't at a party. You don't remember what she told you? The other girl fixed them up, the one who was killed."

"Cherise likes her friends thinking she's a hooker, because working on her back is a step up from what she does."

"Depends how you look at it."

"I look at it like she does," Jordan said. "I'd like to catch her act. Stolzfus paid it the ultimate compliment."

"Everything's an act with her. You're lucky your heart didn't give out like his. She must've taken something off her fastball."

"Where are you—you and Beach—sending her tonight?"

"Call her, and ask."

"I want to surprise her."

"You're the one'll be surprised."

"Are you going to tell me, or do I drop a nickel for everything I have on you?"

"Hold your horses," Greenie said. "It so happens there's a housewarming on the beach. Cherise is working a single. It starts out a single, and then…you get the idea. Twenty Ocean Grove Boulevard in Margate City."

"Whose place is it?"

"You'll recognize him when you see him. Figuring no one sees you first, and gives you the boot."

A haircut was in order, and nicer clothes. Considering his chance of making it through the door, shopping would be a waste of time. A trim, a shave, and hot towels didn't do much for what the mirror showed. Probably nothing would.

He woke up starved from a nap. Room service was on the line when he put down the phone. Who crashed a fancy shindig on a full belly?

Jordan hopped a Checker at the head of the hack line, and told the driver to go south. Ten minutes from downtown they'd put the bright lights, every light, behind.

Margate City was nothing to see, if he didn't count a wood elephant sixty-five feet tall and almost as long, first cousin to the Trojan horse. "Lucy" was built in the 1880s, when zoomorphic architecture was the rage, and had been a tavern, a hotel, a post office. Today she stood with nothing to do, a backdrop for tourists' snapshots, and an embarrassment to the town fathers developing the old blue collar Riviera into a modern resort.

Ocean Grove Boulevard was a thin strip of asphalt from the highway to the sea. Shallow pits in the sand looked to Jordan like miners' claims in a boomtown goldfield. A few foundations had been poured, but much of the new construction would go up on stilts. The Jersey Shore was a hurricane landfall subject to fierce tidal surges. Winter storms carried a wallop as well.

The home closest to the water shined as brazenly as a lighthouse. Limousines competed for parking space with a smattering of out-of-state Jaguars and MGs. Jordan put his hand on the cabbie's shoulder. "Stop here."

"It don't cost no more to the door."

"Here's good."

A stockade fence strung with Japanese lanterns enclosed the yard. Through the chinks Jordan saw a crowd milling under a canvas canopy, the centerpiece a grill staffed by a cook in a toque. He went in as if he owned the place, or was holding the note. He pulled a bottle of Trommer's from a barrel of ice. A waiter snatched it away, popped off the cap, and returned it to his hand wrapped in a napkin.

A three-piece combo he didn't care for banged out stale pop hits. Tonight the music didn't matter. He moved through the crowd betrayed by his shabby clothes, aware of something else that marked him as different. He was a young man at a party for older men. Old and middle-aged men, and much younger women done up as if they'd been asked to the prom by a campus hero with vulgar taste, and had dressed to please him. Jordan watched them cluster around the old men, giddy as Sinatra's fan club. In the competition for attention they were in agreement with all points of view, hysterical over every joke.

One or two, closing in on thirty, had the tragic aspect of women beautiful by any standard other than their own. Most were young, several too young even for him, but available to the old men. A paradox: The old men were clumsy with the young women, but confident, and the beautiful women were graceful and unsure. Some were tipsy. No one told them to take it slow.

A slap on the back caused him to crunch down on the bottle. He looked sideways at McAvoy, his former boss. "Why are you hanging around with old farts, Ken?"

"Same Jordan," McAvoy said. "A day late and a dollar short. It's my place. The farts are my friends."

Jordan played the tip of his tongue against a tooth he might have chipped.

"How did you hear about the party?"

"Reporter's luck. Information finds me."

A man wearing a phi beta kappa key on his vest pulled a Piels from the ice. McAvoy said something in his ear, and he dug deeper for a Trommer's.

"Heard about it in New York?"

Jordan, shaking his head, sensed that he was breaking McAvoy's heart.

"That's Henry Felder, isn't it? The public works commissioner?"

"Know him?"

"By reputation only," Jordan said. "He has his hand in more pockets than a tailor."

"Under more skirts, too. He's a jurist at every beauty pageant on the shore." McAvoy confiscated Jordan's bottle. "Get another, this one's cracked," he said. "Want to hear a good one?"

"A gag?" Jordan said. "Since when do you laugh?"

"I've been thinking of coming to you for work. A story for your magazine I'd write under an assumed name. Hub Chase, the pride—make that the former pride—of the Yankees, got himself killed last night." He paused. "You're not surprised?"

"How'd it happen?"

"He was with a married lady when her husband walked in on them, and Hub got in the way of several bullets."

"Can't use it," Jordan said. "There's nothing to it."

"Same Jordan," McAvoy said. "Too impatient to learn how events pan out. The lady and her husband have one of those marriages where they don't give a damn who the other one's sleeping with when they aren't sleeping with each other. The husband found them in bed together, and went to the living room for a good book till the love-making took a wrong turn. Hub was choking her by the time he went to the lady's defense. Hub got the upper hand, and was kicking his ribs in when the loyal bride pulled a Derringer, and put three in Hub's chest. What do you think?"

"I like what I'm hearing. But it needs more."

McAvoy smiled at a woman—Jordan didn't catch the face—and went after her. "Enjoy yourself," he said to Jordan, "only don't bother the other guests with your opinions about—"

"Jazz?"

"Anything."

Jordan walked around the property looking at the girls. Who had appointed him homicide investigator? Why wasn't it his responsibility to lie, flatter, flirt, tell self-aggrandizing stories, find out how far he could get with Miss America?

Politicians, jurists, lawyers, prominent builders and union bosses were McAvoy's friends, tough negotiators praised in his editorials as custodians of the public trust. None couldn't be bought, but even Henry Felder did not come cheap. Tonight's deal-making was out in the open, a grab bag for the City Hall stalwarts.

A redhead backing against Jordan threw her arms around his neck to keep from falling. "You wouldn't be a judge of beauty?" she said. "I mean beauty judge."

"Don't tell my wife."

She raised a glass, dribbling scotch down her chin. Jordan gave her his napkin. She crumpled it into a ball as she waved like a reed in the wind. " 'll be our secret. Wha's a judge know about beautiful? I can use a friend with connections, but might com-comp-compromise for a big spender. Wha's your name?"

"Adam Jordan. Yours?"

"Miss 1952 Jersey Tomato."

"Do you have a first name?"

" 'S Miss Tomato to you."

Mollie hadn't been this tight the night at his place when he'd purportedly, allegedly, reportedly (a good newsman was careful to include qualifiers in a disputed account) taken advantage of her. He doubted Miss Tomato tumbled into a strange bed without asking *What's in it for me?* He'd never believed that Mollie didn't ask herself the same thing.

Beside the grill he saw a colored waiter in conversation with Beach. Beach, or else his double. Prominent Negroes were kept away from the trough by the power brokers. That Beach was white would make him more unwelcome. He had traversed a line few people crossed, barging the wrong way down a lonely one-way street. Jordan had never heard of anyone allowed to cross back.

It was the wrong time for sociology. Maybe he'd sign up for night classes at NYU, and write his thesis on race relations among the grafters. He hid his face behind the redhead as the man who might be Beach looked his way. The waiter who definitely was Narvin started toward him. Miss Tomato was stuck to his arm as he hurried to the house.

The ground floor was walled in glass on the ocean side, carpeted in tile, furnished in cold modern. A new house on the beach was beyond most newsmen's dreams. Whose pockets was McAvoy in? No one had ever tried to buy off Jordan with more than a beer. He wondered what he would have done if he'd been told to name his price.

He'd lost the redhead. Without her he felt exposed. Girls swarmed around a trestle table heaped with food, and picnicked on the stairs. He stepped over them to a second-story gallery, and looked down at Beach and Narvin pushing inside.

He rattled a locked door, then tried one that opened. A parchment shade softened the light around a woman crouched in bed. Legs protruding between hers were grizzled above black socks. She glanced indifferently as the door squeaked, and then gave Jordan a smile. Opportunities were lost with a sour first impression.

Jordan backed out. There were voices next door, but footsteps on the stairs sent him quietly inside. The couple in bed could go on with what they were doing. He wouldn't stay long. If they ever had to run for their lives, he'd be pleased to return the favor.

The man was undressed. The woman sitting up beside him was wearing a broad skirt, and a blouse open to the waist. A bandana was around her head. Jordan didn't see her face, didn't want to.

The man, on his back, was unaware they weren't alone. He said, "Let me hear you say it."

Cherise looked toward Jordan as she had at the bottom of the bay. Saving her from drowning was one thing. His hands were tied now.

"Okay," she said. "I don't know nothing about birthing babies."

The man shook his head. "Make it sound like you're ashamed to admit it."

"I don't sound ashamed?" Cherise said. "Couldn't we skip this part? Wasting precious time."

"Not at all," he said. "It's good fun. Aren't you having fun? Say it again."

Cherise whisked her hand toward the door. Jordan didn't budge. "Girl gotta do what she gotta do," she whispered.

"What?" the man said. "I didn't hear."

"Ah don' know nothin' 'bout birthin' babies."

"Come to Rhett, honey."

Jordan cracked open the door. If anyone was ashamed, it should be him. He backed in again, and swiped at a wall switch.

The man in bed covered his eyes against the light. "Who are you?"

"This room taken," Cherise said. "Get out or we gonna call to have you thrown out."

"My mistake," Jordan said. "I apologize for disturbing you." He was looking up and down the gallery when he heard Cherise say, "Sorry, Mr. Duchesne, I got to leave."

"Now?"

" 'Fraid so."

"We hardly—we haven't started. And you've been paid."

"Not by you," she said. "Lost my concentration."

"I know what to do to make it come back." He grabbed her.

"Once it's gone, it's gone," she said. "Let go, please."

"Who's this man? What's he doing here?"

Cherise pushed at Duchesne, who held her tight. "My partner."

"Partner in what?"

She embraced Duchesne, squeezed his head against her breast. "Show him the camera," she said to Jordan.

Duchesne shoved her away. He raised a pillow in front of his face.

Cherise buttoned her blouse, adjusted her skirt, slipped into her shoes. "Cost me a considerable piece of change," she said walking out with Jordan.

"Go back. No one's keeping you."

"Heard what I said, I lost my concentration. Don't want to discuss it. What're you doing, following me?"

"Beach is trying to kill me. He saw me, and I ducked into the room."

"Just open a door at any old party, and I'm behind it?"

She went to the railing. Jordan pulled her back. He stood on his toes, looking downstairs as Beach led Narvin outside.

"Why Mr. Beach want you dead? I never heard anything like it."

"Another beauty contestant was murdered after he put her on the card at his theater. I tried to talk to him about her, and had to run to save my skin."

"Think he want to murder you 'cause he the cause of that girl being killed?"

"What else?"

"*You* what else. Come bothering him, snooping around his business, he definitely gonna put a licking on you. I ain't convinced he'd kill you."

"He convinced me."

"All right, kill you. I don't believe he had anything to do with killing a girl. Ain't in his nature. Killing her, and killing you, two separate items."

"Do you know how ridiculous you are?"

"Was ridiculous when I was playing Prissy from *Gone with the Wind*. You ridiculous all the time. Like to play detective, but put two and two together and get a hundred forty-three. Mr. Beach didn't kill that girl, and you went ahead and give him reason for wanting you out of the picture."

"Not at all."

"You a big-time magazine editor in New York, ain't you?"

"So?"

"Big-time detective magazine editor think he killed that poor girl, what could be worse? He don't need you accusing him to the police. Easier to take care of you himself than rent a lawyer. Save trouble down the road on the murder he *didn't* do."

"That's one way of looking at it."

"The right way," Cherise said. "Mr. Beach a sweet man. You should apologize, intrudin' on his private matters."

On the stairs Jordan snatched off her bandana.

"Give it back," she said. "I got another date."

"Do you always play the same part?"

"White men who seen that damn movie before they grew up never have enough Prissy. Thinkin' up a juicy role you want me to play?"

"I was born grown up, Cherise."

"Been regressin' ever since, have you? Not much I ain't game for, but no more slave girls please. Had my fill of 'em."

"I do have a fantasy about you," Jordan said.

"Don't be shy. Can't say it, whisper in my ear."

"I'm not convinced you've got what it takes."

"Must be sick, sick, sick, you won't tell me."

"Some other time."

"What's wrong with now? Worst can happen is you get laughed at to your face, and I let on to Beach and Greenie and everybody here that knows you."

"No," he said. "No, it's not."

A thundershower moving up the coast cleared out the yard. Jordan, pinned beside the food table, took Cherise by the hand. "There's someone you should meet."

Squeezing through the crowd, they approached a pretty young woman at the window. Every woman at the party was attractive, most on the arm of an older gent. This one's escort, slight and smooth-shaven, seemed out of place among adults. A camera was around his neck. Sighting through the viewfinder, he directed the woman with her back to the surf. "Hold the pose," he said, and she stiffened when she saw Jordan.

"The whole world must be here," she said while the flashbulbs popped.

A smile bubbled on the little man's lips as he turned around. "*My* world. You, me, and Adam. And his friend. Are you going to introduce her, Adam, or are you keeping her for yourself?"

"I told you about Cherise," Jordan said. "You're going to help make her famous."

"Indeed I am. I'll get off a few shots now."

"She isn't dressed for it," Jordan said.

" 'Scuse him," Cherise said. "He don't own me, just looks that way. How do you want me?"

While Pixley squared her in the viewfinder, Jordan took Mollie aside. "Your roommate says you might not be coming back."

"Wishful thinking."

"Hers?"

"Hers and mine."

"How did you hook up with Pix?"

"He called. If I had to wait for you, I'd never have a portfolio. He's been very good to me, and knows all the right people. What are you doing here?"

"I'm another right person."

"Your friend, too? What's her name?"

"Cherise."

"I thought you'd brought the maid. I don't need to see a doctor, do I Adam? To have myself tested for various diseases?"

"I couldn't tell you," Jordan said. "I don't know who you've been sleeping with."

"You're a contemptible son of a bitch."

Pixley reloaded. He pulled Jordan in front of the camera, and the flash went off.

"You didn't give me a chance to say cheese."

"I've already seen your smile."

"Pix is gonna have me at his studio tomorrow," Cherise said, "after he's back from shooting Mollie on the beach."

"The ladies will need a stick to beat back their new fans," Pixley said.

"Are you on the colored beauty circuit, Cherise?" Mollie asked.

"Cherise is a performer," Jordan said.

"Has she performed many times for you?"

Jordan glanced at Pixley, who said, "I see Vaughn Rogers from the Boardwalk Commission. You should get to know him, Mollie." He hustled her away. "I'll talk to you soon, Adam. And I'll see you tomorrow at five, Cherise."

"Nice little fella," Cherise said. "Shouldn't've smoked when he was a kid. It stunted his growth."

"Is that what he said?"

"Don't think I got more tact than to ask? More'n Mollie?"

"What's wrong with Mollie isn't tactlessness," Jordan said.

"Ain't what you think it is either. Not too much. She tryin' to get under my skin to get under yours."

"Is that so?"

"Don't play ignorant. She don't want under it 'cause it black. She think you in love with her, and she entitled to make you sweat."

"I'm not in love with her, Cherise. Take my word for it."

"Stopped takin' it before Mollie did. Didn't I say?"

CHAPTER 13

It wasn't her place to tell Pixley how to do his job, but he was missing a terrific shot: a self-portrait in an apron several sizes too large with the three little pigs across the chest, the photographer using a bone-handled fork to poke a pig that wasn't pink and cuddly on a platter. An apple in the pig's mouth didn't alter a pained expression that Pixley had taken for his own.

"Do you know anything about pork, Cherise?" he said.

"Trick question?"

"Aren't you sly? No, I'm serious. Have you ever prepared roast suckling pig? This looks dry."

"I like mine with his eyes lookin' away," she said. "I didn't expect dinner."

"We'll have it at a restaurant," he said. "But before I get to you I've got to finish this shoot. I've been toying with the presentation for so long, he dried out."

"Sweet pet startin' to shrivel. Long as we ain't gonna eat him, got baby oil?"

"I should."

"Whyn't you give him a rubdown? Works wonders on *my* skin."

Pixley kissed her cheek, tickling her with a sparse moustache she hadn't noticed the night before. Sad excuse for a moustache. The baby pig had stiff dark bristles around his snout.

The platter—no surprise—was picture perfect. But the loft wasn't nice at all, most of it given over to Pixley's camerawork. He slept and ate inside his darkroom. There were few books, no TV or Victrola, and the chairs, the bed, and floor were littered with photographs. Someone—not her—might find the set-up romantic. Pixley was an artist, after all, and she expected artists to be eccentric, though he gave her the creeps.

"Not too much," she said as he slathered the pig in baby oil, "or he gonna look like he come in from an afternoon sunnin' on the beach. Reminds me, seen Mollie?"

"Uh-huh."

"Get good pictures?"

Pixley squirted oil onto the back of his hands, which were scratched, crusting in fresh scabs.

"Nothing special," he said. "*She's* nothing special, a pretty girl who'd be advised not to stray far from her clothes. Seeing her in her bathing suit…well, I knew what I was getting. I did her strictly as a favor to Adam."

"Shootin' me as a favor to him also."

"A favor for myself."

"How do you mean?"

"I've always wondered what results I would get using a colored girl."

"Some around," she said. "What were you waitin' for?"

"The right one."

He washed his hands fastidiously. Patting them dry, he reminded her of a surgeon preparing to operate. He mounted a camera on a tripod, and looked through the viewfinder shaking his head, and then he put up a tea kettle on his hotplate, filled three cups, placed them behind the pig where they wouldn't be seen, and squeezed off several shots with steam from the hot water rising over the platter.

"Lost my appetite for roast pig," Cherise said.

"Certain things are not meant to be seen until the photographer is done in the darkroom. Fix your hair. I'm ready for you."

He took her comb and brush away, and made her over again to his liking. When she asked for a mirror, he refused.

"When you sit for me, you put yourself completely in my hands," he said.

"Like Mr. Pig?"

"That's not how I'd choose to put it. But yes."

She anticipated the flashbulb that suddenly went off, and had a smile waiting. Pixley wasn't pleased, but needed to understand that she never let her guard down completely.

He positioned her in front of a white screen, and asked for emotion. He didn't say what kind. She flashed anger, which she had plenty of, and the coyness she believed showed her off well. Then she let her feelings run wild, vamping the little man who looked through the viewfinder shouting encouragement.

"That's fine," he said. "Excellent. Now let me see the face of an innocent schoolgirl."

"Talkin' to me?"

"You can do it."

"Wouldn't count on it."

He got her best wide-eyed look with her mouth slightly agape. "Terrific," he said, "you don't know what an actress you are."

It made her laugh. He got that, too. She liked being in his hands so long as she retained a say in how they shaped her. He popped out the roll of film, threaded another, and caught her unprepared, winking to let her know it was a shot he wanted all along.

"Let's try something different," he said.

"You the boss."

"Not really. I just work here."

She gave him another laugh. He liked it so much he snapped it twice.

"Sit on the bed."

The linens were rumpled, and she thought she smelled them across the loft. It was hard to picture the shot he had in mind, but she wouldn't object to something that might turn out great. She held still while he sighted through the camera lens, and then he reached over and opened her blouse.

"Don't need advertisin'."

"What's that?"

"Jokin' with you," she said. "You didn't hear it."

"Hike up your skirt. Let's see some leg."

"This much?" She stopped an inch or two above the knee. "How high you want to go?"

"Let me have all you've got."

The portfolio was her ticket to a new life. Showing too much flesh in an unmade bed meant punching it for a round trip. Pixley was the artist, but she had the final word. She lifted the skirt to the middle of her thigh, which seemed to disappoint him and excite him at the same time. It was as much as he was going to get.

"Bunch the pillow behind your head, and lie back."

She inched away from a grimy sack leaking feathers. She had come to the loft to pose for glamour shots, but Pixley viewed her as a creature of bed. She didn't care how desirable he made her look. Nothing was gained in bed. Didn't she know?

"How about tryin' something else?"

"I know what I'm doing, Cherise. If you're going to get ahead in show business you have to present yourself as poised and attractive, yet attainable."

"Lyin' in bed makes me feel *too* attainable, you get my drift."

"Everything will be tasteful," he said. "Trust my judgment."

"I trust mine more."

Her foot was on the floor when he pushed her back. The flash went off in her face, and as her eyes slammed shut he jumped her. His hands were between her legs, and inside her blouse. Another—he was on her so fast that it felt like he had three, three at least—squeezed her cheeks as his mouth came down over hers.

She snapped at his tongue, tossed a wild haymaker under his eye as he pulled away. It wasn't the first time someone had tried to rape her. Wouldn't be the first time she made him pay a heavy price.

He wasn't expecting a fight. She slithered away as he sized

her up again, was almost out of bed when she was dizzied by a blow to the side of her head.

Other men hit harder, but none had fooled her as well. She'd thought she could let down her guard around Pixley. Thought he was a fairy, and had been wrong about that also. He wasn't muscular, but knew how to hurt her. Probably he'd been picked on as a kid, and learned never to stop hitting back. She was like that herself.

"Lie still," he said. "Do you want me to break that pretty face?"

"I'll bust you up worse, you don't lay off."

The schoolyard posturing came with a purpose. Without letting him know he was in for a fight, she might as well give in now.

She swung a lamp. He blocked it with his arm. As she ducked away from flying glass, he pinned her shoulders.

"Don't you think I know what you are?" he said.

"Never claimed to be nothing else."

"You've had hundreds of men. What difference does one more make?"

"Overstatin' it," she said. "But it ain't about numbers."

"If I offered money, you wouldn't say no."

"Little bitty squirt like yourself, what can you do with a woman?"

"Shut up, you stupid cunt."

"Don't think I don't know what *you* are? A weasel pretendin' to be a sissy? Imagine a man so low to the ground he'd do that to get close to women."

He hit her in the belly. The breath went out of her, and she thought she'd die. Clawing at his face, she got a thumb in his eye, twisted it while he howled. There was a chair beside the bed, and nothing to stop her from braining him. Maybe if she wasn't in a hurry. She needed to get out of the loft right away, and put this awful experience behind.

As she ran for the door, he hooked a foot between hers and

brought her down on all fours. The chair was out of reach; she was furious with herself for not using it when she had the chance. He made a grab for it himself, showering photos and negatives and contact sheets over her back, and was ready to bring it down on her when she snatched up his camera.

"Be careful, Cherise, I'll kill you if you damage it."

"Rather you did than let you touch me."

"I'm not exaggerating. Put it down."

"I ain't either. You don't let me out, the camera gonna be like Humphrey Dumpty, won't be no one can put all the pieces back together."

She drew back her arm, freezing him.

"Let me have it," he said.

"It'll be waitin' by the stairs."

"I want it now."

"Okay, you asked for it."

Her arm was coming forward when he put down the chair. She walked away keeping an eye on him, moving faster as he trailed after her. At the door he lunged for her, and she fired the camera into his chest.

It bounced away, and he caught it at his knees, bobbled it before he had it securely in his hands. Cherise ran down one flight of stairs to the dance studio where half a dozen couples were exploring the mambo. No one broke step when she barged in. She had an idea that she wasn't the first refugee from Pixley's loft to take cover with them.

An old man in powder blue pants came over after the music stopped, and pressed a handkerchief to her forehead. "You're bleeding," he said.

"Wasn't paying attention when I should've been."

"You have to be more careful."

The music started again, a lame rhumba, and he returned to his instructor. Cherise stood at the window, watching the street.

When the class was over, the old man came by for his handker-chief, and she left the building on his arm.

It was too bad that she'd never see her pictures. Pixley seemed to know what he was doing behind the camera.

The elevator jockey had a discreet case of the giggles. His eyes were red and glassy, and he was tapping his foot to a tune that only he could hear. "Whatever you're smoking, I'd like some," Jordan said.

"You mean these Old Golds?" He slid a pack from his breast pocket. "Get some from the machine in the lobby."

He made a swipe for them as Jordan grabbed them out of his hand. Under the lid were two hand-rolled cigarettes. They were thin, not wrapped tight, leaking seeds and greenish flecks.

"They're all I've got," the elevator jockey said. "Have to last till I score more, and who knows when that will be?"

"How about I buy them from you, and we smoke them to-gether?"

He wanted five dollars, but settled for three. It wasn't bad dope. Jordan, coming down the hall in time to the unheard music, saw light under his door. He thought he'd killed the lights before he went out, but wasn't sure of anything now. He let him-self inside, crawled across the bed a moment before Cherise came out of the bathroom wrapped in a towel.

"How'd you get in?"

"Ain't the first time I sneaked inside a hotel," she said. "In or out."

She took away the roach, and flicked it into the toilet.

"Hey—"

"Need to talk sense."

"We can smoke and talk sense."

"Hard enough under regular circumstances," she said.

He fit the other joint between his lips. Before he could light up he noticed a scratch on her forehead, swelling around her jaw. "Bad actor?"

"Bad actor's me. Went to Pixley to have my picture took. Didn't know I was auditioning to be raped. I thought he was a fairy."

"It's the impression he wants to put over. It took me a while to realize he wasn't."

"What you're saying, he never tried to jump you. Biggest surprise is how strong he is. Strong and determined."

"He wouldn't take no for an answer?"

"He didn't take it about ten times. Wouldn't have taken yes, if I was of a mind to say yes, which I wasn't. Had me there to hurt me. Sex was the batting practice."

"He's plenty weird."

"Queer, you mean? Ain't we agreed he ain't?"

"Peculiar. I never…didn't…think he could turn violent."

"Need to get straight." She opened the windows. "Talkin' bout *you*. Nasty stuff you been smokin' got your brain in a tangle."

"I'm sorry, Cherise, I thought I was doing you a favor."

"First time you sorry for anything."

He patted the mattress, made room for her beside him.

"In the mood for romance?" She ran a finger across her swollen jaw. "Makes one of us. Don't suppose you can get my pictures. I'd still like to have 'em. No hard feelings, not too many, if you can."

Jordan didn't answer.

"Anything penetrate? Or do I need to run the cold water over your head?"

"You're not the only girl I sent to him."

"Other one know how to fight dirty?"

"With her mouth."

"Might want to tell her to cancel the appointment."

"It's too late."

"Could be things didn't turn out bad for her."

"Is that what you think?"

"Might've turned out worse." She dropped the towel, and slipped under the covers, stiff-arming Jordan before she relented, and let him kiss her cheek, the back of her neck, her shoulders. She was squirming into his arms when he dangled his legs over the side of the bed.

"Put you in mind to be with her?"

"Her and Pixley."

"Makin' me laugh."

"Mollie wouldn't know how to fight back."

"She'll figure out what she got to do to satisfy him. She can do that, huh? Do it good enough?"

"You told me yourself, that's not what Pixley wants."

"Don't give a good goddamn about her. All I been through, I'm still shaking. *I* need you now."

"I just want to know she's okay."

"Ain't that fine and dandy?"

He tried to stand, then sat down again.

"So stoned you can hardly move."

He tied his shoes, reached back for her.

"Don't kiss me, don't touch me, don't say nothin' more." She turned her back as he stood over the bed. "Don't bother comin' back."

He left the joint on the night table, and went out.

He hurried past the empty hack line to the next block. Outside an all-night hash joint he got into a parked taxi displaying an off-duty sign, and leaned on the horn. It brought him to the Alcazaba, the cabbie chewing a ham sandwich while Jordan stepped under the darkened marquee and let a match flicker against the glass showcase. The credit beside the portrait of Anita Coburn was hidden behind the frame. The match burned out, and he returned to the cab. "Let me have your tire iron," he said.

"What for?" the cabbie said.

"For a bigger tip."

Three sailors staggered by arm-in-arm while he held the jack handle behind his back. They were almost out of sight when he smashed the glass. Picking through the shards, he fished out the card. The beautiful murder victim had been posed artfully. The picture would make for a fine cover for *Real Detective*, and sell thousands of additional newsstand copies. The photographer would see his name in bold type, but wouldn't collect a fee. *Photo by PixleyPix*.

"Next stop is New York Avenue," he told the cabbie. "A block from the Central Pier."

Murders were piling up faster than he could make room in the magazine. But this case had it all. No woman who wasn't a knockout need apply to join the victims. It was a story to make his name, put him on the best-seller lists, even on track to Hollywood. All that was required to soothe his conscience was to get to the damn killer ahead of the damn cops, and before the next next Miss America.

Pixley's building was unlocked, but not his loft. Jordan rattled the door, threw his shoulder against it, hammered the knob with his heel. The second floor dance studio was sealed, too, but the transom had been left open to allow fresh air. Jordan ran back up a flight, removed two quarts from Pixley's milk box, and lugged the box downstairs, used it as a platform to hoist himself up to the transom.

B&Es would never be his day job. Squeezing inside the studio, he found little that wasn't nailed down aside from a stack of scratchy records he didn't want. A rusted fire escape enclosed the windows. As he dropped over the sill, the twanging of decayed metal brought forebodings of doom. Three stories below, a cat scrounged in a garbage can. When he didn't crash down onto it, he ran up the ladder to the third floor.

Pixley's loft, behind a barricade of geraniums, was too dark to see inside. He forced a window a couple of inches before it stuck, then hurled a flowerpot through the glass. He was a bull in a china shop tonight. A stoned bull, but not a reckless one. A quick tour of the loft turned up nothing. He needed light, but feared ending up on the wrong side of a burglary rap. He reprimanded himself for being paranoid, allowing dope to influence his thinking. Nothing more than that making him sweat. *Well, wasn't it?*

He poked around the living area, went back, and looked under the bed, expanded his search to the darkroom and closets. A white backdrop suspended from ceiling hooks shielded pantry shelves bowed under jugs of chemicals and photographic paper. Discarded backdrops were tangled on the floor, blue, black, red, green, and another, which, as he raised a corner, he saw was painted to look like a sunset over Monument Valley, a convincing trompe l'oeil. The foot swaddled inside it, colorless aside from red toenails, was not designed to fool the eye, but rather, it seemed, to turn the stomach.

It was time—well past time—to bring in the cops. Noticing a phone beside Pixley's bed, he reached around it for a camera, a 35mm Leica with fourteen shots remaining. He used two on the pantry before unraveling the backdrops on the floor.

The foot was a woman's, cold, not stiff, a woman dead less than twelve hours or more than twenty-four. Nicks on her bare leg told him she had shaved it shortly before she died. On the other leg was a nylon. Its partner, a tourniquet almost invisible around her throat, was only a contributing cause of death. A gummy trickle was stalled below a small hole next to her ear. In profile she looked like no one in particular. He preferred that to the finality that came with seeing her face.

It didn't matter to his readers who she was. They were in the know that she'd been beautiful, saintly as well as seductive, trusting his appraisal. *Real Detective* readers were hard-nosed connoisseurs of facts the newspapers were too squeamish to reveal. For these they depended on Adam Jordan, who portrayed murder honestly while keeping the nightmares for himself. This case was no different despite his own involvement. Regarding Mollie Gordon readers might share his sleepless nights, but without a full measure of his guilt.

He cupped her chin as if to steal a kiss. Her eyes were open, dull and dry. He made a mental note of it, and of the way she felt, the cool vacancy of beauty robbed of life, observations which would be attributed in his story to an unbiased witness. He snapped two pictures of her face, and then finished the roll, an intimate album to consult when he was overwhelmed with murder, and its victims lost their individuality. He pocketed the roll. The used flashbulbs went into the alley, frightening away the cat. He was returning the camera to its shelf when he slipped on some photos scattered face down around the body.

Several flipped over as he kicked them, one a shot of a restaurant with MACKIE'S in bright neon in the window. He didn't recognize the faces, but remembered the case, the Virginia Beach stickup-murder and fake suicide. Downstairs he shouted at the cabbie, "The beach—get going."

"It's four-thirty, I need to go home."

"Take me there, and leave. You can do that."

"Pay me first." The engine didn't start till Jordan pulled out his wallet. "Which beach?" the cabbie said. "All we got is beaches."

"Little Egg Harbor. Try there."

The sand belonged to two barefoot runners, a man toweling off after a moonlit swim, a couple under a blanket oblivious to the sun creeping out of the ocean. Jordan kicked off his shoes, and tramped across fluffy dunes bound by beach grass. A small fishing boat teetered on the horizon. The sun rose into the sky. Sea ducks skimmed the waves. That was all there was to see.

He was playing a weak hunch without a fallback if it didn't pan out. At least he would have an invigorating walk to start the day.

The dope filtering from his system left a sense of calm clarity. A flash of light near the place where he'd found Suzie Chase brought him higher into the dunes, and he looked down into the sun reflected from a windshield. Trampled grass led away from the car to a cove where the ocean fell apart on a rock shelf.

A man was dragging a bulky object toward the water, stopping to rest each time he advanced a few feet. Above the tide line a cloth bundle was sheltered in a depression scooped from the sand. The bulky object was also a man. He wasn't big, Jordan noticed, the same size as the man pulling him on his back. The pair were well-matched, the man on his feet grunting and cursing with sweat rolling down his forehead as he struggled to move the other man—who was nude—by the legs, a tug of war the man on his back couldn't win. He was dead.

Jordan circled toward the bundle, a tangle of men's clothing, the outfit Pixley was wearing the last time he'd seen him. A camera anchored it to the sand, and between the camera and the clothes a sheet of paper flapped in the breeze. Jordan had an idea what was written on it.

Bent over the corpse, Pixley reached into his pocket as Jordan came up on him. "Grab a drumstick. I've been expecting you."

The body was that of a blond man with the face of an impish boy, about 120 pounds or so, Jordan estimated, or would be when he was soaking wet.

"Who is he?"

"Marcel," Pixley said. "Sacrificed in the service of a higher cause."

"To save your neck."

"It's better if people think he shot himself. Or rather that I did. Shot myself, I mean. You're doing the story? I don't see a notepad."

"I know how it turns out."

"I've added a twist," Pixley said. "The bad guy, and he's a very, very bad guy, Adam—no excuses—the bad guy gets away scot-free. It's a story without a moral. You've never done one like it."

Jordan studied a ragged exit wound in the back of Marcel's head.

"Marcel was my biggest fan. He loved my pictures, even posed for some of them. He was under the illusion I'd brought him here to photograph him. He loved *me*. If you must know, he was that way." Pixley fluttered his wrist. "A pest who won't be missed."

"And looked enough like you to be your twin."

"Goodness, no, I'm *much* better looking," Pixley said. "Marcel tried to imitate everything about me. He'd hate me for giving away his secret, but he colored his hair. There, see for yourself. He wanted to *be* me. Now he is. Did you happen to read the note?" His hand came out of the pocket wrapped around the grip of a gun, and then he put it back. "It's the last testament of the tormented artist and loveable roué Pix Pixley, in which he admits to the murders of four women, expresses his shame and regret, begs forgiveness, and consigns his body to the sea, and his soul to God. I got the idea from one of your stories. Do you remember the dope who couldn't stage his own suicide without landing behind bars? I've made improvements to the plot. I've supplied proof that I'm dead, and Marcel will look so much more like me—rather he'll look less like himself after he's been in the water." He heaved at the body. "I've done the hard part. It's your turn to pitch in."

"Why'd you kill the girls?"

"Motives, shmotives. I gave your readers the best crime photos. That's all I owe them."

"You owe *me*."

"Let's quit kidding." Pixley pulled the gun. "You aren't going to write my story. I have to shoot you, which is a lousy way to end a friendship. I always liked you, and admired you, although

I wouldn't want to be you. Not now. Trust me to give you a dignified burial in a beautiful place."

"Why did you kill them?"

"Why do you think?" Pixley said. "Actually, you'd be wrong. I do fine with women, always have. And not because they pity me. No sympathy sex—I don't play that game. They find me… um, understanding. But a real man. They love me. Adore me. I do better with them, I bet, than you."

"So you kill them."

"Being understanding is a bore. Snapping gorgeous women, sleeping with any I want, that becomes boring, too. Controlling them never grows old. Destroying them—there's something new and exciting every time. Don't assume I never give it a thought. But you won't find me on a psychiatrist's couch."

"He'd say you're a remorseless predator."

"You're no better," Pixley said. "A vulture. The vulture and the wolf, that's us, feeding off the same carcasses. Put Marcel in the water."

"The tide will wash him back."

"I don't want to sail him to China. The body will be found near my suicide note, my wallet, my clothes, my favorite camera. No one will doubt I shot myself."

"What's in it for me?"

"Another minute or two to enjoy my company." The gun pointed across the corpse. "Lots can happen in a couple of minutes. I could be hit by lightning, have a heart attack. God might strike me dead, though I'm skeptical. In two minutes perhaps you can talk me into giving you thirty seconds more. You see, I also enjoy controlling you. What's it going to be, Adam? I know what I'd do."

Jordan took Marcel under the arms, and backed toward the water. One of the dead man's heels dug into the sand. Pixley raised it, used it as a tiller to steer Jordan to the surf.

Waves thundered into the cove, and died at Jordan's ankles.

Whitecaps boiled over the shoal. A series of combers scoured the beach up to the tide line. As they retreated, Pixley tumbled the body into the trough, and saw it float away before the wind and waves returned it to the sand.

"Carry him deep. We'll send him off on the next big one," Pixley said. "Do you know what the surfboard riders say in the Hawaiian islands? Every seventh wave is from heaven."

He held Marcel back from a knee-high curler as giants stacked up on the horizon. One angled into the cove, a green Niagara swelling until its sheer size brought it down. "Now!" he shouted, and hurled Marcel into the foam.

Jordan dived after the body as a shot rang out. His arm burned from his shoulder to his wrist, while he ground his teeth to keep from shouting into the sea. Using a compact kick he swam underwater, surfaced to see Pixley fire at a red slick, dived again.

Another big wave rolled in. Ten feet behind Pixley, Jordan watched the photographer raise the gun above the redness sweeping around him.

"Adam?" Pixley said. "Adam, where are you? Don't tell me you're alive."

He aimed into a swell, held fire as a wave knocked him off his feet. Treading water with the gun above his head, he spun a 360. Jordan dived, and Pixley fired at his heels, put two bullets dead center in a pattern of concentric circles.

The surface churned. As Pixley turned the gun, Jordan hurtled out of the water, and butted him under the jaw. Pixley's teeth coming together through his tongue stifled a scream. Jordan stripped the gun from his hand, and forced his head under the waves. Pixley touched the shallow bottom, pulled in his legs, and swam away.

"It's not a beach day," Jordan said. "Come in."

Pixley flipped onto his side. Marcel floated toward him, and he stiff-armed the body, which drifted off caught in the tide. Jordan examined a wound bleeding freely above his elbow. A good thing there were no sharks in the water, he was thinking. None as dangerous as Pixley and himself.

"What'll you do with me?" Pixley said.

"I need a memorable finish for my story," Jordan said. "What do you suggest?"

"You can't shoot me. I'm the wolf. You're a...just a writer."

Jordan held the gun over chest-high waves rushing in in rapid order. Pixley remained where he was with Marcel bobbing face-up between them. His eyes squeezed shut, and he flinched each time Jordan pulled the trigger.

"That's your idea of a joke?" he said when the shooting stopped. "You've got a cruel streak, Adam. I didn't know that about you. All I do know is you aren't capable of killing me. You have to let me go."

Jordan poured water on his head, which was ringing from the collision with Pixley's chin. "Look at Marcel."

"Why would I? He's a dreadful sight now. If you must know, I always thought he was."

"Look anyway."

Pixley spit gobs of blood. He turned distastefully toward the floating body. "Not just cruel," he said. "You're an evil bastard."

"Would you like it better if I'd shot *you*?"

"You might as well have."

Jordan heaved the gun as far as he could. "You're creative, Pix. An artist. By the time the cops get here, you'll know what to say."

"There's nothing."

"Tell them you're Marcel, and Marcel's Pix Pixley, who shot himself in the face three times after taking a bullet to the mouth to avoid the chair for murdering those girls whose pictures are all over your—his studio."

"That's not funny."

Jordan waded to shore, shook himself like a dog. "Everybody out of the pool. It's starting to blow."

Pixley turned onto his back, and rode the current away from shore.

"You're out too far," Jordan said. "You'll drown."

The wind shifting out of the north prickled his skin. He hugged himself, but couldn't stop shivering. When he looked back, Pixley was swallowed by the chop. Shading his eyes, he watched the ocean spill over the horizon, the fleeting silhouette of a swimmer receding against the sun.

CHAPTER 14

He called detectives to tell them where to find Mollie, refusing to identify himself. He'd done their job for them; they'd have to settle for leftovers. There would be time to fill them in about Pixley when his body washed up.

After seeing a doctor, he went to the Columbus, and drew up his notes on hotel stationery. Two stories began to take shape, a first-person account for the glossies, an extended hard news piece to sell himself to a big city daily. If no one bit, he could always go back to New York. Crafting the leads, he couldn't find the proper voice, something eating at him till he was forced to put the work aside.

The Checker at the head of the hack line was the same cab from last night. Jordan wondered if the driver ever slept, but didn't ask. He was tired of asking questions, an odd feeling when he didn't have all the answers. "Missouri Avenue," he said.

The cabbie eyed him in the mirror, the soiled face under a soiled newsboy's cap with a pencil stub against the brim. "Nothing but trouble there," he said. "Interested in a piece of ass, I got connections. How much you looking to spend?"

"Thanks the same," Jordan said. "Take a right at the corner."

He crouched on the jump seat, gazing out at shabby blocks that all seemed the same. The radio crackled with a syrupy crooner boasting about the teen queen sporting his fraternity pin. "Kill it," Jordan said. "Another right. I mean left. No, *here*."

On a street dead-ending at a curb beside the beach the cabbie said, "You don't know where you want to go, do you?"

"Did I ever?" Jordan smelled saltwater, glanced toward the ocean through the cool darkness under the boardwalk.

As they backed into a broken U-turn a girl in a red coat jumped a puddle in the pot-holed gutter, and hit the curb without breaking stride. Jordan's door was open before the cab stopped rolling.

"Cherise," he shouted. "Hey, Cherise, wait up."

Her head jerked, and she held it higher. He called to her again, and she spun around pushing one hand away from her chest like a traffic cop at a light stuck on green. "Adam Jordan, don't come near."

She backed off as Jordan edged away from the cab, a slow-motion tango at thirty paces.

"Come to tell me again how sorry you are?" she said. "I had it to here with you, hear?" She hacked at her throat with the side of her hand. "Up to here."

Words were Jordan's best friends, but all but the wrong ones had deserted him. He tried a couple of baby steps reaching out to her. Another sent her bolting up the boardwalk stairs.

"Not so fast," the cabbie said as Jordan started after her. "Fifty-five cents for the ride."

Jordan patted himself down, and flung a bill through the window.

"Got something smaller? This is a twenty."

"Keep the change." Jordan ran.

"You crazy? You can have any woman in this town for twenty bucks."

A bum was camped under the boardwalk, caged in shadow. Sand drizzling between the planks showered his ragged blanket, and built dunes on the stairs. The bottom steps were buried. Jordan vaulted over them running harder, took the rest two and three at a time, three and then four, flying.